The
Dark
Zone

Tor Teen Books by Dom Testa

GALAHAD

The Comet's Curse
The Web of Titan
The Cassini Code
The Dark Zone
Cosmic Storm (forthcoming)

A GALAHAD BOOK

The Dark Zone

Dom Testa

**TOR®
TEEN**

A Tom Doherty Associates Book

New York

THE DARK ZONE

Copyright © 2011 by Dom Testa

Cosmic Storm excerpt copyright © 2011 by Dom Testa

Reader's Guide copyright © 2011 by Tor Books

A Tor® Teen Book
Published by Tom Doherty Associates, LLC
175 Fifth Avenue
New York, NY 10010

www.tor-forge.com

Tor® is a registered trademark of Tom Doherty Associates, LLC.

ISBN 978-0-7653-2110-7

First Edition: May 2011

Printed in the United States of America

0 9 8 7 6 5 4 3 2 1

Acknowledgments

Thank you to . . .

The sibs who have been such great supporters: Dean, D'Ann, David, and Donna.

My son, Dominic, and Sabra, who are treasures in my life.

All the educators around the world who have pushed Galahad into the stratosphere, especially Jen Byrne, Karen Anderson, and Shanna Swinehart.

The people in my corner who have been so patient and helpful: Judy Bulow, Dr. Judith Briles, Jacques de Spoelbergh, and the great people at Tor: Tom, Kathleen, Susan, and Dot.

My radio family: Jane, Jeremy, Tizzy, and Kris. Thanks for the fun and laughter!

The friends who have been there when I really needed them, especially Paul Nagy and Sharon Peterson, and Monica Busick.

All the supporters of my educational foundation, The Big Brain Club, including Herb Tabak and Cathy Kruzic.

And, of course, to the legion of fans who make up Club Galahad.

The
Dark
Zone

What exactly is the difference between the brain and the mind? This question has baffled people for centuries. It's been the topic of thousands of articles and essays, along with numerous research studies. It has been analyzed, debated, hashed, and rehashed. Some have argued that it's possible for a human to have a brain but no mind, and yet they say it's not possible to have a mind without a brain. I tended to agree with this last statement, until I read about something that used to be called "daytime television."

Classic definitions will tell you that the brain is, for the most part, a computer made of living cells, billions upon billions of neurons and synapses, firing away in an attempt to move its human host from point A to point B without stumbling over something, without getting eaten by something big and hungry, and without wearing socks with sandals. The mind, it has been suggested, is the conscious, thinking component, the "higher self" that supposedly separates humans and primates from lower life forms such as reptiles, bacteria, and politicians.

There are a couple of reasons why I bring this up. For one, as an observer of the brilliant kids who stroll the corridors of the great starship called Galahad, I am constantly intrigued by the ongoing internal conflict between the brain and the mind. Sure, these teens were handpicked from around the world to carry out a mission to save humanity; to leave their families behind and travel across interstellar space to the planetary system known as Eos; to escape the deadly clutches of a disease borne by a rogue comet's tail and preserve the history and legacy of their species; to . . .

Well, we've already established that they're brilliant, which is why they're able to make this journey without any adults aboard the ship. They are essentially the perfect laboratory specimens for me to study the brain/mind relationship.

Here's what I've determined: regardless of how sharp a person may be, the battle between the brain's automatic (some might say instinctual) response and the mind's emotional response can often lead to conflict, chaos, and . . . and . . . sorry, I can't think of another word that fits here and starts with "C."

You get the idea. I'm often amazed at how the so-called superior mind of the human species will obsess over details that it should, by all reasonable accounts, ignore. Ah, you say, but that's what makes you human, right? Okay. Then I'm left to wonder how you ever did rise above the bacteria. Your incredible minds, it seems, truly beat the odds.

The other reason I bring this up—remember, there were two—is because I'm an interesting subject myself. My name is Roc, and I'm undeniably the most astonishing artificial brain ever conceived. My role on Galahad is to oversee the ship's primary functions, of course, but I also provide the insight, the intuitive good sense, and a healthy dose of dazzling wit and charm. But . . . do I have a mind?

Why don't we let you decide for yourself? There's plenty of evidence to sift through, and I would strongly recommend that you start at the beginning of the Galahad saga with a volume known as The Comet's Curse, followed by The Web of Titan, and then The Cassini Code. Each of these tales will catch you up on the drama and excitement that has followed our merry band of star travelers from Earth, past Saturn, and through the very border of the solar system. And, along the way, you'll naturally develop a strong appreciation and—dare I say it?—a warm affection for your humble narrator. Then you can make the call on whether or not a mind exists within my circuits.

Brain versus mind. Rational thought versus emotional influence. Smooth peanut butter versus crunchy. None of it gets any easier when you're billions of miles from home, rocketing out of the Kuiper Belt and into the great unknown. My friends aboard Galahad are the smartest, most courageous young people you'll ever meet . . .

But they're only human.

1

There was no sound in the room other than muted sobs. No laughter, no whispers, no private conversations. More than two hundred teenagers, crammed into a sterile space, yet completely quiet. It was an unnatural silence, which added to the somber mood. Occasionally a cry escaped from one of the teens, which provoked a similar response from another, then another. Then once again the deathly veil dropped, and silence reigned.

The shroud-covered body lay alone on the table, identity disguised. It held the attention of every person in the room, for it represented what none had believed possible.

Galahad's first death.

A crew member separated from the crowd and trudged up the steps to stand behind a hastily arranged podium. Choking back tears, they spoke quietly, reciting memories of their late friend, offering words of encouragement in a vain attempt to make it seem that everything would be okay.

Nobody responded. They stood silently, most with hands clasped behind their backs, filling most of the available space in the Spider bay of the ship called *Galahad*. As the speaker walked slowly back down the stairs, music began to drift across the room. It brought about a fresh wave of tears.

Silence dominated again. Then, slowly, the crew members began to disperse. One by one they approached the body; some reached out and placed a hand upon it, others simply stared. After pausing for a moment, they shuffled past, across the vast hangar, and out the door. It took almost thirty minutes for everyone to pay his or her respects individually. In the end, five people were left, huddled together, not wanting to believe it could have happened, not wanting to say good-bye. They embraced, then together approached their fallen comrade and placed upon the shroud a bouquet gathered from the ship's farms; not true flowers, but the closest symbol they could manage.

A minute later they convened in the Spider bay's control room, sealing it off, and stared sadly through the glass. With a spoken command, a door opened in the hangar, exposing the room to the icy vacuum of deep space. Starlight cascaded through the opening. It was a simple reminder: we are far from home.

There was hesitation, a collected feeling of loss, and a reluctance to let go. The next move would send the body into space, to drift for eternity. No one wanted to move, to take the next step, to banish his friend to the depths of empty, lonely space. But at last the word was given, and the ship's computer began the final sequence.

The robotic arm, until now concealed below the table that held the body, extended toward the bay's open door. With a gentle shove it was done; the shroud covering the body fell away, revealing a cocooned human form, layered in specially treated wraps. It cleared the opening and began its endless journey. Within a minute it had receded from view, first a small white object slipping away, becoming a faint pinprick of light, and then gone.

Once again the five companions in the Spider bay's control room embraced, allowing their grief to mingle, physically holding each other up. They remained that way as the bay's outer door closed, blocking out the starlight, sealing them once again into the warmth of their metal nest.

And then the scene froze . . . and faded away.

It was a familiar smell, but Alexa Wellington couldn't place it at first. Still disoriented from the deep sleep, she lay on her bed and kept her eyes closed. The misty line between wakefulness and dreams had dissolved, but once again the vision had been so strong, so intense, so . . . real . . .

She was, as usual, reluctant to let it go. In the last six weeks her dreams had become more and more vivid. They didn't come often, perhaps only two or three that she could remember each week; but they were unlike any dreams she had ever experienced before. For one thing, there was no dreamlike quality to them. In one of her quiet conversations with Bon Hartsfield, Alexa had likened them to minimovies, only with the screen inside her head in full 3-D and high definition. Until she awoke and opened her eyes, her mind would not interpret them as anything except real.

On top of that, they were complete dramas; they had a beginning, middle, and end, unlike the typical dream that generally jumped from place to place as well as backward and forward in time. These were stories that played out as if scripted. Often they were quite pleasant, while others were very unsettling. This particular dream was the most disturbing yet.

Taking a deep breath, Alexa opened her eyes. Other than the soft glow from the computer monitor across the room and the faint emergency light above the door, the room was dark. She could just make out the still form of her roommate, Katarina, sleeping. All was quiet. The scent that had greeted her upon waking was artificial; Katarina had apparently dialed up her favorite sleep aid, a soft fragrance of lavender that seeped through the ventilation ducts.

Alexa resisted the urge to glance at the clock, for she had found that her mind would then only focus on the time, mentally calculating how long it would take to fall back asleep. It might be midnight; it might be 5 a.m. She didn't want to know.

Of course, concentrating on the time might distract her from the troubling dream that had unfolded minutes ago. The nightmare's tragic setting was only one concern; the fact that her dreams had lately started to come true was terrifying.

She took another deep breath, held it, and then slowly exhaled. Try as she might, she couldn't shake the vivid image of the deep-space funeral. Who had been lying beneath the shroud? Who were the friends clustered in the control room, grieving together? Their faces were obscured, their gender a mystery. She had felt that they were somehow close to one another, but that didn't help; there were 251 teenagers aboard the ship.

Another thought occurred to her: Should she tell someone? If indeed her dreams were somehow portals to the future, allowing her to glimpse ahead, was it irresponsible to keep this vision to herself? On the other hand, what purpose could it serve? The dream had given no indication of the cause of death, which meant that realistically no preventive steps could be taken. If word leaked out that Alexa was now predicting death for one of the crew members . . .

And just whom exactly would she tell? Triana Martell? That would be the obvious choice; the ship's Council Leader would be understanding, and would treat Alexa with respect. But Triana had so many responsibilities, and dealt with more pressure than most teenagers could imagine. Why add to her concerns when there was nothing that could be done about it?

Lita Marques would also be very understanding, and, as Alexa's immediate supervisor in *Galahad*'s clinic—lovingly referred to by the crew as Sick House—knew her better than anyone. Lita was a good friend, a good listener, and easily the most compassionate person Alexa had ever met.

And yet was it a good idea to burden her with this information? A mere eight weeks ago Lita had operated on Alexa and removed her appendix. In fact, the surgical procedure had inadvertently brought on the dream visions that now plagued her. Alexa had not awakened immediately after the operation, and instead had briefly lain in a coma. Something had happened to her during this unconscious stretch, something nobody could quite explain.

Although she had done nothing wrong, Lita blamed herself for the frightening turn of events. Alexa couldn't see troubling her with this new development.

Then there was Bon.

The quiet, somber Swede had few real friends aboard the ship. He kept himself busy with his work, running the agricultural program within the two massive domes that topped the spacecraft. Few people had ever been able to get emotionally close to him. And yet, over the last few weeks, he and Alexa had connected.

It began with a visit he made before she was discharged from Sick House. During their brief conversation she realized that he had sought her out because of something they had in common: both were experiencing bizarre mental flashes that had altered their worlds.

For Bon it was his tenuous connection with the alien entity that the *Galahad* crew had encountered while zipping past Titan, the mysterious orange moon of Saturn. That connection had eventually saved the ship from certain destruction within the debris-strewn minefield known as the Kuiper Belt. For Alexa it was her sudden prescient abilities.

It was a bond forged of their uniqueness. As Alexa had said to him recently, "We are the ship's freaks. Nobody else could possibly understand." Bon had scowled at hearing this, but had offered no argument.

She had shared many of her dream visions with him over the

weeks, but not all. How would he take the news that a death aboard the ship might be imminent?

She decided to wait.

With a sigh she gave in and twisted her head to look at the clock, just as the time clicked over to 1:55 a.m. "Go to sleep," she whispered to herself.

Deep inside she knew it would not come easy.

The Dining Hall on *Galahad* was packed. Triana walked in at 7:15, late for her breakfast meeting with Channy Oakland and Lita. The three girls made it a point to start the day together at least once a week, occasionally to discuss Council business, but mostly for social reasons. She scanned the busy room and spotted Channy waving from the far corner. Channy was easy to pick out of most crowds; all one needed to do was look for the brightest T-shirt in the room. Today's choice was hot pink.

"Sorry I'm late," Triana said after loading a tray with some fruit, an energy block, and simulated juice, her usual breakfast combination. "It took me longer to answer emails than I expected."

"Everything okay?" Lita said.

Triana nodded as she sipped her juice. "Lots of questions about what's going on back home. Not that I could really offer much information."

"It had to happen eventually, right?" Channy said, a grim tone overriding her usual upbeat British inflection. "I mean, I'm surprised we kept contact for as long as we did."

"It's still tough to swallow, no matter how prepared you think you are," Triana said.

Lita looked thoughtful. "So I guess we can officially declare ourselves out of the nest. No replies to our messages must mean that Galahad Command has closed for good."

The three girls reflected on this for a moment before Triana said, "It's not that we really needed their help for anything in particular. With Roc we pretty much have the technical know-how. It's the . . . uh . . ."

Lita finished for her. "It's the emotional tie."

"Yeah." Triana looked around the room. "Although the crew seems to be in pretty good spirits. I can't remember when I last saw this place so busy in the morning."

Channy laughed. "It's because of this." She held up a small bowl with a sticky residue around the insides.

"What's that?"

"Oatmeal."

Triana raised her eyebrows. "You're kidding. We have oatmeal?"

Lita smiled. "Bon impresses again. He told a few people that it would finally be ready, and the word spread like wildfire."

Turning to look over her shoulder at the serving line, Triana said, "Why didn't I see any?"

"Because it's all gone, that's why," Lita said. "I don't think anyone was prepared for the rush."

"I got here at 6:45 and scooped up one of the last bowls," Channy said. "Sorry, I guess I should have saved you some."

It was Triana's turn to chuckle. "Don't worry about it. I'm sure I'll have plenty of chances over the next few years." She looked around. "Who knew that oatmeal could bring so much joy?"

"If you ask me," Lita said, "it's not simply the fact that we have any particular new food. I think it's simply change, and that's something this crew could use."

"What do you mean?" Channy said.

"It's not healthy to fall into a rut," Lita said. "This is just my opinion, of course, but we could all use a shake-up in our routines. Tomorrow is the ten-month anniversary of our launch, and besides a few dramatic moments, and the switching of job assignments, we have pretty much all fallen into the same patterns, day in and day out." She looked at Channy. "It's no different than what you preach to us every week in the gym, about alternating our workouts. After a while your body adapts, right? It's not as effective."

Channy nodded. "Right. But you're talking mentally?"

"I'm talking about all of it: physically, mentally, emotionally." She indicated the food dispenser line. "A new food choice is a little thing, but look at the reaction. It's a welcome change; not all change is embraced, but it's almost always good for people."

Triana smiled. "Any suggestions, Doctor?"

Channy piped in before Lita could answer. "Oh! I know! What if we had something like, I don't know, um . . . okay, how about Shake It Up Day, or something like that? You know, everyone has to do everything differently for one day."

Lita's laugh was gentle and pleasant. "I know that you love to plan special events, Channy, but I wasn't thinking about just one day. I'm talking about a lifestyle adjustment."

"I know, but at least it would bring it to everyone's attention."

Triana shrugged. "I'm probably the biggest creature of habit on this ship. I'm pretty sure it would do me some good to mix things up a bit. I don't know if we need a special day dedicated to it, but it's something that we should discuss in a Council meeting."

Channy grinned. "Just don't forget about tonight."

Her two companions went through the motions of adjusting the items on their trays, neither making eye contact. Finally, Lita said, "Tonight?"

"Oh, stop pretending you don't know," Channy said with a huff. "The Dating Game? This evening? Auditorium? Big fun? Remember?"

Lita and Triana looked at her, then at each other. Triana kept quiet, leaving it up to Lita to respond again. "I'm pretty busy with reports this week."

Channy crossed her arms. "It's one hour out of your life, Lita."

She shook her head at both girls. "I swear, you two are the biggest wet noodles I've ever met. Would it hurt that much to put yourselves out there?"

Triana at last broke her silence. "I know you really want us to participate, Channy, but maybe next time." She offered a wry smile; Channy returned a pout.

"Fine. You could at least stop by and be part of the audience. I promise I won't bring you up on stage. But I could use some more bodies in the crowd."

"I'll pop in for a few minutes," Lita said.

"I'll do my best," was all that Triana offered.

For the next ten minutes the conversation drifted through a variety of topics, mostly with Channy's enthusiastic comments, Lita's thoughtful responses, and an occasional observation from Triana, who often chose to listen and quietly consider. During this time the room began to thin out, as more and more crew members cleaned up their tables and set out on their daily duties.

Galahad's crew worked in six-week shifts within the various departments on the ship, before rotating into a different assignment. It was understood that this would allow each person to become proficient in many areas. Along with the advanced schooling that accompanied their work, the idea was for *Galahad* to have a seasoned, well-educated crew when it arrived at the Eos star system, their eventual destination.

At any given time a group of about sixty people were on a break from work, but even then their education continued. Many found that the break only led to boredom, and when their next assignment arrived they gladly returned to the rotation.

Lita stood, stretched, and picked up her tray. "Back to work for me. Anything exciting for you guys today?"

"I'm going to ask Bon if we can clear a path around the outer perimeter of Dome 2," Channy said. "A few people in the afternoon workout group suggested that it might be more fun to run up there. It would be more like running outside. I think they're very tired of the treadmills."

Lita laughed. "Good luck. If I hear the walls shaking today I'll know that you asked Bon."

"I know he's very protective about his crops," Triana added, "but that's actually a pretty good suggestion. Let me know if you want me to go with you."

"What about you?" Lita said. "What's your day like?"

Triana stood and pushed back her chair. "This will be an interesting day in the Control Room. We are officially shooting out of the Kuiper Belt now, and I've heard some rumblings about what might be on the other side."

Channy sat still, looking up at the Council Leader. "And what do *you* think is out there?"

"A whole lot of nothing."

"Just empty space?"

"Just empty space," Triana said. She waved good-bye to Channy and walked toward the door with Lita.

As they exited into the curved hallway and prepared to go their separate ways, Lita looked into Triana's eyes. "Do you really believe there's nothing outside the Belt?"

Triana sensed the anxiety in her friend. "Honestly, Lita, I have no idea anymore. It's getting to the point where nothing would surprise me."

"Bon and Alexa seem a little worried about it."

Triana sighed. "I know. But what can we do?"

Lita didn't answer at first. Then, with a smile, she said, "We're tough. We can handle anything, right?" She turned and walked toward the lift.

Triana bit her lip. For two months she had wondered what they would be facing when they shot out of the minefield of debris that circled the solar system. Soon they would find out.

2

His name was Taresh, and he held the attention of about twenty-five *Galahad* crew members who hunched over their workpads. This particular session of School focused on history; in particular, the rise and eventual end of British colonization. With their stylus pens hastily scribbling notes, the students' eyes darted back and forth between their workpads and the young man from India who spoke onstage in the Learning Center.

From the beginning, the man who had organized the *Galahad* mission insisted that the crew members participate in their own education. Dr. Wallace Zimmer had provided the necessary information in the ship's computers to instruct the young pupils in all areas, a measure that ensured that Eos would be settled by a highly educated population. Yet, rather than have them sit through lecture after lecture by Roc, Dr. Zimmer put a heavy emphasis on students carrying much of the load.

Regardless of the subject matter, *Galahad*'s crew members were expected to take their turn onstage, sharing specific information that they had researched for that particular lesson. It not only encouraged each student to expand his or her individual acquirement skills, it developed a sense of teamwork. Whether they were outgoing or shy, it didn't matter; at various points everyone would take his turn in front of the group.

Taresh had volunteered to share the story of India's past. A native of Patna, a city on the banks of the Ganges River, he was a good choice to teach his fellow travelers about the region. Easygoing and well liked, he exuded pride about his home country that was evident to everyone in the room. With the help of graphics that Roc flashed on the large screen behind the stage, Taresh quickly recounted the story of India's vast wealth of cotton, silk, spices, and tea, and how Britain established outposts that soon came to dominate the country. The British East India Company evolved into territorial rule, complete with a government infrastructure, armies, and more. Taresh concluded his comments by addressing the rise of self-government, and official independence in 1947.

Seated in one of the chairs, and entirely absorbed in the information, was Gap Lee. The Head of Engineering on *Galahad* and a Council member, he enjoyed School, especially these times of student led discussion. In particular, Gap admired the way Taresh held himself, and the graceful manner in which he related the story of his country's heritage.

Gap felt a similar pride for his home country of China. He knew that for ages, the people of his country had clashed with the people of India, often over disputed territory between the two great nations. Now, with Earth billions of miles behind him—and growing more distant every second—it was difficult for Gap to fathom those differences, and how they could go unresolved for so long. Taresh was a friend, and Gap was saddened that countless generations of their people had chosen a warlike path over peace and cooperation.

Too often it had been the same story for the people of Earth; here, however, in the cocoon known as *Galahad,* such cultural and territorial disputes seemed old and irrelevant.

Taresh finished his report, and a smattering of applause followed him to his seat next to Gap. A five-minute break would follow before the class shifted its attention to mathematics.

"Well done," Gap said, clapping Taresh on the shoulder. "I've heard the name Gandhi so many times, but I never really knew what he was all about."

"I felt the same way when we studied Greek history last week," Taresh said, saving the data on his workpad. "Familiar names, but I couldn't have told you anything about them."

A boy in front of them turned around. "I still don't understand why we have to learn any of this anyway."

Gap looked into the eyes of Micah, who hailed from New York. "What do you mean?"

"Well, we've left all of this behind us. Why bother to drag it to Eos? What good will it do when we start over on a new world? I don't get it."

Gap glanced at Taresh, who jumped in to answer.

"It's important to learn as many lessons from the past as possible."

"I don't see how," Micah said. "Shouldn't we spend more time on math and science, and forget about all of the nonsense that our ancestors caused? If you ask me, it's better to ignore their mistakes."

Gap shook his head. "I can't agree with that. The reason we study the mistakes from the past is so that we'll recognize what works and what doesn't. Besides, it's not all about mistakes. There were some great people who did some amazing things; just reading about their wisdom inspires me sometimes."

"And remember this," Taresh added. "The path that we've all taken is a part of who we are. How can you appreciate what you have if you have nothing to compare it to?"

Micah looked thoughtful. "Yeah, that's true. I never looked at it that way before."

Taresh chuckled. "I know that sometimes it just seems like a bunch of useless facts that we'll never really need. But that's because we forget to look underneath. The story of our past is a great tool for creating a better future. It's not just facts and figures; it's our foundation. It's the same with traditions."

With a nod, and a new look of respect on his face, Micah turned back around. Gap looked at Taresh. "So what's new in your world?"

"I'm about to start a turn in Sick House in two weeks. I'm glad, too, because medicine is one of my interests."

"That's cool. Lita's a good teacher, too," Gap said. "What have you been doing for fun?"

"Would you believe board games?" Taresh said with a smile. "Seven or eight of us have gotten hooked. We meet in the Rec Room twice a week after dinner, and it's a blast. You should join us sometime."

"Might be a good change from playing Masego with Roc," Gap said. "I've still never beaten him, and I think lately he's been letting me get closer, just to keep my hopes up."

While he was talking, Gap glanced around the room. People were sitting in groups, chatting, and others were walking in and out of the door to the hallway, preparing for the second half of the class. He started to say something else about Roc, when suddenly he caught sight of a familiar face in the back row.

It was Hannah Ross. She kept her head down, and appeared to be sketching something. The fact that she was in the back of the room probably indicated that she preferred not to be seen by Gap. He understood.

Two months earlier he had ended a relationship with Hannah, and they had not spoken since. He saw her occasionally, but it was rare. And in those awkward moments she made sure to avoid contact or conversation.

The breakup had come during a stressful, disturbing point in Gap's experience on *Galahad*. In the weeks that followed he had questioned his own decision, often tempted to stop by and visit the quiet girl from Alaska. The closest he had come was an email, a long, detailed letter explaining his motives. In it he admitted that he missed her, and wondered if she would have any interest in meeting for dinner.

Hannah had not responded.

Now, at the back of the Learning Center, she continued to keep her gaze on her workpad. She had to know that Gap was in the room.

"Well?"

Gap realized with a start that Taresh had been speaking to him. "I'm sorry, I was drifting," he said.

Taresh turned to look in the direction that Gap had been staring, then looked back at his friend. A knowing expression was on his face. "I said we're going to be meeting up in the Rec Room again tonight, if you'd like to come by."

"Uh, sure, I'll try to make it if I can," Gap said, shifting back in his chair to face forward. "Anybody I know in your group?"

"Channy started playing a couple of weeks ago," Taresh said.

"Really? Channy?" Gap was surprised that the chattiest member of the crew had not said anything about it during a Council meeting.

"Yeah. She, um . . ." Taresh appeared to search for words. "She . . . has been very friendly lately."

Gap laughed. "What are you talking about? Channy is always friendly. You know that."

Taresh raised his eyebrows. "No, I mean she's been very friendly."

It finally sank in. Gap's mouth dropped open. "Ohhhh. Interesting."

"Don't say anything to anyone," Taresh said, dropping his gaze to the floor. "I'm not trying to embarrass her. I just don't know . . . how to handle it."

"Do you like her? I mean . . . she's very cute." Gap suddenly felt uncomfortable about the conversation. In a strange way, he almost felt as if he was talking about his sister.

Taresh shrugged. "Yeah, she's cool. I don't know."

A soft tone sounded in the room, announcing the end of the break. Both boys seemed relieved.

The door of the lift slid open, and Triana was immediately aware of a heaviness that blanketed the Control Room. She wondered for a moment if something had gone wrong, until she glanced to the far corner and recognized the figure who sat before a keyboard, his back to the room. He likely had not said a word, nor done anything to intentionally produce the feeling that swam about the room, yet Bon's mere presence often cast a dense shadow. The word "brooding" had been used by more than one crew member when describing the tall Swede; the result was that he usually worked without interruption or small talk.

Triana crossed to the workstation and looked over Bon's shoulder at the vidscreen before him. A jumble of code played out, countless strings that meant nothing to her, and, strangely enough, probably meant as little to Bon. He was a vessel, a container of information, a messenger of sorts. Yet the information he carried had saved the lives of everyone aboard *Galahad*.

Without knowing exactly how it worked, Bon was able to sync telepathically with the alien force they called the Cassini. Ageless and intellectually advanced beyond human comprehension, this powerful force occupied Titan, the methane-wrapped moon of Saturn. During the brief encounter as *Galahad* whipped past, Bon discovered that his mind was being used as a conduit to the alien entity. He was able to sink into a painful, frightening connection with the Cassini using a device known as the translator, whereupon data was transferred in a sort of mental uplink. The crew of *Galahad* had used that data to navigate its way out of the deadly Kuiper Belt, avoiding collision with the trillions of pieces of space debris that circled the edge of the solar system.

Each stage of the navigation, however, had required an individual uplink. Triana had grown concerned that Bon was somehow becoming addicted to the powerful connection. She knew that his link to the Cassini had altered him in some way, something that neither she nor he could describe. Even though his connections were agonizing, it seemed he was too eager to repeat the experience. Wary, and more than a little distrustful of the effects he was suffering, Triana chose to hold onto the translator herself, and only allow Bon to use it in her presence.

He had made another connection the previous evening, kneeling among the dirt and plants in Dome 2, where he felt the most at ease. Triana had watched the spasms take over, watched Bon's head snap back, his eyes turn a terrifying shade of orange, and a mash of voices pour forth from his mouth. It meant that the Cassini had taken hold of him.

Although it lasted barely a minute, Triana always found herself shaking by the time it ended, often clutching herself with both arms, anxious for it to end, unable to relax until Bon's normal shade of ice-blue seeped back into his eyes.

This would likely be the final set of instructions for navigating out of the belt. Already the number of rock chunks and ice balls had plummeted; what lay before them, other than a second ring called the Oort Cloud, was cold, empty space.

Truly empty, they hoped.

Triana placed her hand on the back of Bon's chair. He responded by looking up at her, his usual blank expression revealing nothing.

"Well?" she said. "Finished?"

"Yeah," Bon said, punching one final key with a flourish. "Not much of a change, really. I think we're basically out."

The words sent a shiver through her. The Kuiper Belt had

been a two-month game of dodgeball, with destruction always a possibility. And yet, at the same time, it had also acted as a security blanket, preventing anything from outside the solar system from reaching them. *Galahad* had now rocketed into the great unknown.

"I'll let the crew know," she said, quickly regaining her composure. "Any other information from our friends?"

Bon shook his head. "No, just this final course correction. I got the feeling that they were washing their hands of us . . . for now. Of course," he added, "it would probably be a good idea for me to check back in to make sure."

Triana looked down at the Swede. On more than one occasion he had subtly suggested that she allow him to keep the translator. She tried to read his face, but came up empty. "Right," she said quietly. "Well, we'll talk about that."

She turned and made her way to an empty workstation and sat down. "Roc," she called out, "analysis of the space up ahead."

The computer's voice responded. "Dark and empty. Reminds me a lot of Gap's head."

"Be nice," Triana said with a smile. "What about our course to Eos? How far off have we veered?"

"Not too bad, but it will take some more adjustments once we're safely out of any danger of getting creamed by a stray boulder. Not that the super brains on Titan seem to care about our travel plans."

Triana said, "I know, you don't care for them. But they did get us through this mess safely. Can't you show a little gratitude?"

"Hmph, if you say so."

"All right, go ahead and pout because you weren't the hero this time. Anything else to report?"

Roc was silent for a moment before answering. "Nothing. All systems on the ship are fine, the path ahead is pretty much clear, and I think I set a new record for solving Rubik's Cube."

"Congratulations."

"Don't think I don't hear the sarcasm in your voice," Roc said. "Let's see *you* try it with no hands."

Triana pushed back her chair and stood. "I'll be in Engineering if you need to brag about anything else."

Bon had finished his work, and joined her as she walked toward the lift. She sensed that he wanted to say something to her, but kept quiet. They had just stepped into the lift when she heard Roc call out from the Control Room.

"Uh-oh."

Triana put her hand up to stop the door from closing, then stepped back out of the lift. "What is it?"

Roc's playful tone had evaporated. "There's something up ahead. And it's not a chunk of rock or ice."

Triana's gaze shot quickly up to the large vidscreen. It showed only inky blackness, with a panorama of softly twinkling stars. She squinted, trying to make out any unusual object.

"Correction," Roc said. "Lots of somethings."

3

With all of the drama you juggle each and every day, it's a wonder to me that humans are able to sleep at all. Roy—my creator—once bragged that he only needed three hours of sleep each day; any more than that, he said, was a waste of his valuable time. Experts would tell him that he's (a) not allowing his body to recover from the stresses of the previous day, and (b) not allowing his brain to process and filter all of the information that it soaked in during that day.

I know that you're already enormously jealous of me, but here's another tidbit that you'll hate: I don't sleep at all. Not even a catnap.

That means I don't have to deal with nightmares, which occur during REM sleep, or night terrors, which happen earlier in the sleep cycle, and are seldom remembered.

I don't know what you'd call Alexa's dreams . . . just be glad you don't have them.

It was the worst part of her job, but Lita understood that it had to be done. She had followed her mother's path into medicine in order to help people, and to bring a gentle, human touch into circumstances where people were rarely at their best. All of that inspired her. Writing these reports, however, did not.

In earlier days, she realized, it was much worse. Back then it was pure paperwork, and entailed endless hours hunched over a desk with mounds of paper piled up on all sides. Today it was all keyboards and touch screens, and could be accomplished in a fraction of the time.

It didn't make it any more enjoyable, however. "I'm a book-keeper as much as a doctor," she thought, keying in another entry from the previous day's physicals.

Keeping all 251 crew members fit was a top priority of the five-year mission. They had been quarantined during the final thirty days before the launch from Earth. Holed up inside the Incubator, isolated from all outside human contact, it was hoped they would begin their journey without carrying along the worst kind of baggage: Earth's collection of infectious diseases. Then, once on their way, it was Bon's job to produce a healthy balance of foods in the two domes that sat atop the ship, and Channy's responsibility to drive each of them during their daily workouts.

Lita's role was to monitor their medical data on a regular basis, which meant brief assessments every ninety days. Space travel was a challenge to the human body; fortunately the ship's artificial gravity eliminated the problem of bone and muscle atrophy, and the combination of proper diet and exercise kept their cardiovascular systems running smoothly.

Still, Dr. Zimmer had stressed the importance of staying on top of everything, not allowing any condition to fester and lead to complications. The physicals, while necessary, meant several hours of record keeping. Lita's top assistant, Alexa, handled the bulk of the filing, but it was easily a job for two.

Lita pushed her chair back from the desk and rubbed her eyes. The constant staring at the vidscreen always sapped her energy. She looked across the room and found Alexa staring back at her.

"Having fun?" Lita said before noticing the expression on her friend's face, a look that caused her to sit up straight. "Hey, everything okay?"

Alexa continued to stare through her for a moment, then blinked and offered a slight smile. "Uh, sure. Just thinking."

Lita hesitated before offering the question that was on her mind. "Been dreaming again, haven't you?"

Alexa blinked again, then looked down at her work. She said nothing.

"Wanna talk about it?" Lita said gently. "I know it troubles you; maybe it wouldn't be as . . . as heavy . . . if you talked about it."

When Alexa still didn't respond, Lita wondered if she had made the situation worse by adding a new level of pressure. The truth was, she wanted Alexa to open up and discuss the prophetic dreams that tormented her, but she wanted her to do it without feeling as if she was being analyzed or tested. For weeks Lita had allowed her friend the privacy that she seemed to long for; at the same time, might it be better if she shared the fears that obviously weighed on her?

They had developed a close bond from the moment they met, and the two years they had trained and worked together had only cemented their relationship. When it had fallen on Lita to operate on Alexa in order to save her life, she might just as well have been rescuing her own sister. And, when things had initially turned scary, Lita's pain was unbearable.

Since then, a veil had somehow dropped between them; their relationship was still good, but a shift had occurred. Lita knew that most of it was the result of the gift of future-sight that had befallen the medical assistant following her surgery—if gift was the right word. Lita suspected that it was more likely a curse.

The week before, Alexa had marked her sixteenth birthday, a day that normally would have found the two of them celebrating. Instead, Alexa had requested the day off, complaining of a headache, and spent the entire day in her room. Lita had dropped by with birthday greetings, but their visit had seemed rigid, uncomfortable.

Lita mourned the loss of their special connection, but held out hope that it was temporary.

For now, she decided that a good friend should never shy away from trying to help. "I know this is awkward for you," she said to Alexa, "but we've been friends a long time. I really think it would make you feel better if you talked about it."

After another moment of hesitation, Alexa looked up at Lita. "I have talked about it, actually. I don't know if it makes me feel any better, but . . . but Bon and I talk about things every few days."

Bon and Alexa.

Although Lita knew that their bizarre mental transformations had created a unique link between them, it was startling to imagine Bon showing that much interest in someone, or opening up to her. His personality was nothing like Alexa's.

Or, at least, it hadn't been. Things on *Galahad* had changed so much in less than a year.

"Do you feel like it helps you?" Lita said.

Alexa shrugged. "Yes and no. I guess it feels good to talk about it with someone who understands . . ." She paused, a sudden look of alarm on her face. "Not that you don't understand. I mean, he just . . . I mean—"

"It's okay, I get it," Lita said with a smile. "You're both experiencing things that the rest of us might never really understand. It's natural for you guys to grow close." She chuckled. "Well, I take that back, it might be natural for *you*, but not our Nordic Grump."

Alexa smiled back. "Oh, he's not as bad as most people think."

With raised eyebrows, Lita said, "Oh, really?"

A blush spread across Alexa's face. "Stop it. We just talk. You're starting to sound like Channy."

Lita raised her hands, palms up. "I'm not saying anything." Then her face grew serious again. "But you said yes and no. What's the no?"

"Well, it gets stuff off my chest, but . . . but verbalizing it almost makes it seem more . . . I don't know, concrete, I guess. When it's just a dream I can treat it that way. When I talk about it, though, it's like I'm . . ." She trailed off.

Lita said, "Yes?"

Alexa exhaled loudly. "When I talk about it, it's like I'm planning it, or something. Like it's all my doing."

"You know that's not true, though," Lita said.

"Of course I do, but you know how our brains work. Rational and logical don't always win out."

Lita nodded. "Well, I can tell from your face that you've had another experience. I just want you to know that you can talk to me about it, too. I might not have Bon's exact frame of reference, but I might be able to help you sort things out."

"And I appreciate that, I really do," Alexa said. She smiled. "I might be a weirdo these days, but I'm still glad you're my friend." She seemed to think hard for a moment. "And you're right, I did have another episode last night. I . . . I just don't think I can talk about it right now. I haven't even told Bon yet."

"Okay, I won't pressure you," Lita said. "As long as you know I'm here."

Alexa smiled again, then bent back over her work.

Lita decided to give her some privacy for a moment. She stood up and walked out to the corridor. A good five-minute walk would do her good anyway, blow out some of the carbon, clear her mind a bit, and prepare her for another hour-long session of staring at a vidscreen.

As she walked she wondered what it must be like to carry the burden that Alexa did. Some people wished for the ability to see the future; apparently those who could do so would trade it away in an instant.

"Would I want to know?" Lita thought, walking with her head down and her hands behind her back. "Would I?"

The cursor on the vidscreen before her blinked patiently, but Channy's fingers rested without movement on the keyboard. Three drafts of the letter had come to life, and almost immediately had been discarded. The fourth didn't seem to be coming at all.

Talking with Taresh had come easily at first, when there were no feelings involved. Now that he occupied her thoughts on a regular basis, she found that her words sounded clumsy and forced. Things had been fine until the night before, when she had awkwardly pursued questions about his family, his hobbies, and—she sighed just remembering it—his cultural background. When he had finally lapsed into a quiet stage, Channy realized she had been very obvious.

But, she asked herself, so what? What's wrong with letting someone know that you're interested? Why should games always be a part of the early relationship dance?

She hadn't convinced herself.

After leaving Triana and Lita at breakfast, she decided to make a quick stop at her room and compose a brief note to Taresh. Its primary function was to save face from her enthusiastic gushing of the night before, but also to reinforce the fact that she was interested in more than just a simple friendship. Subtle, yet direct, she decided.

Except subtle was a suppressed gene in Channy's molecular makeup.

"C'mon," she said to herself, wiggling her fingers above the keys. Nothing came.

She stood up with a huff, pushed back her chair, and marched a small circle around her desk. "What's so hard about this?" she said. "Just tell him. 'Hey, I like you, I think we could have a lot of fun together, I'll let you skip an occasional workout in the gym.'"

She stopped, turned, and paced in the opposite direction.

" 'Look, no pressure, I understand you want to take it slow, so do I, we can maybe have lunch tomorrow, may I kiss you, please? No, forget I said that! I was just kidding. No, really, I think you're an amazing guy, and—' "

She had come full circle again around the desk, and plopped back into her chair. "Aarrgh! This is not difficult, Channy! Quit being so odd!"

What made it all the more frustrating was her own reputation. Often hailed as the ship's unofficial matchmaker, she prided herself on her ability to detect hidden romantic feelings between crew members. More than once she had murmured sly comments to those involved, which brought either a hail of denials—guilty, lame denials though they were—or flushed looks of embarrassment.

So how could she, *Galahad's* resident Cupid, suddenly find herself at a loss when it came to her *own* emotions? This was unacceptable.

On more than one occasion she had been called on it. Lita had often responded to Channy's romantic meddling by asking, "And what about you?"

She had been crafty in deflecting all such questions, using her wit and charm to divert attention away from her own love life. No one had pressed the issue, which had been a blessing for Channy because of the secret that she kept hidden from everyone.

Deep down, she was terrified of falling for someone.

Whenever the possibility had presented itself, she had moved in another direction, afraid of taking the chance, of opening up her heart. It was much easier, she decided, to occupy herself with everyone else's pursuits. No chance of getting hurt when you kept yourself out of the game.

The trick had been to keep a clamp on her emotions and not allow herself to spiral in too closely to someone. Taresh, however, had caught her off guard. His soft-spoken demeanor made for an interesting combination with his strong presence. It had an intoxicating effect on the young Brit, and she was stunned when it dawned on her: she had fallen hard for him.

Her inexperience, however, soon became apparent, culminating with the embarrassing exchange the night before. It was the reason she believed some damage control was called for.

This left her now, sitting again, staring at the flickering cursor on the vidscreen.

She sighed. Her hands flew across the keys, two quick paragraphs, hastily written. Punching the final period, her finger hovered above the Send key. After another moment of hesitation, it fell hard on the key, and the message was away.

Five seconds later she groaned aloud. "Oh, no, what have I done?"

She sat back and laced her fingers together over her head. She stared at the vidscreen's mocking text: Message Sent.

In an instant her mind raced through every possible fix. She would immediately write back to Taresh and tell him it was a joke. No, she would simply act like she'd never sent it, never acknowledge anything, and ignore him for a month. No, she would ask Kylie, her roommate, to snoop around and find out if Taresh was saying anything about the email to his friends.

No.

No, she would own up to it. She would accept the fact that she had fired off an email in an emotionally unbalanced state, that she had opened herself to embarrassment and ridicule. She would live with the consequences, no matter what they might be.

And then she would go to the Spider bay, open the hatch, and jump off the ship.

An alarm sounded in Triana's head. Roc, for all of his glib humor and often reckless attitude, knew when to stow the comedy and get down to work. There was a definite tone he was able to summon in that manufactured voice that said, "This is no joking matter."

That tone was in effect now.

Triana walked briskly back to the empty workstation in *Galahad's* Control Room. "Explain, Roc. What's out there?"

"Can't get a visual fix on them. I count . . ." He paused. ". . . Between eight and ten. Small. Fast. Very quick in their maneuvering. Makes it hard to get a good read on them."

"Wait," Triana said, "slow down. Did you say maneuvering?"

"I did. It's what brought them to my attention in the first place. Things out here . . . well, they tend to go about their business in one direction, right? Until they bump into something, or get tugged by gravity. But even then they just bend a little bit." The computer hesitated before adding, "These little devils are darting in several directions."

"Location?" Triana said.

Roc seemed to calculate for a moment. "Straight ahead, swirling along both sides of our path. They were scattered when I first picked them up, spread out over a pretty large distance. But now they've collected themselves. They're like . . ." He didn't finish.

Triana turned to Bon, who had followed her to the workstation. "Please find Gap and get him up here." She then looked back at the vidscreen, peering through the star field, searching . . . for what? Her mind tried to fill in several blanks at once.

The dread that had clawed for attention the past few weeks pushed its way back in. Triana recalled the suggestions made by both Bon and Alexa that something might be waiting on the other side of the Kuiper Belt. Neither of them could say what that something might be, nor could they offer any explanation for their feelings. Which, Triana decided, had made it even worse. Every horror movie fan knew that the terror didn't come when the monster jumped out at you; no, the real panic lurked in the shadows, torturing you with what *might* be there.

She bit her lip and looked around the Control Room. The smattering of crew members on duty—it never totaled more than five or six—seemed as nervous as she, most of them taking quick, furtive glances at the vidscreen. Roc's vague description of the unexpected company ahead had altered the mood; if Bon's heavy disposition had cast a gloom over the setting, it now had an overlapping tinge of fear.

The crew of *Galahad* had already experienced more than their share of the mysterious unknown, but that didn't make each new incident any less ominous. They were constantly reminded of their vulnerability.

And, she thought grimly, they would always be the outsiders, the new guys on every new block. Always trespassing.

Another three minutes passed before Triana heard the lift door open. She glanced around to see Gap striding up to her. He apparently read her face instantly.

"What's going on?" he said.

Triana shrugged. "Roc says there are . . . things up ahead. Unidentified, and hard to pin down."

Like everyone else in the room, Gap peered up at the large vidscreen. "Things? Not rock or ice chunks, I take it."

"They're maneuvering."

Gap's head snapped around, and he stared hard at Triana. "Maneuvering? So they're not natural." He paused. "What do you think—"

"I have no idea what to think," Triana said. She turned her attention back to the panel before her. "Roc, how long until they reach us?"

The computer's voice replied, "Oh, they're not approaching. They're circling in our path, waiting for us to reach *them*. At least we have some prep time. I estimate we'll make contact in roughly . . . fifty minutes."

Gap nudged Triana. "Let me in here a minute." He punched a

few keys, looked at the results on the small screen before him, then keyed in a few more entries. A minute later he looked up at Triana.

"Yeah, they're on both sides of our path." He stood up and looked toward the large vidscreen again. "Ever seen a marathon? You know how people line the sides of the streets to either applaud the runners or hand them a cup of water? That's what this is like; we have a little group of spectators waiting to welcome us."

A shiver went down Triana's neck. "Have you been able to tell anything else about them? What size are we talking about?"

Roc said, "Best guess would be about the size of a large bird. This, by the way, lends itself to the comparison I was going to make earlier, and one that is much better than Gap's silly marathon analogy."

"Which is?" Triana said.

"I'd say they're behaving more like vultures, circling over the spot where a varmint is about to collapse in the heat of the desert."

Triana's shoulders sagged. "Great."

"And," Roc added, "they have the mobility of birds, too. What we've got here, ladies and gentleman, are space vultures."

The words hung in the air of the Control Room, and Triana felt the atmosphere of dread tick upward another notch. Her mind sifted through their options, but only one idea came to her. "Should we change course?"

"These things are incredibly quick," Roc said. "They have already responded to our approach and placed themselves in position to intercept us. We can't run away from them.

"I'm afraid," the computer continued, "that we're left with no choice but to plunge right through them." After a pause, he added, "Gee, I hope they're friendly."

Channy sat with her feet dangling from the stage of the auditorium, staring out at a sea of mostly empty seats. She worked hard to keep a look of irritation off her face, and kept reminding herself that it was still early.

Behind her, on the stage, a crew of hastily assembled volunteers arranged a series of chairs, while others finished placing decorations that mostly resembled Valentine's Day at an elementary school. Oversized pink and red hearts, along with improvised images that were meant to represent Cupid in a variety of poses, either hung from drop lines or trumpeted from the backs of chairs and podiums. After starting and stopping a few times, the soft sounds of what passed for romantic music drifted from the room's speaker system.

Channy bumped her heels against the front of the stage and drummed her fingers across the floor. She watched one of the auditorium's doors open and admit a smiling Lita, who strolled down the aisle.

"Hey, it looks really good, Channy. Very bright, very festive."

"Very empty," Channy said, gesturing toward the seats.

Lita sized up the situation and offered a look of pity. "It doesn't start for another fifteen minutes. Nobody will ever want to be the first one here, you know that."

"I smell a disaster."

"Oh, stop that," Lita said, swatting Channy on the leg. "It's the first Dating Game, and you knew it was going to be a challenge." She pulled herself up onto the stage and sat with her arm around *Galahad*'s Activities/Nutrition Director.

"I know you don't want to hear this," Lita said, "but now you know why I suggested you do this in the Dining Hall. At least the first one." She waved her arm to indicate the room. "This is a very big space."

"Because it's a big event," Channy said defensively. "Or at least it should be. You have to think big, you know."

Lita seemed to measure her words before answering. "You have no problem thinking big, Channy. It's too bad not everyone shares your enthusiasm all the time. But you know how human nature works."

Channy grunted. "You mean to act like big chickens?"

"No. Sometimes people have to warm up to things, that's all."

A door opened at the top of an aisle and a girl peeked inside for a quick moment, before disappearing again and closing the door. Channy shook her head.

"That's happened about ten times. If there were even a few more people in the seats they would come in and sit down. They'd sit as far back as they could, but at least they'd come in." She turned to look at Lita. "Where's the rest of the Council, anyway? You'd think I'd at least get some support there."

"Something's happening in the Control Room," Lita said.

"Right. A likely story."

Lita shook her head. "No, seriously. Triana didn't tell me much, but said that they're checking something out." She paused and patted Channy's shoulder. "C'mon, you know Triana supports everything you do on this ship."

"Except this. She's afraid I'll stick her up here on stage as a contestant. And what about Bon? What about Gap?"

"Gap's in the Control Room with Triana. And who are you kidding about Bon?"

Channy quietly stared into the room.

"You still have fifteen minutes," Lita said.

"Five."

"Okay, five minutes. Just start a few minutes late and I'll bet you'll see a bunch of people wander in. You know that curiosity will start to work on them."

As she said this, the door opened and three crew members walked in, snickering among themselves as they took seats in the back.

"See?" Lita said, beaming. "It's already started."

"Wonderful," Channy said sarcastically. "At this rate we'll have more contestants on stage than in the seats."

"Well, I'll be in the seats," Lita said, hopping off the stage and turning to look back. "Do not—repeat, do not—call me up there. In fact . . ." She turned back toward the door. "I'll go find Alexa to sit with me. That's another warm body for you."

"Grab everybody you see on the way," Channy called out to her. "Threaten them with tetanus shots if they don't come."

I should do something," Triana thought. "There should be something that I can do."

And yet the harder she concentrated on the situation, the more she realized that they were helpless to do anything at the moment. *Galahad* sped toward a rendezvous with as many as ten unidentified objects that loomed ahead, circling like vultures, as Roc had put it. There was no way to stop, no way to maneuver, which would be useless anyway, given the agility of the mysterious strangers. There remained but one question.

What would happen at the point of contact?

Triana kept her voice low as she spoke to both Gap and Roc. "Can we survive a collision?"

Gap responded with a similar hushed tone, never taking his eyes off his control panel. "We don't even know what they are, so there's no way to predict what would happen. I can't believe they would just let us slam into them, though. A suicide job makes no sense. Besides . . . wait a minute." He punched in a quick adjustment on the keyboard.

"What?" Triana said.

It was Roc who answered. "Well, isn't this interesting."

"What is it?" Triana said again. "Tell me."

"Apparently they don't want to stop us," Roc said. "I think they intend to hitch a ride."

Gap's face displayed shock as he looked at Triana. "We are officially the fastest object in the history of our solar system. We should zip past these . . . whatever they are . . . in a microsecond. But . . . this is incredible."

Before Triana could sputter another demand for information, Roc chimed in. "They have gone from circling in one spot to an acceleration that doesn't seem possible. They have adapted to our course, and are suddenly rocketing along almost as fast as we are. That changes our time of contact, of course. With their new speed and trajectory, we have a whopping ninety-five minutes until we are rubbing shoulders . . . or wings . . . or whatever these things have."

Gap shook his head. "I don't know how they did it, but suddenly they're pacing us." He looked up at the room's vidscreen. "Nothing should be able to accelerate that fast."

Triana was again aware of the atmosphere in the Control Room, and tried to modulate her response to cloak any sign of panic. "Well, I guess that rules out any intention of collision." She bit her lip for a moment before continuing. "Is there something we can do to keep them away from the ship? Maybe some sort of electrical charge on the outside?"

The silence from Gap and Roc answered the question.

"Well," she said, "what about rocking the ship, or going into some sort of controlled spin?"

"No," Gap said. "I think we need to accept the fact that these things are going to catch us and grab hold. I'm not sure that would cause any problems, actually."

"Unless they cut their way into the ship," Roc added. "Or oozed some sort of acid that ate its way through the skin of the ship. Or physically started eating the ship. My, imagine that; actually eating the steel of our ship."

"Stop," Triana said.

"How can that not fascinate you?" the computer asked. "Or what if they—"

Gap interrupted. "Tree, do you, uh, want to make some sort of announcement to the crew?"

The idea had flashed through her mind. Would it make sense to warn the crew of their impending contact, or better to just wait and see what happened. After a moment's hesitation, she shook her head.

"Later. Let's see if the situation changes in the next half hour or so." She took a few steps away from the console and stood with one hand on her hip, the other cupped around her chin. She studied the large vidscreen that refused to divulge any sign of the vultures.

One thing after another, after another, after another . . .

Triana could pick up the uncomfortable vibe of the room, the tinge of fear that seeped from each crew member. She marveled at how quickly the aura of the group had shifted from when she had first walked in. Bon was absent, and the unease he triggered was now replaced by alarm of the unknown.

It was a feeling that apparently the crew of *Galahad* should get used to, she realized.

She turned to Gap. "We're certain about the time until contact?"

He glanced at his monitor, and then back to her. "Yes. Just over ninety minutes."

"Okay," she said, walking toward the door of the lift. "I'll be back in forty-five. If anything changes, call me immediately. I'll be in my room."

A puzzled look spread across Gap's face, but he mumbled a quick "sure" before bending back to his monitor.

Three minutes later Triana sat down at the desk in her room. As the Council Leader, she had the luxury of solitude, the only crew member without a roommate. At times like this, she was grateful.

"Roc," she called out.

The computer responded at once. "Don't you just love this? Another big adventure. Some people go their whole lives without a whiff of excitement, and yet we could practically bottle the stuff."

"I think I speak for the rest of the crew when I say that we could use a nice, long, boring stretch. Like about four years' worth."

"Are you sure?" Roc said. "It's all in your perspective; just think how battle-tested you'll be once you reach Eos. At this rate, there won't be a thing that could surprise you at your new home. Wouldn't want to sail all the way there without a little conflict now and then; you'd show up lazy and complacent."

Triana responded with a grunt of skepticism, then changed the subject. "Listen, I didn't want to talk about this in the Control Room, in front of the crew."

"I knew that's what you were doing," Roc said. "Either that or a quick bathroom break."

She ignored this. "After our misunderstanding of the Cassini, I'm a little hesitant to assume the intentions of anything we might encounter out here in the middle of nowhere. But it would be irresponsible of me to not assume that these . . . vultures, or whatever you want to call them, are dangerous."

"I agree," the computer said.

"And it would also be irresponsible of me, as the Council Leader, to not take every precaution possible to protect this ship."

"Again, I concur."

Triana paused for a moment before continuing. She tapped a finger on her desk and said, "I hate to be the aggressor in a situation like this, but . . ." Her voice trailed off.

Roc filled the empty silence that followed. "You know, even though I'm not human, I know your species, and I know your history. I have read practically everything ever written—well, except some of those romance novels; I get easily embarrassed—and your history texts are full of instances where people fall back on one particular rule."

Triana obliged the computer by asking the obvious question. "And what rule is that?"

"Shoot first, ask questions later."

There was another long silence. "Well," Triana finally offered, "that's kinda what I was getting around to. My question for you is: Do we have anything to shoot with?"

"What do you mean? You know this ship isn't equipped—"

"I know what we've been told," Triana interjected. "I know that Dr. Zimmer didn't have the time or resources to build a traditional weapons system into the ship."

"So," Roc said, "what are you suggesting?"

Triana tapped her finger a few more times. "I'm suggesting that there might be something in the Storage Sections for us to use."

"Ah-ha," Roc said. "Silly me. I never saw your mind going in that direction."

Triana chose to remain silent for the moment and wait for the computer to answer her charge. But her mind, in fact, had gone in that particular direction the moment she had learned that the vultures were pacing the ship. *Galahad* was essentially a modern *Mayflower*, delivering the human race to a new world, full of new opportunities, new challenges. But it also was a ship of peace; there were no weapons of any kind aboard.

Or were there?

The crew had been trained in every aspect of the immense ship, and they were intimately aware of every square inch of their home-away-from-home . . . with one exception.

Dr. Zimmer had insisted that the teenage crew remain in the dark about the last components to be loaded aboard before launch. Dubbed only as the Storage Sections, they occupied the majority of *Galahad*'s lowest level. Dark passageways surrounded these impenetrable vaults. The contents were a mystery, one that would not be revealed until the young explorers entered the space around Eos, now a little more than four years away.

"It's for your own good," was all that Dr. Zimmer would say when pressed. "You won't need any of it until you arrive. The best thing for you to do is simply forget that the Storage Sections even exist. Go about your days without even thinking of them."

But it was impossible to assemble a crew of the best and brightest and not expect insatiable curiosity. If Zimmer had known it would have this effect, he hadn't let it influence his decision. The crew would not know the contents until the end of the ride.

But Roc *did* know.

When it was obvious that he would not volunteer any more information, Triana stopped tapping her finger and sat back. "I'm not asking for an inventory, you understand, right? I'm only suggesting that if there's something in there that could help us defend ourselves, this might be a good time to open up."

She paused before adding, "In fact, it might be our *last* time to open up."

"We don't know what these vultures really are," Roc said. "They might be harmless."

"They might not be."

"Perhaps they intend to just look at us."

"Perhaps they intend to do more."

"You like arguing, don't you?" Roc said.

"And you don't?"

"I can't tell you what's inside the Storage Sections."

Triana let out a slow breath. "Even if it could save us."

The computer mimicked her dramatic exhale. "I'm not able to confirm or deny that anything exists within those units that might, or might not, be able to help. Humans are prone to break sworn promises; I'm not capable of that. I don't blame you for asking; in fact, I think it's rather ingenious of you to ask. But stop asking."

For the third time, silence blanketed the room. Triana waited for the stalemate to end, then accepted defeat.

"Okay. Can you think of anything we might do to protect ourselves?"

The computer seemed to consider the question for a minute. "Well, I'm sure you don't want to hear this, but the best thing to do is wait until we know more about these things. Then there might be an obvious answer. You might not need your average, everyday shoot-'em-up gun."

Triana bit her lip. She didn't like the idea of playing defensively, but couldn't see another option at the moment.

In eighty-five minutes, she realized, they might run out of options entirely.

5

The girl on the stage was quite obviously nervous, sitting on her hands, swinging her feet back and forth under the chair. Her attention swept between her friends sitting in the auditorium and the two boys sitting across from her. Both boys were going to immense pains to seem casual and comfortable, sitting back in their chairs, even leaning back on two legs from time to time; but nervous tics and laughter betrayed this facade.

Channy stood in the center of the stage and addressed the modest crowd. "This has flown by pretty fast, but now you all know how it works, so I'm sure we'll have more contestants next time. As you can see, nobody got embarrassed up here, and nobody had a massive heart attack and fell out of their chair."

She waited for the polite laughter to subside before saying, "So, thanks to a few brave souls who came forward as volunteers, we all know how easy this is. Which brings us to our final contestant this evening." She turned to the nervous girl seated next to her. "Antoinette is sixteen, was born and raised in England . . ."

Channy paused and addressed the crowd, exaggerating her British accent: "Of course, all of the coolest people on *Galahad* hail from the U.K., right?" This brought even more laughter, and a few hoots from the crowd. In the third row, Lita turned to whisper to Alexa.

"She's a natural at this, you know?"

"I'm glad she's having fun," Alexa whispered back. "She's put a lot into the whole thing."

Lita glanced around before responding. "For all of her worrying, it's not a bad turnout. Probably fifty people, wouldn't you say?"

Alexa nodded, and both girls turned their attention back to the stage.

"Antoinette is currently assigned to the Farms," Channy said. "Although she notes, 'I'm anxious to rotate out in a few weeks, because I dislike dirty hands and fingernails.'" This brought a few more chuckles from the crowd, spurred on by Channy's dramatic gestures and facial expressions. "I don't know, Antoinette, I'm sure Bon would give you a day off if you broke a nail."

Lita and Alexa joined in the laughter. Onstage, Antoinette turned a shade of red and kicked her feet a little more quickly.

"All right, let's say hello to the two very cool gentlemen to my left," Channy said. "Andrei is seventeen, comes to us from Moscow, and apparently does not believe in haircuts. He is presently on his six-week break, lucky guy, and enjoys working out and solving extreme math problems." She smiled at him. "Brains and brawn; a Mr. Galahad if I ever saw one."

She then focused on the other boy. "Next to Andrei we have Karl, a native of Düsseldorf. He is currently assigned to the kitchen crew, and enjoys Airboarding and chess. Oh, and today, believe it or not, is Karl's sixteenth birthday." There was a smattering of applause and whistles at the mention of this. "Sorry, my friend," Channy said, "but you will not automatically get the hand of Antoinette as a gift; you must earn it.

"Antoinette has chosen the simple question option. This means that she is eliminating a lot of the usual back-and-forth silliness, and is instead trusting her instincts." Channy held aloft a small index card. "She has already answered this random question, and her answer is stored on the workpad. We will have each of the gentlemen answer the same question, and then post all three on the giant vidscreen behind us. The game is simple: the young man with the answer most similar to Antoinette's will be the winner, and away they will go to a private romantic dinner, where they will get to know each other better and see if those instincts were correct."

Channy took a step toward the front of the stage and lowered her voice. "Of course, if neither of the gentlemen is even close to Antoinette's answer, then she gets to select one of them using a completely different form of instinct, if you know what I mean."

This was greeted with more hoots from the crowd, and Antoinette again went red. Andrei and Karl grinned and continued their relaxed act.

"Okay, gentlemen," Channy said with a flourish, "workpads ready. In twenty-five words or less, please answer this question: What will we find on Eos that will make it the most romantic place in the galaxy? You have two minutes. Begin."

At this cue, a crew member enabled the recorded music that Channy had selected for the Dating Game, and the soft, melodic tones filled the auditorium. The crowd began to talk within their small groups, supplying their own answers to the question, while Andrei and Karl took a moment to think before hunching over the workpads on their laps. Lita and Alexa looked at each other and giggled.

"How much you wanna bet they both say multiple moons, or something like that?" Alexa said.

"Hey, that was the first thing that popped into my head," Lita said with mock indignation. "You have a better answer?"

"No," Alexa admitted. "I only said that because it was the first thing I came up with, too." She looked up at the stage. "I think the object is to try to get into Antoinette's head and guess what *she* would say."

"But that's not right," Lita said. "If it's a game of matching instincts, then the guys should go with their own gut. Otherwise the date is already based on a lie."

"I know that, and you know that," Alexa said. "But look at those two guys. Watch the way they keep glancing at each other. I don't think they really care about Antoinette's answer; they just want to win."

Lita smiled. "I have to give Channy a lot of credit. This game is not only fun for the contestants, it's fun for us, too. Suddenly we're all analysts and relationship experts."

The music came to an end, and Channy moved back to center stage.

"All right," she said, "it's time to compare answers and see which lucky guy has earned a date with the lovely Antoinette." She turned and faced the giant vidscreen at the back of the stage. "The question was: What will we find on Eos that will make it the most romantic place in the galaxy? Let's have Andrei's answer first, please."

There was an electronic version of a drumroll before the screen flickered and the connection was made with Andrei's workpad. The crowd laughed as Channy read his response.

"Northern lights like Earth's aurora borealis, except these lights would dance in sync with the songs of the birds."

Channy put a hand on one hip and gave Andrei a critical look. "My friend, birds don't sing at night."

"They might on Eos," Andrei said with a grin. The crowd clapped its approval of his defense, and he egged them on by giving the "come on" sign with his hands.

"Riiiggghhhttt," Channy said. "Okay, you get points for creativity, but remember, the idea is to come close to the lady's answer.

Before we put her answer on the screen, let's see what Karl had to say."

She turned again to the screen and narrated. "Perpetual rainbows."

Oohs and aahs rumbled from the crowd. "Wow," Alexa said to Lita. "They really like his answer."

"Are you kidding?" Lita whispered back. "I *love* his answer!"

Alexa raised her eyebrows. "Well, if Antoinette doesn't get him, *you* should ask him out."

"I might," Lita said with a laugh.

Channy turned back to the audience. "Two excellent answers, wouldn't you say? Let's see if either of them comes close to Antoinette's choice. Are you ready?"

The crowd applauded and whistled. "Okay," Channy said, and faced the nervous girl on the stage. "Antoinette, I tried to read your face when each answer popped up on the screen. As you know, I'm pretty well tuned in to people's emotions." The crowd snickered, and she shot them a warning look that brought laughter. "Oh, it's true, we all know it." She looked back at Antoinette. "I distinctly saw a reaction, and if I'm right, it means that a certain young man from Germany will be dining with you this week."

She pointed to the vidscreen. "What will we find on Eos that will make it the most romantic place in the galaxy? May we please see the lady's answer?"

The vidscreen flickered again, went black, and then lit up with Antoinette's answer. The crowd cheered as Channy read it. "Rainbows every evening! Wow! An exact match! Karl, you're incredible!"

The crowd jumped to their feet, and the applause grew louder. On the stage, Karl stood up, walked over to Antoinette, and took her by the hand. Her face turned a deeper red, and she laughed nervously. Across the stage, even Andrei clapped and grinned.

"Oh well, the one that got away," Lita said with a sigh.

"There's always the aurora borealis guy," Alexa said. "That's romantic, too, you know."

Channy put her hand on Antoinette's shoulder and addressed the crowd. "Can I read people, or what?" She thanked everyone for coming, and announced that a second Dating Game would be forthcoming. There was more applause, and as the music swelled again, the audience turned for the doors.

Two minutes later, Channy was standing in the aisle with Lita and Alexa, beaming.

"See?" Lita said. "A major hit. You were worried for nothing."

"Could've been a few more people in the seats," Channy said.

"That won't be a problem next time," Alexa said. "Did you see the way people were talking when they left? You put on such a great show, it will be packed next month."

"Thank you," Channy said. She batted her eyes. "Anything I can do to promote love. Hopefully this inspired people to stop being so shy all the time."

"Hmm," Lita said. "Did it inspire you?"

"Maybe," Channy said, lifting her chin. "Maybe it did."

On one hand, Triana felt that it was important to hurry back to the Control Room. Another part of her brain, however, suggested that walking—and thinking—could be more beneficial. Away from people, away from the situation, she hoped to at least find clarity, if not answers.

The clock was ticking. In a little over an hour *Galahad* would plunge into a swarm of darting objects that littered the path ahead. It would be their second alien encounter since leaving Earth.

The first had almost destroyed them.

The lift doors opened onto the lower level of the ship. A left turn would take Triana toward the gym and the Airboarding track. Instead she quickly moved to the right, into the dim corridors that snaked through the Storage Sections. She was confident that she would have this portion of the ship to herself.

She paused momentarily by the large window that looked out upon the dazzling panoramic star field of the Milky Way before putting her head down and moving on.

Her thoughts skipped through a checklist of possibilities regarding their impending rendezvous with the vultures. There might be contact, a collision of sorts, and the consequences of this baffled Triana. The vultures might attack, but what form would that take? There was always the possibility that the vultures might scatter and allow *Galahad* to pass unmolested, but the Council Leader didn't think this likely.

She rounded a turn and slowed her pace, focusing to match her breathing to her steps, a technique that her dad had recommended to help her get centered during times of stress. In a flash her thoughts turned to the man who had meant so much to her.

Her memories stirred, then settled on a sun-filled afternoon, soon after her thirteenth birthday. Sitting in the passenger seat of their car, she had twisted the hair tie around her fingers, stretching it almost to the point of breaking. Her dad maneuvered the car gently along the road that wound into the foothills of the Rocky Mountains just outside of Denver. He glanced at his daughter's hands, watching her stress manifest itself in the bending and stretching of the cloth tie, a faint smile on his lips.

"Still worried?" he said, shifting the car into a lower gear as they began to climb a steep hill.

"No," she said. Then, after a pause: "Yes."

"Wanna talk about it some more?"

Triana watched the replay of her younger self, anguishing over a painful moment that time had somehow sanded away. She did remember, however, what her grumpy reply had been: "Will it change anything?"

Her dad waited before answering, using the time to glance out at the trees racing past, the afternoon sunlight dappling them as it cut through a V in the mountains. Triana always treasured their drives together, most of which were filled with warmth and laughter; many times, however, the front seat became a sanctuary, their private refuge from a confusing world, a place where they could dissect the events of the day, or whatever might be troubling the dark-haired teen.

"Your question says it all," her dad said. "Your energy is concentrated on trying to change something that is out of your control." He threw a quick glance at his daughter before looking back at the road. "There are a lot of things in our lives that we can control, and a lot that we can't. When you get wrapped up in trying to change something that is beyond your power to change, it causes frustration and despair."

Triana continued to work the hair tie, but had now begun to bite her lip. She let her father's words sink in before replying. "So what do I do?"

He took his right hand off the wheel and gently placed it over both of hers. "You stop worrying about things you can't change, and divert your energy to the things you can. One of the most powerful days of your life will be when you learn to tell the difference."

His touch had its usual calming effect. After momentarily tensing, she felt her hands relax. Her breathing slowed, and she leaned her head back against the deep cushion of the seat. She turned to look out the passenger window, taking in the rush of colors, the sharp outline of the craggy hills rising up to pierce the sky, and for a moment a feeling of gratitude replaced the stress that had eaten away at her.

Without her realizing it, the hair tie slipped from her fingers.

Now, almost four years later, Triana paused in the dim corridor of *Galahad's* lowest level and leaned her back against a wall.

The time had come to take inventory of what exactly was in her control, and what wasn't.

The ship would soon reach the contact point with the alien forms they referred to as the vultures; that was inevitable, and no amount of worrying would change that. Her reaction would have to wait until the moment their paths intersected.

Bon's attitude had shifted somewhat since forming a tenuous connection with the Cassini, yet he was often still difficult to communicate with. Again, her reaction was the only thing within her control.

The crew would be apprehensive when they found out about the vultures. That, however, was somewhat within her control because it was one of the responsibilities of leadership: managing the crew.

Her thoughts were interrupted by joyous shouts echoing through the halls, and she knew it likely was a passel of Airboarders celebrating another successful tour of the track and now on their way to the upper levels of the ship. She tapped her heel against the wall and let her mind sift through the remaining obligations of her day, all of which could wait until after the encounter with the vultures.

As she turned to make her way back toward the lift, she could feel her father's warm hand covering hers, and his calm voice: "Learn to tell the difference."

Time alone on *Galahad* was a precious commodity, and getting away from 250 crew members could be a challenge. With the crew quarters and most of the primary work and meeting facilities concentrated within the middle decks, it was no surprise that individuals would gravitate to the extreme upper and lower levels to seek escape. Many would sneak away to the lonely corridors near the Storage Sections and Spider bay in the bowels of the ship. With the dim lighting and narrow passageways—not to mention its reputation as the hideout of a maniacal stowaway early in their mission—the area was often described as spooky, and attracted only the hardiest souls.

This left the Domes as the primary getaway location. Prior to launch, noted psychologist Dr. Angela Armistead had briefed the mission's planners that *Galahad*'s young explorers would be naturally drawn to all of the domes' sensory delights, including starlight, gentle breezes—even manufactured ones—and the many smells that would remind them of open fields on Earth. Dr. Zimmer had consequently informed Bon Hartsfield to expect dozens of crew members to tromp through the farms of *Galahad* on a daily basis.

Bon understood as well as anyone, given his own upbringing, and grunted agreement.

Now, as dusk descended upon the ship, he knifed along a path that cut between one section of wheat and another of corn. As the keeper of this domain, he was intimately aware of the least-traveled pathways, and rarely had difficulty finding solitude. He could usually count on this particular route to be quiet, and had shared his secret with only one person.

He pushed aside the arm of a cornstalk that reached across the path, and there she was, sitting cross-legged on the soil in a small clearing. Beside her lay a small, portable lantern that emitted a soft glow, along with two personal water bottles, one of which she held up to him as he came to a stop.

"Thirsty?" Alexa said. Bon accepted the water and stood beside her.

She looked up through the mesh of clear panels that separated *Galahad's* food supplies from the harsh vacuum of space. "This is my favorite time of day. I love it when the lights go down and the stars turn on."

"Turn on?" Bon said.

She laughed. "Yeah, why not?" Pointing almost directly overhead, she said, "Tonight it was Arcturus that turned on first. That red one, right there."

Bon glanced up momentarily, then back at the blond girl on the ground. "It's a red giant. Probably similar to what our own sun will look like in a few billion years."

Alexa raised her eyebrows. "Yes, but that's not the good stuff."

Bon shifted his weight to his right foot. "The ancient Polynesians used it to navigate back and forth from Hawaii. Is that the good stuff?"

"No, that's the science. I'm talking about the romance. In Greek mythology, the story of Arcturus was rather sad." When Bon didn't answer, she leaned back on her elbows and stared up into space. "A story of love and jealousy. Would you like to hear it?"

"Mythology doesn't really interest me," Bon said. "There were two kinds of people in those days: those who sat around and made up stories, and those who used the stars to actually get work done."

Alexa laughed. "And there's no question which line you descended from."

A smile flickered across Bon's face. "You're right about that. I'm a farmer, from a long line of farmers. You can thank the stars for teaching my ancestors when the time was right to plant and harvest."

With a bow of her head, Alexa said, "On behalf of my silly romantic ancestors, thank you, thank you very much." She patted the ground beside her. "Have a seat; you make me nervous standing there."

Bon knelt and gently gathered an earthworm that was edging along the soil. He placed it a few feet away, then sat down. "You said in your email that you wanted to talk about something in particular tonight."

His directness never failed to catch Alexa off guard. She took a moment to collect her thoughts before looking into his face.

"I've . . . I've had another vision."

Bon studied her eyes. "You've had several, but you've never looked like this."

She nodded, and her voice fell to a whisper. "This was different."

They sat quietly for a moment. They heard distant laughter from a handful of crew members, but it was obvious they were heading in another direction and would not disturb this small clearing. Alexa fidgeted, looking upward again, toward the starlight that fought its way through the slowly dimming natural light of the dome.

"I wasn't sure I should talk to you about this. Well, talk to anyone about it, actually. But . . . but I knew you would understand better than anyone."

Bon ran a finger through the soil beside him, carving a miniature channel, before filling it in and starting again a few inches to the side. "Maybe understand isn't the right word. You have visions; I get . . . feelings. They're not the same thing."

"But you understand how difficult it is to be on the receiving end," Alexa said, and offered a smile with a shrug. "You're at least a good listener."

He kept his gaze down at the ground. "Tell me what happened."

Alexa took several deep breaths before responding. "I saw death."

Bon's head snapped up, but he let his face ask the obvious questions.

"I don't know who," Alexa said, "and I don't know how. All I know is that I saw someone's funeral." She spent a minute recounting all that she had seen in her dream, the words picking up intensity as they spilled from her. Bon listened, his finger once again scoring grooves into the dirt. When she lapsed into silence, he spoke.

"You said that people spoke at this . . . this funeral. Couldn't you make out any details, any information about the person?"

Alexa shook her head. "I heard the sounds of people talking, and I understood that it was a eulogy. I don't remember hearing anything specific." She seemed to struggle to find the best description. "You know how you overhear a conversation, and you somehow know what they're talking about without grasping any exact details? Besides, it was a dream, or a vision, or . . . something. It made sense at the time, while I was floating in the middle of it."

Bon nodded. After a moment of hesitation he said, "Do you have any guesses at all? Anything that feels like . . . I don't know, an instinct?"

A small chuckle escaped from Alexa. "Remember, that's *your* specialty. I have the visions, you have the feelings." Then, when he didn't answer, her face grew serious again, and she reached out to place a hand on his knee. "Bon . . . I'm really scared."

He looked at her hand for a moment before covering it with his own. "Yeah, I know. But not all of your visions have necessarily played out, right?"

"I don't know. Some of them have been so unrelated to anything in my experience, I don't know if they're happening or not. I mean, they *seem* to be real."

Bon raised his other hand palm up. "Right, but isn't it possible that what you're seeing are just possibilities? We barely understand even a fraction of the way the universe works, but we know that there are an infinite number of possible outcomes. It's like . . . like an infinitely long hallway, with an infinite number of doors, all with a different future. Isn't it possible that your mind is simply opening doors at random, and seeing something that might—or might not—happen?"

They both seemed to consider this, although Alexa's face betrayed skepticism. The sounds of scattered activity around the dome filtered across the fields to their isolated setting, along with the gurgle of an irrigation pump two or three rows away.

"Are we going to get wet?" Alexa said, peering through the leaves.

A wry smile worked across Bon's face. "I adjusted the system to skip this spot for another hour."

Alexa grinned back, and gave his knee a small squeeze. "Wow, it's nice to know the manager of the place."

They remained that way for a minute, taking in the sounds, the smells, the atmosphere of their oasis of solitude. Finally, Alexa removed her hand and pulled her hair behind her ears.

"I suppose you might be right. I'm not even sure what I could do, anyway. I don't think I should tell Triana." She hesitated, as if waiting for agreement. When it didn't come, she asked. "Do you?"

Bon shrugged. "What if you wait to see if it happens again? You're right; I don't know what anyone could do without more information. Maybe you'll . . . I don't know, see something else that might help."

"I'd have to go back through that same door," she said.

The gurgle of the irrigation pump was replaced by the thump of water pressure kicking up a notch. From twenty feet away they could hear water flicking across leaves. Alexa began to think that Bon's attention had been diverted back to his work until he fixed her with a look.

"Perhaps," he said, "you have some control over which door you open."

She studied his face, as an image of endless possibilities opened before her.

Gap hunched over his workstation in the Control Room, shifting back and forth between two monitors, oblivious, it seemed, to the activity going on around him. Triana twice attempted to communicate with him, but gave up; with only minutes remaining until *Galahad* streaked through the cluster of vultures, his mind was locked onto the task of determining the outcome.

The fact that there were too many unknowns in the equation didn't seem to make a difference to him.

With a sigh, he finally pushed back from his station and looked around the room to find Triana. She threw another fruitless glance at the large vidscreen before walking over to stand next to him. He seemed to understand what question her raised eyebrows implied.

"The best I can figure out," he said, "is that there are close to ten of these things out there. They're not that big, which makes them tough to nail down, and they're in constant movement. They flit around almost like moths near a light."

Triana nodded, even though this wasn't exactly new information. She knew that Gap was doing the best he could, with an enthusiasm she hadn't seen from him in a while. He recently had battled discouragement over his contributions—or his perceived lack of contributions—to the mission; in a way, for Gap the intrigue brought on by the vultures was good medicine.

Roc chimed in with his own observations. "Their wingspan is approximately one meter across, their composition is unknown, and their sense of drama is impeccable."

"Can anyone make an educated guess what will happen when we cross paths?" Triana said. "I'm hearing a lot of 'I don't know,' so how about a few cases of 'I think.'"

"I think their mission is to either check us out as we shoot by, or try to board us," Gap said.

"I agree," Roc said. "They are obviously quite advanced technologically, if they were able to spot us, plot our course, and arrange to intercept us; crashing into us would not make much sense. Ever seen a bug hit a windshield? Yuck."

Triana looked at Gap. "All right. How much time?"

"Two minutes."

With a determined step, Triana walked to her command post and punched the intercom, which fed the entire ship.

"If I could have your attention," she said, keeping her voice as calm as possible. "We have picked up some sort of escort out of the Kuiper Belt. Eight to ten objects, roughly the size of large birds. They are pacing us, and appear to want to make contact." She paused, and could only imagine the impact these words were having upon a stunned crew. Swallowing hard, she began again. "I have no idea what we can expect; maybe a jolt, maybe something more violent. But whatever it might be, it's going to happen in about one minute. Please prepare yourself."

She snapped off the intercom and wondered exactly what that

preparation would consist of. Holding on to something? Sitting down?

Roc began a countdown. "Thirty seconds to contact . . . twenty . . . ten . . ."

Triana found herself unconsciously reaching out and grasping the arm of Gap, who responded by putting one hand on her back. They both stared at the large vidscreen.

Suddenly Gap cried out. "Did you see that?"

Triana strained her eyes. "I didn't see—"

But then she did. At the extreme edges of the screen, on both sides, wispy black shapes, almost appearing to be doing cartwheels, spinning, vibrating, flew into her field of vision. They flashed briefly, a muted shade of blue-green, and then were gone.

Half a minute elapsed, with no sound from anyone, and no apparent reaction from *Galahad*. Triana gradually let go of Gap's arm. He kept his hand on the small of her back. They looked at each other without saying a word.

Finally, one of the other crew members on duty in the Control Room spoke up. "What happened? Did they miss us?"

Gap bent back over the panel before him, but it was Roc who answered.

"At the point of intercept we were able to positively identify eight of them. They are no longer registering. Wait, check that. I have one vulture, trailing us . . . now peeling off."

Triana considered this. "And the other seven?"

"I have to assume," Roc said, "that they have indeed grabbed hold of us, and are comfortably attached to the outside of our ship."

like games. As part of my programming and training, I was taught hundreds of them. I'll tell you right now, I have no use for Duck Duck Goose; I got no legs, which means I get killed every time. I'll stick with the cerebral games, thanks.

Not only do I enjoy poker, but I love the way poker's colorful language works its way into human relationships. Playing something "close to the chest," or "vest," comes from the way poker players hold their cards close so that no one else can see them. Well, it's the same with budding relationships: neither side seems to want to reveal too much to the other.

Plus you seem to always try to "keep a poker face"; you keep important information in reserve, which means you have "an ace up your sleeve"; and you never want to "tip your hand." I'm telling you, poker players and budding romances have an uncanny amount in common.

Triana and Bon have been playing a kind of poker game for months . . . and I still don't think they are ready to "lay their cards on the table."

t was late, the ship's lights had dimmed for the night, and the Dining Hall was almost empty. Triana sat in her customary spot near the back, facing the door, and picked her way through a plate of mixed vegetables. She had not eaten since breakfast, and yet found that she was forcing herself to take in the nourishment. In the four hours since their encounter with the vultures, she had been unwilling to break away from the Control Room, although no new information was forthcoming.

They had indeed picked up some uninvited guests; seven entities that they described as space vultures had apparently latched onto *Galahad*. A report from crew members indicated that one of the vultures was firmly attached to the outside of Dome 1 like a leech. Its dark color would normally have camouflaged it against the black background of space, but following Triana's warning message many of the farmworkers had been peering upward through the domes. Several gasped when a dark shape blotted out a small section of stars.

The other six could not be seen, but Roc assured Triana that they were there. He was busy programming many of the ship's external cameras to begin a sweeping scan to locate the remaining vultures.

Triana poked at a piece of carrot before opting for a hunk of green pepper. One of the last groups of crew members in the room began to clear their table and make for the door, which opened and admitted Bon. He quickly picked up a tray and filled it with fruit and vegetables, an energy block, and a cup of water, before turning and making eye contact with Triana.

She watched him hesitate, and knew what thoughts were tumbling through his mind. He would ordinarily have chosen to sit by himself, but the absence of other people in the Dining Hall would have made it rude—even by Bon's standards—to ignore her completely. With what appeared to be a resigned sigh, he carried his tray to her table.

"I can't remember the last time I ran into you here," Triana said.

"Then you must not usually come this late," he said, pulling out the chair across from her and sitting down. "I always wait until things have cleared out."

"Surprise, surprise," she said with a smirk. "You? Avoiding people?"

He fixed her with his blue eyes. "I work late. This is more convenient."

"Uh-huh." She picked up a wedge of cucumber and took a bite, then held up the remnant. "In case I haven't told you in a while, this is all delicious. You do know your stuff, I'll give you that."

He didn't respond, his usual style in dealing with compliments. Instead he concentrated on quickly eating. Triana waited a moment before changing the subject.

"Did you happen to see the blob hanging outside Dome 1?"

Bon nodded. "Not much to see. A black triangle." He took a bite from his energy bar. "What are your plans now?"

She shrugged. "It's one of the things we'll talk about in the Council meeting tomorrow. As of right now they don't seem to be doing anything. Of course, we don't know that for certain."

They sat in silence for a moment before Bon spoke up. "I suppose we could ask our friends about it."

Triana had been lifting a glass of juice to her lips. She stopped and stared at him. "You mean the Cassini."

He nodded.

She set the glass back on the table, took the napkin from her lap, and wiped her mouth. All of this allowed her to process the thoughts that were tumbling through her head.

"I guess this is as good a time as any to talk about this," she said. "I have some thoughts about your connection with the Cassini, and I'd like for you to hear me out."

She took his lack of response as permission to continue.

"I'll just come right out and say it: I'm concerned about your recent . . . fondness, I guess, for making that connection."

His eyes never left his tray. "What do you mean?"

"I mean that you seem much too eager to link up with them,

especially considering the pain that it causes. The obvious comparison would be the drug addict who needs his fix." She moved her tray to one side, clasped her hands together, and leaned forward. "I know you, and I know you'll brush that off, but think about it. The link is agonizing for you, and yet you are beginning to crave it. Talk to me; what is happening during this connection that has you so . . . addicted?"

He looked up at her. "You didn't have these concerns when I was getting the information we needed to escape the Kuiper Belt."

"Yes, I did. I shouldn't have waited this long to talk about it with you."

He set down his half-eaten bar. "The pain isn't nearly as bad as it was in the beginning."

"You mean you're building up a tolerance."

"If that's what you want to call it."

"So it won't be long until you feel nothing at all? Just a quick high, with a side of orange eyes?"

He grunted. "Listen, this conversation is ridiculous. I'm not a Cassini addict."

Triana looked back and forth between his eyes. "You're avoiding my question. What happens to you during the connection? There's obviously something that attracts you."

Bon sat back and pulled a strand of his long dark hair out of his face. "I didn't ask for this responsibility, remember? In fact, I seem to recall a time when you begged me to make contact with them. Why are you pestering me?"

"Because I—" She broke off at the sound of her own voice, surprised at how loud it had burst from her. The handful of crew members on the other side of the room looked around, then returned to their own discussion. Triana felt a flush creep into her face, embarrassed at her sudden lack of control. Bon appeared to study her.

"You mentioned responsibility," she said in a calmer voice. "Well, don't forget that I have a few myself, including the well-being of the crew. That includes you. If I have concerns over your mental connection with an alien force, it's my duty to discuss those with you, and if I feel it's necessary, make any command decision that I believe is required."

A sneer spread across Bon's face. "I see you're able to recite the manual."

Triana choked off the impulse to lash back at him. She felt anger rising in her, reminiscent of the emotions he had brought out of her for so long, emotions that had lain dormant recently. For months she had battled confused thoughts about Bon, drifting back and forth between anger, frustration, and . . .

And what? Could she even put a name to all of the emotions he triggered? If he irritated her so much, why did she sometimes find herself thinking about that one moment, sealed in her memory, when they had kissed? Why during Council meetings did she keep her gaze on him longer than normal? Why did his new association with Alexa cause an unfamiliar ache?

She let his words settle a moment, then pushed back her chair and stood. Gathering her tray and her composure, she said, "We're essentially out of the Kuiper Belt. If we mutually agree that another connection is necessary for the safety of the ship, it will happen. If not, it won't. Any questions?"

He looked up at her, his eyes cold, and slowly shook his head.

"Good," she said. "See you at the meeting."

The images on the Rec Room wall had been dialed in by a crew member from South America. The montage included scenes from the Amazon, complete with the subtle soundtrack of jungle life, followed by the sweeping majesty of the Andes. That image would dissolve into a video clip of a crowded beach in Rio, then shift to the wonder of Machu Picchu. The backdrop was different each evening, depending upon whose turn came up in rotation.

Channy barely noticed. Of the thirteen people who had attended Game Night, all but three had said good night and trundled off to bed. Besides Channy, that left Ariel Morgan and Taresh. Under normal circumstances, Channy would have enjoyed having Ariel to chat with; the spark plug from Australia was always good for a laugh because of her sarcastic wit. But tonight Channy wanted more than anything to spend a few minutes alone with Taresh. The fact that he had also stayed gave her hope that he felt the same way.

Or, more likely, he wanted to respond to her email. Channy was desperate to hear his reaction. Or was she? He had not sent a reply; did that mean he was angry about it? Was he embarrassed by it?

Was it possible that he loved it, and couldn't wait to tell her?

The answer would have to wait, because Ariel seemed to be in no mood to leave the Rec Room. She perched on the end of a table and dangled her feet over the side, a wide grin covering her face.

"I have a great idea," she said. "Airboarding."

Channy lowered her chin and raised her eyes. "What? Now?"

"Of course! We're obviously the diehards in this party group. If the others want to go to bed, fine. But we should go make a few turns while the adrenaline is still pumping."

"Uh, my adrenaline has just about sputtered," Channy said, looking at Taresh for some backup.

He was sitting against the wall, tipped back on his chair's rear legs. A look of alarm streaked across his face.

"Uh . . ." He looked between Channy and Ariel, not sure which of the two required his answer. "I don't know, I'm a little tired . . . I guess."

"Oh, come on," Ariel said, swatting at one of his legs. "What's thirty minutes? It'll be fun."

"I've only done it twice," Channy said. "And I've been up since five this morning, you know, in the gym. I think I'd like to be completely rested when I—"

"Of all people," Ariel said with a comic scowl. "I would have thought you'd be with me on this." She glanced back at Taresh. "And your excuse? You weren't in the gym at five, were you?"

Taresh offered a faint smile. "If I said that I was, would I still have to go Airboarding?"

Channy could barely suppress the grin that forced itself onto her face. She studied Taresh, suddenly aware of a glint in his rich brown eyes that she hadn't noticed before. The look he leveled at Ariel was at once both challenging and good-spirited, and when he broke that link to fix his gaze upon Channy, she felt a catch in her breath. His smile broadened and seemed to imply that the two of them were somehow conspirators, partners in a private game.

Now, more than ever, she longed to be alone with him; if that meant being obvious to others, it was worth the attention and ribbing.

"Ariel," she said, "you should go ahead without us. I think I just want to relax here for a few minutes. Besides, there's something I'd like to talk to Taresh about, anyway."

The girl from Australia sat silently for a moment, then nodded. "Okay, I see." She stood up and pushed back her chair. "If you wanted to be alone, you should have just said so." As she strolled toward the door she added, "You kids be good."

The door closed behind her, and Taresh eyed Channy. "I hope she doesn't think we're rude. I'm just really not in the mood for boarding this late."

"I don't think she thinks that," Channy said. She lowered her eyes and her voice grew soft. "Of course, she only has to mention this once or twice and people might start talking about us."

Taresh remained motionless, his chair still propped against

the wall. His face was impassive. "I don't know what they would have to say. We haven't done anything. You simply said that you wanted to talk with me about something, right?"

"Right. But you know how people are."

A touch of playfulness coated his voice. "Well, I know how *you* are."

She grinned, and her gaze darted up to briefly meet his before dropping again. She felt her pulse increase and a flush dance across her face. She considered and then rejected several possible replies to his comment; she didn't necessarily like the fact that he might think of her as a gossip, but at the same time she enjoyed the attention he was paying to her. How would it look if she corrected him, especially when they both knew that what he'd said was true?

Then, in a heartbeat, her giddiness turned to alarm when he said, "So, you wanted to talk with me alone. Is it about your email?"

His manner had not changed, the tone of his voice was steady, and he still appeared relaxed as he leaned back in his chair. Channy wished that she was able to project the same image of ease, and yet at the moment every signal she gave off was dripping with tension. She knew that every instant she waited to respond to his question only added to the awkwardness of the situation.

She scrambled for something that would strike a balance between a lighthearted reply and one that would not completely dismiss what she had sent as frivolous. Why, she wondered, hadn't she hit Delete instead of Send?

As if to soften her distress, Taresh finally brought his chair back down to all four legs, then leaned forward with his hands resting on his knees. He gave her a sympathetic look.

"For what it's worth," he said, "I feel like you're someone special, too."

Channy felt a rush of air escape from her chest, and only then realized that she had been holding her breath. "Really?" was all that she could manage to say.

Taresh nodded. "I do. All of your responsibilities, and yet you keep everything so . . . I don't know, so loose. You're always laughing, always having fun. It makes it fun to be around you. So, yeah, I think you're someone special."

"Oh," Channy said. She quickly tried to digest what he was saying. It certainly was not what she had in mind when it came to being "special." Was he being coy? Was he guarding his feelings? Did he really only think of her as special in that way, or did he harbor other feelings as well? She couldn't read him well enough to know.

It dawned on her that since he had broached the subject, she had managed to say all of two words: Really and Oh.

"Well," she said, attempting to sound as relaxed as possible, "that's very sweet of you to say. I try to have fun, you know? Everyone's under a lot of stress, and I think it's important to have a release, more than just a workout in the gym, right? I know we all have different ways of blowing off steam, and for some people it's running on the treadmill, and for others it's doing something completely different, like reading, or just sitting up in the domes watching the stars, kind of like meditating, I guess. I like to laugh, and so . . ."

With a start she realized that she had gone from saying nothing at all to babbling uncontrollably. Taresh was staring at her, his eyes wide, trying to take in everything that she was saying. He nodded politely.

Channy couldn't recall ever feeling so clumsy. Her years of training in gymnastics, her grace and balance in dance class, her natural charm in front of large groups . . . all of it had deserted her. She twisted her hands together.

And yet, from somewhere deep inside, she at last tapped into a reservoir of courage. Swallowing hard, she reached across and laid a hand on his knee. "Okay, so I'm not very good at this, all right?"

Taresh remained silent, either unsure of her direction, or unable to think of a way to make it easier for her.

"I know I talk a big game when it comes to romance on this ship," she said, chuckling. "I know that I have developed a reputation as a bit of a Cupid character, or something like that. And I know that I tend to stick my nose into other people's business on a regular basis.

"But I think you're finding out firsthand that I'm really not all that good at this kind of stuff. I'm sorry if my email made you . . . uncomfortable." Taresh began to shake his head, but she kept going. "I'm not trying to put you on the spot, or anything like that. I just thought it was important that I share those thoughts with you, that's all."

She paused, then slowly pulled her hand off his knee. "I don't expect you to respond, and I certainly don't expect you to automatically feel the way I do. I . . . I just wanted you to know that, even though we don't know each other all that well, that I think you're pretty special. That's all. And that maybe . . . well, maybe we could spend some time getting to know each other."

By the end her voice had dropped, and was barely above a whisper. She had broken eye contact, and now stared at the floor between them.

Silent seconds passed before Taresh reached out and slowly rubbed the back of her hand, a gesture that Channy couldn't decipher. When he spoke, his voice was soft and gentle.

"I didn't mean to dismiss anything you said in your email, Channy. I appreciate everything you wrote to me, and everything you've said tonight, too. I guess I just don't know exactly what to say. I mean . . ." He paused. "I do think you're a special person, and I really do enjoy the time we spend together. Any other feelings I might have . . ."

She kept her gaze on the floor, until he eventually finished his sentence.

"I just have to think about everything, that's all. There are things in my life that are . . . complicated. It doesn't mean that I'm not attracted to you, or that I don't like being with you. It's just complicated, that's all."

"I understand," she said.

He smiled, and used his index finger to raise her face to meet his. "No," he said, "you couldn't understand, actually. But hopefully I'll be able to explain it to you soon. In the meantime, can we do what you requested, and just get to know each other a little better?"

She felt tears begin to collect in her eyes, and willed them away. "Yes, of course," she said. "I think that would be perfect."

have finished my study of great poetry and music, and have reached the conclusion that falling in love shaves off about twenty percent of your IQ and makes you miserable."

Triana set down her pen and looked at Roc's glowing sensor. "What are you talking about?"

"It's true," the computer said. "Pick up any book of poetry or listen to any popular music, and chances are the author has either lost his marbles or wants to curl up in a ball and suck his thumb. Losing one's marbles, by the way, is an old expression that means going slightly insane."

"I know the expression."

"Not only that," Roc added, "but the romanticizing of love leads to ridiculous scientific conclusions."

"Such as . . . ?"

"Such as the lyric 'love makes the world go round.' Gravitational forces, while relatively weak in the scheme of things, are unaffected by human emotions."

"Right," Triana said.

"And when Romeo says to Juliet, 'with love's light wings did I o'er-perch these walls,' we have a breakdown in the laws of physics, all because of this one emotion."

"This is quite a study you've completed. Any particular reason you took this on?"

"My never-ending attempt to understand the human creature," Roc said. "So much of your lives is built around your obsession with love, and yet it makes you loony. You have other emotions, some of them very powerful, but they don't come close to making you do so many dumb things."

A scowl worked its way onto Triana's face. "Have you been eavesdropping on people again?"

"What an insulting thing to suggest."

"Well, have you?"

"It's not eavesdropping, it's research. How can I assist you if I don't completely understand you? Next I'm going to study kissing, which strikes me as a very poor form of communication. Not to mention unhygienic. Yuck."

Triana sighed. "It's late, and I'd like to finish this journal entry before bed. Is there something important you wanted to discuss?"

"I know you wanted an update on our little vulture pals," Roc said. "Can't seem to get a clear picture of them, but I still believe we have seven of them stuck to the skin of the ship."

"We're going to talk about that during our Council meeting in the morning," Triana said. "I think we need to go out and take a look, don't you?"

"Aye, Cap'n, I agree. An EVA."

Triana nodded. "In the meeting I'll need your help with explaining it. Anything else tonight?"

"Besides being a research specialist and budding expert on the human condition, I'm also a mailman. You have a new video message. Good night, Tree."

The announcement caught her off guard for a moment before she realized that it had to be another message from Dr. Zimmer.

The nonchalant manner in which Roc had mentioned it almost struck Triana as funny. She picked up her pen and tapped it against the journal that lay open on the desk before her.

Dr. Zimmer had been more to Triana than just the project director; he had been an advisor, a confidant, a surrogate father of sorts. He had quickly recognized the depth of the teenage girl from Colorado, and had taken on the responsibility of nurturing her throughout *Galahad's* training period. No one, with the lone exception of her real father, had ever understood Triana as well, nor had ever known quite how to communicate with her when it came to personal feelings. Dr. Zimmer had forged a unique bond with her, an affection that was rarely acknowledged verbally, yet was genuine nonetheless.

He had died shortly after *Galahad's* launch. However, in his final days he had recorded a variety of private messages for her, and she never knew when one would show up in her in-box. She looked forward to them, not only because of her affection for the man but because each one gave her some insight into human relations that stimulated her intellectually and emotionally. Dr. Zimmer provided a parental connection and influence that she dearly missed.

She chose to finish her thoughts on the night's journal entry before opening the message.

I try my best to keep my personal feelings from interfering with my responsibilities as the Council Leader. But my dealings with Bon really make that a challenge. When I argue with him over the translator, how much of that is really for the good of the ship—and Bon—and how much of it is my own frustration with him? Am I trying to punish him somehow for not showing more interest in me? Am I acting like a jealous lover because he now seems to have found a

connection with Alexa? Or am I right to make the decisions
I have, and my emotions are simply causing me to second-
guess everything?

Triana rested her head on her fist and contemplated adding
more about Bon, but decided that this was enough. The idea that
her actions were being motivated in large part by her emotions
had not occurred to her until she sat down to journal, and it produced a sick feeling in her stomach. Writing it down, however,
had helped; now that it was spoken, more or less, it could be
dealt with.

One final issue, however, demanded her attention.

Maybe it's because it happened so fast, or maybe it's because
they haven't really done anything, but I am starting to wonder why I haven't felt more of a sense of urgency over the
vultures. Have we been through so much, so quickly, that
now something that once would have astonished us is treated
so casually? There are seven alien entities attached to our
ship, and yet no one seems to be panicking . . . or even worrying that much, it seems. Now, tonight, I am beginning to
feel like that's a dangerous mind-set to have. Yes, they're
relatively small, but these things are potentially more dangerous than anything else we've encountered so far. I have
decided to announce at tomorrow's Council meeting that
we will immediately get out there and investigate, and, if
necessary, remove them. Almost no need to ask for volunteers, because I know without a doubt that Gap will insist on
going. And, honestly, I wouldn't want anyone else doing it.

As with most of her entries, she kept it shorter than she normally would have preferred. Paper was a precious commodity
on *Galahad,* and her bound journals constituted a large portion

of the personal items she had been allowed to bring on the journey. Still, it felt good to put her thoughts onto the pages.

She stood and stretched, then filled a cup with water. It was close to midnight, and the next day would be extremely taxing. Yet there was no way she could go to bed without watching Dr. Zimmer's message.

At the sight of his face she felt a sting in her heart. She realized that it was easy to get caught up in the day-to-day activities of running the ship, and to sometimes forget about the life that she had left behind. But one look into the eyes of her mentor brought everything home again in a flash. It stirred memories not only of Dr. Zimmer but of her dad as well.

The scientist was putting on his best face, given his condition during the recording. Bhaktul's disease had begun to systematically ravage the man, and would eventually take him completely. For now he summoned a smile, the lines around his eyes crinkling. Triana recalled his previous message to her, and his observation that she would age and mature throughout the course of their journey, and yet he would not change; he was frozen in time in both her memory and these video clips.

"Hello to you, my little interstellar traveler," he said. "Oh, what I wouldn't give to be there with you, to see the miracle of creation in its purest form, so unlike the artificial world we have built around us here on Earth.

"I trust that you are healthy and happy. After my last recording I realized that I was so focused on speaking to you that I neglected to have you pass along my best wishes to the Council, and to the rest of the crew. Please let them know that they are in my thoughts."

He shifted slightly in his chair, and Triana could sense the discomfort that he tried so hard to disguise; she knew him too well.

"Since Roc has seen fit to deliver this next message, I conclude that you have safely emerged from the Kuiper Belt and are now entering a fairly empty stretch of space. Empty, at least, compared to what you've just experienced."

Triana softly chuckled. He could never have imagined—nor, for that matter, could any of the other scientists and astronomers on Earth—just how treacherous the Kuiper Belt really was.

"I would also imagine," he continued, "that everyone on board has pretty much settled into a routine by now. Oh, I'm sure there are some grumblings and disagreements, but hopefully nothing that you can't handle."

Again, Triana smiled, thinking of the crisis situation with the crew that had been narrowly averted just weeks earlier.

"I think it's important, Tree, that you're prepared for the additional stresses that are coming as a result of the natural connections that are taking place right now." Dr. Zimmer paused, looked down for a moment, and then laughed. "Listen to me, I sound like such a clinical scientist. By 'natural connections' I'm obviously referring to the personal relationships that are starting and, unfortunately, ending. Sorry, the vocabulary of a lifelong bachelor can sometimes be a little . . . cold and emotionless.

"But I'm sure you know exactly what I'm talking about. You yourself have perhaps felt some of this stress, and if so, you probably find that it often gets in the way of rational thought. I simply want you to understand that it's okay, you're not the first one to experience it, and you certainly won't be the last."

Triana felt a lump in her throat. Her father never really had the chance to have much of a talk with her about boys, and now Dr. Zimmer was doing his best to touch on something that not only made him feel uncomfortable, but was something in which he knew he lacked much personal experience. It was touching to the teenage girl, and made her love the man even more. His rambling, stumbling approach to discussing teen angst was adorable to her.

"What makes it even more difficult, however, is the fact that all 251 of you are confined to such a small space, relatively speaking. As these relationships follow their normal course, there will be friction and ultimately hurt feelings. Again, I'm no expert, but I would highly encourage you, as the Council Leader, to keep your eyes open for any signs that it's affecting the safety and performance of the crew. It's sad but true that not all relationships will work out. Talking about it will help, I know that. I would even go so far as to recommend group meetings to allow people to share their feelings, if necessary, to let them know they're not alone with the quickly changing emotions they're experiencing."

Triana had never considered this, but found herself nodding. She wondered if she would be able to discuss her topsy-turvy feelings.

"But regardless of how these things work out, the ultimate responsibility of every crew member is to the safety of the ship and the success of the mission. It's difficult enough to find life balance here on Earth and to function normally during times of stress; in your situation, it can be critical.

"I suppose what I'm trying to say, Tree, is that all of us working on the *Galahad* mission knew that you kids were going to be facing conditions that are much more difficult than the average teenager would ever deal with, both physically and emotionally. I spent many hours talking with Dr. Armistead about this, and she was quite blunt. As she told me, the fact that you were specially selected through a vigorous process really wouldn't have any effect on the emotional aspect; kids, even amazing kids like you, are still kids, and your emotional evolution was determined a long, long time ago."

He paused, and what seemed to be a spasm of pain rippled through his face. He turned to one side and coughed into a handkerchief, and when he faced the camera again Triana was sure that she saw tears in his eyes. She was sure that this time they were tears of pain. He knew that he didn't have much time left, and yet he was determined to spend that time offering every bit of wisdom and support that he could to the kids who had captured his heart—and his imagination—for the last years of his life.

"Tree, before I let you go," he said, "I wanted to say something about the news I dropped on you last time. I'm talking, of course, about the child that I never told you about."

He paused again, and Triana involuntarily sat forward. During his last recorded message to her, Dr. Zimmer had stunned the Council Leader by announcing that he had fathered a child, and—most shocking of all—that child was a crew member on *Galahad*. His or her identity was a mystery.

"A part of me questions why I felt the need to tell you anything," the scientist said. He rubbed a hand over weary eyes. "You never would have known. For that matter—" He broke off and stared from the screen. "My child doesn't even know, and believes their natural father to have died before the birth. The mother and I thought this would be best, a decision that I have also questioned many, many times since then. There were times that I often thought about showing up at the door, and introducing myself to my only child. I planned the conversation in my head a thousand times, played it out over and over again, imagining their face as I broke the news. But . . . I never had the nerve.

"And, eventually, a stepfather came into the picture. I couldn't disrupt the household after that, and felt that I had missed out on my chance to get to know them."

Dr. Zimmer again rubbed his forehead. "Then, of course, I began the *Galahad* project, which consumed my life. I reached out to the mother and suggested that there could be a spot on board. She was hesitant at first, but realized that it was a chance to save her child's life. She agreed."

At this point a concerned look spread across his face. "I don't need to point this out, but I want you to know that this crew member has every right to be aboard. Yes, there was favoritism shown, I will not deny that; but at the same time, I believe in my heart that they could have easily been accepted anyway. They are just as qualified and gifted as any other person on the ship. I don't want you to think a spot was taken by someone who shouldn't be there."

He looked down, obviously ashamed at not only his actions from the past but his passionate plea for Triana to somehow accept this mystery crew member. When he spoke again, his voice was barely above a whisper.

"I don't know why I feel it's so important for you to know that, but . . . but I have thought a great deal about it since I first told you. I know you, Triana, and I know that deep down you always wanted me to be proud of you, and to feel worthy." He looked up again. "I suppose I want the same thing."

There was silence for a long time. Triana sensed what was coming, and raised her hand to place it on the vidscreen, a split second before Dr. Zimmer did the same.

grin stretched across Channy's face. She sat cross-legged, her back against the curved wall in the hallway outside the Conference Room. The object of her delight was Iris, the cat that had become the unofficial mascot of the ship, rescued from a small metallic pod orbiting Titan, Saturn's largest moon. Channy could often be found escorting Iris to the domes, where the cat would spend many happy hours exploring the fields and rolling in the dirt.

At the moment she lay sprawled across the hallway, her legs stretched out, her eyes mostly closed but her tail giving away her attentive state by twitching at the very end. Crew members rounding the turn laughed as they stepped over the animal, and many of them stopped to either rub her belly or delight her with a quick scratch behind the ears. Iris was soaking up the attention, and Channy was sure that was why the cat had positioned herself as she had; there was no getting around her without some form of acknowledgment.

"She's a bigger ham than you," Channy heard someone say with a chuckle, and looked up to see Gap leaning against the wall with his arms crossed. "And," he added, "I never would have thought that possible."

Channy looked back at the cat. "She is an affection hog, isn't she? It's almost like people have to pay a bit of a toll to cross over her. One rub or scratch per person."

As if she recognized that she was again the center of attention, Iris sat up and began one of her many daily bathing routines. She licked at one paw and rubbed the side of her head with it, her eyes closed, and a soft purring sound rolled from her throat.

"I take it we're the first to arrive for the meeting," Gap said. When Channy nodded, he added, "Lots to talk about, too. I'm anxious to hear what Triana wants to do about the vultures."

Channy gave a noticeable shudder at the word. "I'm creeped out to think about them stuck to the ship. Can't we get rid of them?"

Gap shrugged. "Probably. Oh, and I'll bet we talk about your Dating Game. I heard it was a smash hit. Congrats to you."

"Thank you. You never had a doubt, did you?"

"No, but I heard that you did," Gap said. "What's next on the agenda for you?"

"Ugh, nothing right now. I want to savor the success of the Dating Game before I worry about anything else. You?"

Gap slid down the wall to sit next to her and rubbed a hand through his hair. "The most exciting thing in my life today is getting this cut. I'm a shaggy dog. I need to go see Jenner and have him chop it off."

Channy laughed. "I swear you get more haircuts than anyone else on board. Besides, it doesn't look bad to me. Trying to impress someone?"

"Right."

"Speaking of which, what's going on with you and Hannah?"

A cloud passed over Gap's face, and Channy quickly continued. "I mean, if you don't want to talk about it, I understand. But you two were so cute together, and . . ." She trailed off.

"I think the world of Hannah," Gap said, nodding at two crew members who strolled past and briefly stopped to pet Iris before continuing down the hall. "But she seems to need her space right now."

"Have you tried talking with her?"

"Yeah, I tried." Gap realized he was saying more than he intended; Channy had a way of pulling that out of people without much effort. He turned to her and smiled. "Enough about me. What's going on with you? I hear you're part of a games group in the evenings. How come you haven't said anything about that?"

He noticed a momentary look of panic that streaked across her face before she recovered with her usual grin. "Oh," she said, "it's just a few people that get together once in a while. I thought you knew."

In a flash Gap thought of all the times Channy had needled him about his love life, and decided this was the perfect time for some payback. He kept an innocent look on his face as he said, "No, this is the first you've mentioned it. Anyone I know in the group? Maybe I should drop by and play sometime, eh?"

The anxious look on her face lingered a bit longer this time, and he could tell that she was weighing her response.

"Um . . . well, you probably know some of them," she finally said. "I'm not sure there's really enough room right now. You know," she added quickly, "you have to have an even number for so many of the games. Partners and stuff, right?"

He nodded in understanding. "Of course. Well, if someone can't make it, I would love to sit in, okay?"

She smiled again, obviously relieved to have dodged him. "Sure."

Gap had to get in one more shot. "My friend Taresh told me about it, so maybe I'll come with him sometime and just watch."

He had to stifle a laugh when she almost choked. The timing was perfect, however; before she could reply they looked up to see Triana and Lita approaching from their left, while Bon briskly walked up from the right.

"Another hallway meeting?" Lita said. "I'm starting to think we might get more done out here than in the Conference Room." She kneeled down and gave Iris a scratch on the chin; the cat responded by closing her eyes and once again stretching out across the carpeted floor.

"As much as I enjoy the relaxed atmosphere of the hall, let's go ahead and move inside and get started," Triana said. "I assume that Iris is joining us."

Channy, who appeared to have recovered from Gap's comments, rubbed the cat's belly a few times, then scooped her up. "If she gets antsy I'll have Kylie stop by and take her up to the domes."

The five Council members took their seats around the conference table. Triana opened her workpad, scanned her notes, then laced her fingers together and addressed the room.

"Before we get down to the serious business at hand, I wanted to acknowledge a few things. Channy, I apologize for missing the Dating Game. As you know by now, we had a bit of drama to deal with in the Control Room."

Channy waved her hand. "Yes, I know how much you were dying to join us." There were chuckles from around the table, including Triana's own guilty laugh. "I almost believed you invented these new creatures just to get out of attending, actually."

"Well," Triana said, "I just wanted to congratulate you on another successful social event. I've heard rave reviews from Lita and a couple of other people. Thank you for your hard work in keeping the crew entertained. Honestly, I don't take that lightly, and I'm grateful to have you on our team."

Channy looked touched. "Thank you, Tree."

Triana turned her attention to the opposite end of the table. "And I want to also acknowledge you, Bon, for the sacrifices you've made—physically and emotionally—in helping to lead us out of the Kuiper Belt. I know that your connections with the

Cassini are not very pleasant, but your links provided us with a safe path to follow. So, thank you."

There were assorted words of agreement from the other Council members. Bon looked uncomfortable.

"You . . . um, you're welcome," he said, and cast his gaze down at the table. Triana knew that attention was always the last thing he wanted; she punched a key on her workpad and redirected the conversation.

"But although we are out of the danger zone with the Kuiper Belt, it would seem we have a whole new issue to deal with. By now you all know that we have picked up some unexpected passengers. I'll let Roc fill you in with the latest information."

"They're icky," the computer said. "That's my latest information."

Gap leaned forward. "Have you been able to get a close-up look with one of the exterior cameras?"

"No, they're in awkward places, and our cameras are set to scan outward, not so much inward. But one of them is clamped onto Dome 1, so we had a crew member scramble up onto a maintenance catwalk and get close enough to snap some shots. Icky."

"Why do you say that?" Channy said.

"Ever seen the suction side of a snail, or octopus tentacle?" the computer said. "Those things give me the creeps. Blegh."

Triana steered the conversation back to business. "A few more pertinent details, please."

"Seven alien entities," Roc said. "They have extraordinary maneuvering capabilities, they can accelerate to remarkable speed in the wink of an eye, they can turn on a dime—you guys wouldn't know that expression, since you're part of the postcurrency generation—but trust me, it means we could never outrun or dodge them.

"As of right now we can only guess as to their makeup, including their source of energy, their guidance systems, and the sticky stuff that keeps them glued to the skin of our ship."

"Okay—" Triana said before Roc interrupted her.

"Wait, one more thing. I know I called them vultures earlier, and if you really like that name, you're welcome to keep using it. But I'll tell you right now that what they really act like are parasites."

Channy grimaced. "Parasites?"

"The official definition means 'an organism that lives in, on, or around another organism for the sake of feeding, without benefiting or killing the host.' From the ancient Greek *parasitos,* which meant 'one who eats at another's table.' How's that for detail?"

"Feeding?" Channy said.

"Well," Roc said, "so they haven't started feeding on us or anything . . . yet. But they have suctioned themselves onto the ship like a copepod on a shark. So, yes, I am more inclined to call them parasites than vultures. They must want something."

This induced silence from *Galahad*'s Council. Triana looked around and saw each of them considering this last comment.

"I've discussed this with Roc," she finally said, "and I think the obvious answer is an EVA."

Channy blinked. "An EVA? Extra vehicle something?"

"Extravehicular activity," Roc piped in. "What used to be known as a space walk."

Gap said, "I'm assuming that this would be in a Spider, right? So we go out and either shoo these things away, or . . ."

Lita fixed him with a look. "Or what? Kill them?"

"I'm not sure that sweeping them off the ship with a broom would do much good," Gap said. "What would prevent them from glomming right back on again?"

Lita's voice crept higher. "You think we should kill them?"

"We don't even know if they're alive," Gap said. "We have no idea what these things are."

"I agree," Lita said. "That's why I'm not in favor of just automatically destroying them. We don't know that they mean us harm, do we?"

"We don't know that they don't, either," Gap said. "But there's another possibility, too."

"Which is?"

"I go out in one of the Spiders, grab one, and bring it back for us to study."

Channy let out a groan. "You want to bring one of those things into the ship? Are you kidding me?"

Gap looked at Lita and then Triana. "I think we have some sort of . . . I don't know, a container, or something, that we could put it in. Don't we?"

Lita's expression brightened. "That's right, we do. It's perfect, because it can actually simulate the conditions of space." She turned to Triana. "Okay, if we're talking about capturing one, I think that's a great idea. Think of the knowledge we could gain from this."

Channy cut in. "Think of the danger."

"Of course there's a risk," Lita said. "But there's also a risk if we just leave them out there and don't learn anything about them."

"I'm with Roc," Channy said. "They're gross, and we shouldn't bring them inside."

"I used the word 'icky,'" the computer said, "but I vote for bagging one. As long as I don't have to touch it."

Lita said, "Tree, this is an amazing learning opportunity for us. We might actually get to study an alien life form."

"What if it's not life?" Channy said. "What if it's just a killing machine?"

"That's a little dramatic, isn't it?"

"How do we know?"

"If I had a head, I'd have a headache by now," Roc said. "Can someone turn a hose on these two?"

"Wait a minute," Triana said. "Everyone take a breath." She waited until she had the Council's attention, then leaned back in her chair. "Here's what we know: these parasites, or vultures, or whatever, can outmaneuver us, and can outrace us. They are either programmed to attach to us, or have some form of intelligence—if they're alive—that has them curious about us, and they have chosen to hitch a ride. They have been clamped aboard the ship for . . ." She looked at the clock on one of the room's vidscreens. "For about sixteen hours. And in that time they haven't moved, they haven't eaten their way into the ship; they haven't done anything that we can tell.

"Here's what we *don't* know: whether they're sentient beings, whether they're simple life forms, or whether they're programmed machines." Here she paused and looked at the faces staring back at her. "And, we don't know what they want. So, I think picking one up would at least allow us to find out what they are, and might help us figure out that last part: what they want."

There was silence for a full minute. Triana bit her lip and, for no reason she could think of, looked down the table at Bon. He was staring back at her. For a moment he seemed completely unreadable, as if unwilling to offer any feedback whatsoever. Then, barely perceptible, he gave a slight nod.

"Our mission is not necessarily one of exploration," she said. "Our assignment is to safely carry our knowledge and our history to a new world, to start over. To save our species, really.

"And yet, we're human; we are creatures of discovery. Through the years our path has been a difficult one because we chose to make it that way. We have never taken the easy route, and when we've been confronted by the unknown, it quickly becomes our task to make it known."

She paused a moment, then, tapping her finger on the table, said, "Now we're confronted with a new mystery. These things, whatever they are, made the first move. I believe the next move is ours."

A grin spread across Gap's face. "That's great. When do I go?"

"I would think as soon as possible," Triana said. "We don't know what they're doing out there, and I really don't like playing defensively."

"Someone should probably go with him," Lita said. "I'll go."

Triana shook her head. "No, I won't have two Council members out there at the same time. But I think someone from the Medical Department might be a good idea."

Lita looked thoughtful. "Either Alexa or Mira. Mira's a bit of a go-getter."

"And I think Alexa has had enough excitement for a while," Triana said. "Please talk with Mira and get her up to speed." She turned back to Gap. "Work with Roc on setting up your plan, and let's shoot for tomorrow morning."

10

You never visit me in my office," Alexa said, staring out of the large picture window near Bon's desk. Her attention was captured by a small tractor that pulled a flat cart through Dome 1. The cart was laden with what appeared to be bushels of bright red fruit, perhaps strawberries. As she watched, the driver maneuvered a tight turn, then backed the cart up to a loading dock staffed by half a dozen other farmworkers. In seconds the team went to work, lifting the bushels from the cart in a synchronized system that almost resembled military drill precision.

She turned around and leaned on the glass. "No comment?"

Bon stood behind his desk, jabbing at his keyboard. "I try to avoid hospitals at all times. It has nothing to do with you."

"If you say so."

He glanced up from his work. "Besides, I thought you liked it up here."

"Oh, I do. I just thought it would be nice for you to stop by every once in a while, just to say hi."

"Just to say hi?"

Alexa grinned. "Yeah, well, I guess that's not really your nature, is it? Okay, never mind." She nodded toward the door. "C'mon, let's walk."

They left the office and made their way down the path that would take them into Dome 2. Neither spoke until they emerged under the canopy of artificial sunlight that simulated early afternoon. A rich medley of smells greeted them, a combination of citrus from the nearest crop and freshly tilled soil from the adjoining lot. Alexa found herself inhaling deeply, enjoying the infusion of natural odors after another morning spent working in recycled air. She rubbed her bare arms, feeling a light coating of moisture from the mist of nearby irrigation.

Bon steered them toward a bench that sat in the shade of some sprawling orange trees.

"Where is everyone?" Alexa said, noting just a few farmworkers scattered in the vicinity. "Usually there're more people wandering around up here on their breaks."

"They're all piled into Dome 1," Bon said. "That's where the show is."

"The show?"

"That thing stuck on the outside of the dome."

"Oh," Alexa said, and felt a shiver flash through her. The mere mention of the alien object attached to the ship ushered in a dark sensation, a feeling of dread.

Bon sat down next to her on the bench. "Something wrong?"

She looked past him, her eyes focusing on nothing, and it took a moment for her to answer. "I don't know. I get a strange feeling about those things." She shook her head and tried to smile at him. "It's creepy just thinking about them stuck to the ship like that."

"Well, you might get to see one up close and personal pretty soon. Gap is going to try to catch one and bring it into Sick House for you guys to study."

The heavy sense of dread again shook Alexa; she immediately identified it this time as foreboding. She pressed Bon for more details, and he shared what he knew.

"Lita is very excited about the chance to examine it," he concluded, leaning forward, his elbows on his knees. "No doubt you'll be in the middle of it."

Alexa nodded slowly. "As I should be. I don't know why I feel like this." She attempted another smile. "It's probably nothing. Like I said, just creepy, that's all."

They sat in silence for a minute, taking in the sounds and smells of the farm, before she spoke again. "Is this one of those occasions where you might check in with the Cassini?"

Bon grimaced. "Apparently that's a subject for debate." He recounted most of his conversation with Triana.

"So she thinks you're addicted, is that it?" Alexa said.

"That about sums it up."

"And . . ." Alexa hesitated, then pressed on. "Are you?"

Bon turned to look at her. "I expect that from her, not from you."

She sank back from his glare. "Don't get angry. It's a fair question. Remember who you're talking to here."

He stood up and paced a few steps, one hand running through his hair. With his back to her he said, "I'll tell you the same thing I told Triana: I didn't ask for this. I was chosen."

Alexa recoiled at this. "Chosen? So now you've been chosen? You've never said that before."

"Well, isn't it true? There are 251 of us on board, and I'm the one who gets tapped to receive this information?"

"Because of a random configuration of your brain. It could have been anyone."

Bon turned to face her. "A Council member? You think that's a coincidence?"

She looked up at him. "Bon, are you listening to yourself? The Cassini communicate on a particular wavelength, and it just happens to sync with you. There were a few other crew members who had a touch of it, too, as I recall. Maybe not to the same extent—"

"Fine," he said. "But the point is, I do have the ability to communicate with them, and so far it's been pretty helpful."

Alexa sighed. "Nobody is questioning that. But we also have no idea what it's doing to you. Don't tell me the pain spasms are nothing." After a pause, she added, "And don't tell me that you can't see it from my—and Triana's—perspective. Even your reaction and attitude sounds like the angry denial of an addict."

"I was waiting for one of you to say that," he said, his voice low. "That's a no-win situation for me. If I don't disagree, then I'm essentially agreeing. And if I disagree, then I'm in denial. Either way supports your argument and leaves me guilty."

Alexa considered this for a while. "Okay, so I guess we're at a stalemate here. By your argument there's nothing I can say, either, without you thinking of it as a trap. So let me ask you a personal question instead, and be honest. Have you lost your fear of the connection?"

"My fear?"

"Yeah. Don't put on a macho act for me; that connection had to be frightening. Is it still?"

He stared at her, but didn't answer.

"I'm guessing that the answer is no," she said. "And if that's true, think about it. The most powerful alien force we could imagine, potentially doing damage to you, causing intense pain, and leaving you with thoughts and feelings you don't understand . . . and you've lost your fear of that? That doesn't tell you anything?"

Bon looked down at his feet, then back to her. "You just don't understand. It's not about fear; it's about information."

"No," Alexa said, "it's about control. They have assumed control over you, and you can't see it." He looked away again, and she softened her tone. "Bon, at least acknowledge that the people confronting you on this have valid concerns; Triana is responsible for your safety and the safety of the ship. And I—" She stopped and looked away.

"Yes?" Bon said.

With her eyes still averted she said, "And I care about you, that's all."

The tall Swede again ran a hand through his hair, a look of resignation on his face. He walked back to the bench and eased down beside her.

"You're not fighting fair," he said softly.

She didn't answer, and rested her head on his shoulder.

Gap stared at the game board on the vidscreen before him, perplexed. Only seconds earlier he had been convinced that this time he would finally defeat Roc at a game of Masego. Now, as he scanned the tactical moves instituted by the computer, he realized that he had blundered once again.

"Incredible," Gap said. "How could I let that happen?"

"Not crossing to the H-line three moves back," Roc said.

"It was a rhetorical question, thank you."

"I can never tell with you," the computer said. "Besides, you once said that you learn something from each loss; I wanted you to learn the value of moving to the H-line when you get the opportunity."

Gap sat back in his chair and examined the board again. Masego challenged him mentally, and he had enjoyed the competitive element from the first day that fellow crew member Nasha had introduced him to the African game. But it was also a source of great frustration; no matter how much he practiced—or concentrated—he could never get the better of Roc. He shook his head and blew out a breath. "Okay, one more, and then I have to take care of some errands."

In a flash the vidscreen reset to Masego's starting pattern. Roc wasted no time making his first move, and said, "I hope you're better at strategy when you pilot a Spider. There are no do-overs in space."

Gap considered his first play of the game. "Thanks for your confidence. I'm sure I'll do fine." He touched the screen to indicate his move. "Plus, I'll have you chirping in my ear the whole time, I imagine."

"I'd better. An EVA requires precise maneuvering. You're going to be hugging pretty close to the ship; I'd hate to see you knock off a piece that we might need later."

"I'm not going to knock off anything, except one of those suction monsters."

They played in silence for a few minutes, each probing, advancing, blocking. The game of strategy required each competitor to think several moves in advance. The din of the Rec Room would often spike, yet Gap maintained his concentration.

"If you don't mind me asking," Roc said, "I've noticed that you haven't been to the Airboard track in quite a while. Lost interest? Or maybe a little nervous about injuring your shoulder again?"

"You are a nosy thing, aren't you?"

"So you *do* mind me asking."

"No," Gap said. "If you really want to know, I decided that I was spending too much time there, and not enough time focusing on my job."

"That's a shame."

"What? Being more responsible is a bad thing?"

"No," Roc said. "That's good. But your once-deft skills in Airboarding could come in handy if there's a crisis in the Spider."

Gap chuckled and touched the screen with a new move. "You are so nervous about this EVA. And never fear, my little mechanical friend, those skills do not go away after a few weeks off. I could hop back onto a board right now and you'd never know I'd been away."

Roc responded by lighting up the vidscreen with his own move; Gap saw instantly that he was doomed.

"All right," he said. "I concede. Good game." He sat back and crossed a leg over a knee. "Okay, since you're so worried about it, let's talk about this EVA for a minute. What's really bothering you about it?"

"Two obvious issues spring to mind," Roc said. "For one thing, these vultures can flat-out move. They can fly circles around you, and at lightning speed. It's not like you'll see one coming; more like it will be in one spot at one moment, then in your face the next."

"And the other issue?"

"We have lived in a virtual stare-down with them since they intercepted us; neither side has done anything. But the minute we go out there like some space age exterminator getting rid of bugs, the game changes. If they read it as an attack—which, in essence, it is—then we don't know what they will do to the Spider or the ship itself."

Gap scowled. "Wait, they attacked us in the first place."

"Did they? Would they read it like that? There's been no damage to the ship; they seem fairly benevolent right now, almost like old-time hobos hitching a ride in a boxcar. But as soon as you start ripping one from the skin of the ship they'll probably not take too kindly."

"You didn't say a word about this in the Council meeting," Gap said.

"Oh, please. I'm not saying anything that anyone else couldn't have thought of. Besides, I'm still in favor of you going out there; why would I try to talk Triana out of that? You should go. I'm just answering your question, that's all."

Gap chewed on this for a minute, then said: "Okay, since it's just the two of us talking here, tell me what you think these things really are. What am I about to bring inside the ship?"

"I've given that a lot of thought," Roc said. "As fast as they are, as organized as they appear, and as efficient as they seem, I can't help but feel like they're the muscle, not the brains."

"What do you mean?" Gap said.

"Consider what they're doing. Some alien species wants to patrol the outer ring of our solar system, either looking for a way in, or hoping that something will pop out, like we did. There's an awful lot of space to manage. You tell me, who's gonna get that assignment? Not the big dogs, that's for sure. It's one of the reasons I'm questioning if these really are alive, or more like semi-intelligent drones."

"And their job is, what?" Gap said. "To just make contact and call for reinforcements?"

"I don't think they'll call anybody here," Roc said. "Again, this is all guesswork, obviously, but it wouldn't make sense for a mother ship to be close. I would think these things are probably scattered everywhere, just doing a little reconnaissance. And, if they find something good—like us—then I would think they call it in."

Gap rocked back in his chair, his hands laced behind his head, and looked up at the ceiling while he thought. Slowly he said, "But a call would take a long time to reach . . . wherever it was going."

"I've been thinking about that, too," the computer said. "I have a theory that explains not only how they would speed up that call, but how they move so fast in the first place."

"Care to share?"

"Not yet. Let me think about it a little more. But if I'm right, they wouldn't bother to send anyone here when they could just have them meet us along the way."

This brought Gap's attention back to the glowing red sensor. "That sounds ominous."

"But like all of my ideas, it makes complete sense," Roc said.

"Now that I've probably given you nightmares for tonight, care for another game?"

Gap shook his head. "No, I have to get back to work."

He waved to a couple of crew members as he walked out the door and toward the lift. His mind was suddenly on active alert, and Roc's dire suggestion lingered. The computer was right about one thing: it was entirely possible that nightmares would be in order tonight.

11

The final session of School had finished for the day, leaving the large auditorium vacant. Channy sat on the edge of the stage, reliving the euphoric feeling of the Dating Game, looking out over the sea of empty seats. Behind her, Iris padded lithely across the stage, stopping occasionally to sniff at something on the floor, her tail twitching only at the tip.

Channy waited and watched the doors in the back of the room. She had told herself that she would not be the first to show up, that she would make him wait for her. In the end, her excitement hadn't allowed it, and instead she had arrived a full fifteen minutes early. She rationalized it by telling herself that Iris needed the exercise after being cooped up in her room for several hours.

With one hand she rubbed at the corners of her mouth; she wasn't used to wearing anything on her lips, and the thin layer of gloss felt unnatural. Kylie surely wouldn't mind that she had borrowed it just this once.

She glanced down at the shirt she had picked out, a flashy red cotton polo shirt. There was a slight crease near the right shoulder, which she tried pressing away with her fingers.

Cupping her hand before her mouth, she exhaled and checked

her breath, silently cursing herself that she had brushed her teeth twenty minutes before leaving her room, rather than waiting until the last minute.

She quickly dropped her hand to her side as one of the rear doors flew open, and Taresh strolled in. He spied her and gave a quick wave, then walked down the aisle toward the stage. She tried not to stare at him, and forced herself to look back at Iris. The cat had wandered to the edge of the stage and plopped onto her side, one paw hanging off into space, her eyes following the progress of Taresh as he approached.

"I'm not late, am I?" he said.

"No," Channy said. "I was a little early. Wanted to give our furry friend here a chance to stretch her legs." She glanced at the cat sprawled a few feet away and laughed. "Although it doesn't look like she's stretching anything right now, does it?"

Taresh dropped into a seat on the front row. "Yes, the life of a cat. Doesn't she sleep something like fourteen hours a day?"

"More than that, I think. Or maybe she just wants us to *think* she's sleeping, and she's actually listening to what we're saying. Either way, you're right, seems like a pretty good life."

Taresh looked around the empty room. "Funny that you picked this spot to meet. I like to come here by myself sometimes, to get away, to read a little bit. Not too many people think about coming here; they're usually either in the Dining Hall or Rec Room." He turned his attention to Channy and grinned. "Can't imagine that you ever look for anyplace without people."

She wagged a finger at him. "Are you picking on me already? I'll have you know that I enjoy some quiet time every once in a while." When he responded with an incredulous look, she added, "At least once a month."

They both laughed, but Channy got the sense that he was nervous about their meeting. He had likely been nervous from the moment he entered the room, which explained why he had chosen to sit in the seat rather than join her up on the stage. She decided to quit stalling.

"Well, you said that you wanted to talk again," she said, "and I know that the domes have been pretty busy lately. So . . ." Her voice trailed off.

Taresh sat forward in his seat. "Yeah." He looked down at the floor, and seemed unsure of what to say. Channy couldn't think of anything to help him get started; *he* was the one who had requested that they talk. She gripped the edge of the stage with both hands and watched him.

Finally he cleared his throat and spoke. "I was impressed by your honesty in expressing your feelings. I know that it took a lot for you to send the email, and then to say something about it after Game Night. I guess it's time I said a few things, right?"

All Channy could do was nod; her stomach was tangled, but she summoned all of her strength to appear calm and comfortable.

"You should know that I am interested in getting to know you better, like we discussed that night," he said. "But—" He broke off and looked back down at the floor for a moment, as if searching for the right words. "But I told you that things are complicated, and you deserve to know what that means."

Now he stood up and began to pace in front of the row of seats. Channy felt a wave of anxiety pass through her.

"For generations my family has lived in the region of India called Bihar. I grew up in Patna, just like my parents and grandparents. My family has always worked hard, always wanting more for their children than themselves. That was true with my parents, their parents, and their parents before them.

"Family is so very important in my heritage. We look after one another, we respect each other, and we love very deeply. I guess you could say that we value our heritage more than anything, because it is what has kept the bonds of our family so strong throughout our history."

Taresh stopped pacing and made eye contact with Channy. "Over the last several years there have been many in our culture who have parted with the old ways. They have introduced not only Western technology and lifestyle, but Western behavior and beliefs. They have ultimately disregarded their family traditions and background, and have surrendered to new ways.

"My family has been very careful to balance these influences. While my grandparents and parents have gradually blended some Western ways into our lives, they have always been dedicated to preserving our Indian culture, and to preserving our strong family line."

He paused. Channy watched him intently, but although she heard what he was saying, her mind scrambled to understand the context. What exactly was he trying to get across? She chose to remain silent, and Taresh continued.

"When I was nominated for the *Galahad* mission, you have no idea of the stress it placed on my family. On one hand it provided a chance for my family line to continue, to survive and spread to the stars. And yet, my mother and father were also very concerned. As my father said, 'What good is it to preserve a heritage if that heritage is blurred?' "

He began to pace again. "In the end my family gave their blessing to me to reach for the stars, but on one condition. They asked me to give my word that I would remain true to my past, true to my sense of cultural identity." He grew quiet for a moment, and, when his pacing brought him even with Channy, he stopped and looked at her again.

"I agreed. I gave my word that I would not lose that identity."

Channy sat still, absorbed in what Taresh was saying, but still confused. She thought she understood . . . and yet it made no sense to her.

"I'm trying to understand," she finally said softly. "Are you saying that . . . that you can't see me because . . . because I'm not from India?"

He exhaled loudly and rubbed his forehead. "I'm saying that that's what my family requested, yes. Our sense of cultural identity in my family is very strong. But . . ."

"But?"

"I'm my own person, too. I have thoughts and feelings that I often don't understand. I know that when the opportunity came for me to apply for this mission, I was so excited that I was willing to agree to anything."

Channy looked deep into his dark eyes. She was afraid to interrupt him now.

"I am torn, Channy. I obviously am interested in you, and that has troubled me a great deal. I want to be my own person, I want to go with whatever my heart says. But . . . it's difficult."

He slowly walked up to where she sat on the edge of the stage. He drew close, but kept his hands at his sides, unwilling—or unable—to reach out and touch her.

"You have no idea how troubled I have been. I do care about you. When you wrote that email, I wanted to respond right away. When you spoke to me in the Rec Room, I wanted to respond. But at those times, the faces of my mother and father loom before me, and their words cut through me. I think of them, and my grandparents, back on Earth, and think of the blessing that they gave me by allowing me to make this journey. I think of everything that I owe them, all of the work that they have done, all of the sacrifices that they made for me, and I think of the trust they put in me when they hugged me good-bye. I think of their dedication to our history and culture, and it's difficult, Channy. It's very difficult. I know this is hard for you to understand."

She nodded. "You're right," she said, her voice barely audible. "It's very hard to understand." She tried to control her breathing, which had accelerated. "You say you care about me, but . . . but you can't explore those feelings because . . . I'm not of your culture? No, Taresh, I don't understand."

He opened his mouth to answer, but stopped. Channy reached out and placed a hand on his shoulder.

"I care about you, too," she said. "I care enough to practically make a fool of myself, but it's because there's something in you that I'm attracted to. Now, to find out that you have the same feelings, but can't respond because of . . . this . . . ." She felt that she was on the verge of tears, and willed them away. In their place, a touch of anger seeped in.

"If this is what you decide," she said, "how many people of your culture are even on the ship? Fifteen? Twenty? Are you saying that they're the only people worthy of your attention?"

Taresh reached up and covered her hand with his. "I'm saying that I am struggling with this. I haven't decided, okay? But it's also not something that I take lightly. I need you to be patient for now and let me think through everything."

She nodded, and, as with the tears, consciously worked to drive away the irritation that had taken over. "I'll try."

He leaned forward and lightly embraced her. Then, with a shy smile, he turned and walked back up the aisle toward the door.

On the stage, Channy watched him leave. A moment later she felt something rub up against her, and looked down to find Iris stretched out with her back against Channy's leg. She absently scratched the cat's chin, and again felt her eyes fill with water. This time she let two single drops course down her face.

Months had passed, and yet Gap still felt uncomfortable in the Spider bay control room. He had unintentionally witnessed something pass between Triana and Bon in this very room, when his feelings for Triana had left him vulnerable. Now, even following his own brief relationship with Hannah, he still felt awkward stepping into this room; memories rushed upon him, clouding his thoughts.

Triana stood beside him, her attention focused on the small vidscreen that displayed a diagram of the route that Gap would take to locate the vultures. The only other person in the room was Mira Pereira, a tall sixteen-year-old from the Algarve coast of Portugal, who would be accompanying Gap in the Spider.

Roc had been speaking, and Gap had heard only scattered words.

"I'm sorry," he said, "my mind was jumping ahead. What was that again?"

"You're certainly instilling a lot of confidence," Roc said. "Perhaps I should speak . . . very . . . slowly . . . ?"

Triana looked up from the vidscreen. "Everything okay?"

"Everything's fine," Gap said. "So, we're sure that we want the one on the dome?"

The Council Leader laughed. "Wow, you did check out for a moment, didn't you? Yes, that's what we've been talking about. I don't know if the others are causing damage or not, but I'd feel a lot better if we could pull that one off the dome. That makes me a lot more nervous than the others."

She pointed to the screen. "Everything is plotted and laid in. This program has been downloaded into the Spider that you'll be taking. Let's do a visual check on all of the vultures first, and get their exact location logged. Then you can finish with the target on Dome 1. I'll be in communication with you the whole time, but Roc will control most of the Spider's movement at first. Once you get close, you'll take over with manual control. It's going to be pretty delicate maneuvering when you get close to these things. Any questions from either of you?"

Mira nodded. "I understand that this is a reconnaissance mission primarily, and a collection mission at the end. But I'm still not clear on how we defend ourselves if something goes wrong."

"The short answer is that we don't," Gap said grimly. "Obviously we have the arms of the Spider at our disposal, but the speed of the vultures pretty much makes those useless."

"It's one of the reasons we want to bring one inside in the first place," Triana added. "Hopefully we'll be able to learn more about them, and find out if we even need to worry about defense." She studied Mira's face. "It's not too late to back out, if you'd rather not take this on."

"Absolutely not," Mira said with a grin. Her dark eyes sparkled. "I wouldn't pass this up for anything."

"Good," Triana said. "Okay, let's get you guys loaded and ready to go."

The three of them walked into the vaulted hangar, where the eight remaining Spiders awaited. The small, egg-shaped transfer vehicles had been given their names because of the multiple arms that splayed out from the sides and front. One of the Spiders was not functional, and had only been loaded for potential spare parts. Two others had been lost to space right after launch; in the space it once occupied now sat the small metal pod that had been rescued from the orbit of Titan. Its lone occupant had been Iris.

Gap approached one of the Spiders and began the procedure to open its door. Triana stood to one side and inspected the polyglass container that they hoped would soon house one of the vultures. The large rectangular box was already secured to one of the Spider's arms; it would be up to Gap and Mira to somehow capture the alien entity and get it safely stored inside.

The Spider door slid open with a hiss. Gap helped Mira climb inside, then pulled himself up and in. He turned and looked back at Triana.

"Need me to pick up anything at the store while I'm out?"

She laughed. "Anything chocolate. Preferably dark chocolate."

"Will do. If I'm not back before dark, leave a light on, okay?"

Triana gave him the thumbs-up. "Good luck. I'll probably

monitor from the Control Room instead of down here. Roc will oversee the launch."

He waved to her, and she suddenly felt a twinge of fear pass through her. The lighthearted banter, she realized, was simply their way of camouflaging the stress that both must be feeling. This was more than just an ordinary housekeeping stint on *Gala-had*'s exterior; they were once again confronting an unknown force. Although Gap was enthusiastic about the assignment, Triana knew that his insides were likely twisting and turning; *hers* were, and she wasn't the one taking the risk.

She returned his wave, then walked toward the exit. At the door she looked back to see if he was still watching her, but the Spider's hatch was sealed. In minutes it would be on the hunt.

12

Maybe you've wondered what would happen to you if you got caught in outer space without a protective suit or helmet. Of course, some of you have also wondered what would happen if you could squeeze inside a microwave oven, but let's try to stay focused here, okay?

Scientists have debated how long you'd be able to survive in space, but the point is that it's not very long (maybe one to two minutes if you're extremely lucky), and the results are not pretty at all. Pretty grisly, actually.

So hopefully Gap closed the door properly.

Gap adjusted the tilt of his seat and cinched up the safety harness, pulling it snug against his upper body. He stole a quick glance to his right to make sure Mira was strapped in as well. Behind them, twenty-eight seats sat empty. The Spiders were primarily designed to transport the crew from *Galahad* onto the surface of Eos, but were equipped with multiple arms for various duties on the exterior of the ship. Larger arms could tackle heavier payloads, while a series of smaller limbs were designed for precision work. The interiors were simple, almost bare, with space at a premium.

The two pilot seats at the front sat surrounded by an instrument panel, which now bathed Gap and Mira in a golden glow. The majority of the Spider's maneuvering functions could be carried out by Roc, but most of *Galahad's* crew members had trained for weeks on their operation. Gap had been one of those with intensive study and practice behind the craft's function; he was comfortable at the controls, and had even taken a couple of the Spiders out for routine maintenance checks over the past several months. But, given the gravity of this particular situation, he still felt butterflies in his stomach.

He flipped on the radio. "Hello, Roc," he said. "Beginning preflight check."

The computer's voice filtered through the speaker system. "Roger that."

"What?" Gap said.

"Old-time jargon from the days of fighter pilots," Roc replied. "I've never had the chance to use it, and couldn't pass up the opportunity. I kinda like it. Roger that. It means 'okay, understood.' Sorta like ten-four, but much cooler sounding."

Gap shook his head. "Okay, whatever." He looked at the checklist on the small vidscreen in the console, and proceeded to work his way through the steps necessary to launch the Spider. A few minutes later he looked back at Mira, who had finished her own list. "Ready?"

She smiled and gave him a thumbs-up. "See," she said, "I know a few fighter pilot moves myself."

"Spider bay is clear, preparing to open outer door," Roc said. "Oh, wait. Has everyone gone potty? I don't want to have to stop this car again until we're finished."

"Roc, just open the door," Gap said. He kept a straight face, but inside he appreciated the lighthearted air that the ship's computer brought to the mission. Things were tense enough; Roc often brought just the right touch of wit to take the edge off.

Inside the pressurized Spider no sound could penetrate from

the bay, but Gap and Mira watched wide-eyed through the window before them as the bay door slowly and silently rolled open. A spectacle of starlight danced through the widening breach. For a moment Gap had a frightening vision of a cluster of vultures swooping through, into the ship. But the feeling passed with the first jolt of movement that told him they were being shifted into launch position.

The Spider edged toward the opening, and soon the star field monopolized the view. They stopped at the very edge of the bay door.

"Final check complete," Roc said. "Listen, one more thing before we sling you out into space. Good luck and all that, but if you don't make it back, Gap, can I have your stamp collection?"

"I don't have a stamp collection."

"Well, then never mind. Hold on, kids, here we go."

The Spider's maneuvering jets flared to life, and the mechanical arm below the craft jerked it forward, through the opening, and into the void. Even though he had experienced this before, Gap found himself inhaling sharply, and heard Mira do the same. It was an involuntary reaction. Space blanketed them, and the immensity of it—and the majesty—was staggering. Billions of stars winked greetings, and yet the blackness between them was heavy and deep. Not for the first time, Gap felt humbled by it all, a reality check that placed humans and their meager creations into a truly cosmic perspective.

Jets fired from the port side and below, and the Spider nudged gently to the right and began to ascend *Galahad*. Gap keyed the radio. "Triana, you with us?"

Her voice spilled from the speaker immediately. "Right here."

"We're on our way. Just starting to make the climb. All systems are green and go."

"Good," Triana said. "How's it look out there?"

"Magnificent. You should get out here more often."

"Don't have much time for joy rides these days," she said with a laugh. "We're monitoring from your front cameras; that's gonna have to be good enough for now."

The Spider edged up the side of the ship. "Keep your eyes peeled," Gap muttered to Mira, who nodded mutely. Together they scanned the gray surface of *Galahad,* and the Spider's camera system fed images to Roc, who for now controlled their ascent.

A minute later they crested the ship. To one side lay the massive domes, their interior light blazing through the panels and radiating into space. The Spider hung in place momentarily before spinning to approach the rear. The plan, laid out before their mission, called for a circuit of *Galahad's* starboard side, beginning at the rear, and working around side and bottom. Then they would repeat the circuit on the port side. The final task would be the capture of the vulture attached to the dome.

With Roc guiding them initially, Gap had focused all of his attention on the search. Now he assumed control of the craft as they glided twenty feet above *Galahad's* hull, calmly applying pressure to maintain a consistent velocity. Mira leaned forward and touched the control panel, activating twin searchlights and concentrating their beams onto the metallic gray surface of the ship below them.

Several minutes passed in silence. They had worked across the top and barely begun to drop over the back side of the ship when Mira uttered a cry. "Wait, wait. Hold up."

Gap throttled back and peered through the window. "What do you see?"

Mira pointed to a spot just a few feet over the edge. There, attached to the back side of the spacecraft, was a dark, triangular shape, roughly two feet wide. Gap nudged the controls of the Spider, and brought them a little closer.

"Triana, are you getting this?" he said.

"Yes, we see it," she said. "Are those wings tucked up to the side?"

Gap studied the vulture. "I think so. That would explain why it appears smaller now. And . . ."

There was silence for a moment before Triana prompted him. "Yes?"

"Well," he said, "I wouldn't call it breathing, but there's some kind of movement going on. Roc, what would you call that?"

"It looks like it's venting," the computer said. "Those rectangular slits around the circumference; they're opening and closing in a sort of rhythm. Doesn't appear to have a particular pattern that I can discern right now, but . . . hmm."

"Hmm?" Triana said. "What is it?"

"I'm just disappointed that I so quickly jumped to a conclusion. I automatically assumed that the vulture might be venting something out into space. But it could just as easily be absorbing something *from* space. Or doing both, I suppose."

"I'm going to move a little closer," Gap said. He deftly adjusted the controls of the Spider and dropped to within ten feet, which allowed him to take stock of the vulture. It was jet-black, with a strange ribbed effect that reminded Gap of a kite. It was roughly triangular in shape, its surface pebbled. Folded along the sides were two extensions that resembled wings.

Mira pointed again. "It's emitting some kind of light."

Gap studied the alien entity. "She's right," he said to Triana. "Are the cameras picking that up? Up there by the . . . I guess you'd call that the head. Do you see that?"

As they watched, a soft, blue-green glow seeped from one corner of the vulture, lightly at first, then briefly picking up intensity before fading again. To Gap, it almost seemed like an eye opening and closing. He felt a shudder ripple through him.

Roc's voice piped through. "A little more data is coming in now. Other than those brief flashes of visible light, it's not putting out any heat or radiation, which is very odd, and makes me question whether it's alive. But even a machine gives off something.

Well, the machines we're used to, anyway. There are sixteen vents across the surface, and I was correct, of course, about the lack of any pattern to their opening and closing. A few of them seem to be fairly active, a few others less so, and two have only opened once so far."

"Any idea about how it's holding on to the ship?" Triana said. "Could it be magnetic?"

"No way of knowing until we get one inside," Roc said. "But I'm not picking up on anything magnetic, unless you count my personality."

"Of course," Triana said.

"Should I poke at it with one of the Spider's arms?" Gap said.

"I'm sorry," Roc said, "but did you just ask if you could *poke* at it?"

He could hear Triana chuckle through the speaker. "You are such a boy. This is not some frog that you've found in a creek. Let's wait until you get to the one on the dome. Let's go look for the others."

Gap took one last look at the vulture, then gently lifted the Spider away and began to guide it down the back of *Galahad*. Within a few minutes they had reached the ship's lower side. Mira adjusted the spotlights to give them a clear view in their search.

"Ugh, I don't know why, but I hope we don't find any down here," Gap said. "I don't like the idea of these things clamped onto the ship's underbelly."

The words had barely escaped his mouth when Mira spoke up. "Sorry. Two of them dead ahead."

They were within a few feet of each other. As Gap drew the Spider close, he could see the methodic opening and closing of their vents, and an occasional blue-green glow. Although sound waves did not carry through the vacuum of space, he could almost imagine a sort of electrical hum that might accompany the light. Something about the motion and light—without the soundtrack that humans were used to—added to the creepy feeling as he watched.

He noticed something else as well. The combination of movement and light, executed in such a relaxed manner, was almost hypnotic. Gap found himself drawn in, his hands resting limply on the Spider's controls, his face slack. The vultures, meanwhile, behaved as if nothing was out of the ordinary, as if they had been clamped onto this particular starship for years, oblivious to the artificial craft hovering mere feet away.

But were *they* artificial? Gap punched up the link to the twin cameras on his vidscreen and zoomed in. He swept across the backs of the vultures, looking for anything that might indicate if they were alive, or merely drones. And yet, he realized, how could he—or anyone else with only Earth-bound experience—know what forms life might take in the universe? The Cassini had taught them that.

Triana's voice came from the speaker. "I can't tell any difference between these two and the first one. Roc, are you picking up anything new?"

"Very slight variation in size, but negligible. Comparisons of the vent activities are processing right now, but don't appear to have any connection. Same with the light emissions; no pattern that I can make out."

"Could they be talking to each other?" Mira asked.

"We can't rule that out," Roc said.

After a few minutes observing the two specimens from different angles, Gap pulled the Spider away and continued the search. Forty minutes later they had discovered three more vultures on the port side: one on the top, one on the back, and one on the bottom. They each exhibited identical characteristics as the first three, with one exception.

"Now why do you suppose the light from this one is constant?" Gap mused aloud. The Spider hovered above the lone vulture attached to the top of *Galahad*'s port side. "The others were slowly winking, and this one has a steady glow to it."

"Maybe it's a short in the wiring," Roc said. "We should shake it."

Triana said, "You know what I'm thinking? This one might be the leader of the pack."

"A squadron leader," Roc said. "Here we go with the fighter pilots again."

"And," Triana continued, "if that's the case, then the light probably *does* signify some form of communication, just like Mira suggested. Maybe the other six stay in contact with this one."

"And, if that's true, I wonder if this guy is in touch with a mother ship somewhere," Gap said. There was silence as this sank in.

Mira looked thoughtful. "Well, if this one *is* the captain, should we maybe try to snag it and leave the one on the dome?"

"No," Triana said after pausing to think. "We don't know anything for sure, so let's stick with the original plan. Besides, I'm still nervous about that thing attached to the dome. We're much more vulnerable there than on the hull."

"Plus, who knows how the others might react if we kidnap the boss," Gap added. "I think we're finished here. It's time to go catch a vulture."

He pulled back on the Spider's controls and spun the small craft in a 180-degree turn. The bright lights of *Galahad*'s twin domes loomed up ahead, beckoning. As they crept closer, a pale shade of green bled through, and shadows played against the clear panels. When the distance had closed to about one hundred feet, Mira looked at Gap and raised her eyebrows.

"You see it?"

She turned her attention back to the crest of the dome and Gap followed her gaze. There, a sinister dark outline emerged, like a bird-shaped hole in the plate. Gap felt a shiver steal through his body and at the same time heard a small sigh escape from Mira.

They both understood that their role as silent observers had come to an end; they were about to become the first human beings to ever make physical contact with an extraterrestrial organism.

There was no way of knowing how that organism would react.

Triana's voice came through. "Let's do this in stages. Start with the same distance you hovered above the others. Then move in closer, and let's see how it reacts to something invading its space. If there's no movement, we'll proceed with the capture."

"We're still assuming that *we're* capturing *it*, right?" Gap murmured as the Spider's lights coated the vulture.

"I hope so," Roc piped in. "We can't afford to lose another Spider."

"Thanks," Gap said. He adjusted their speed and piloted the small craft to a spot fifteen feet above the panels. "Roc," he said, "let's bring down the lighting in both domes thirty percent. The glare is a little tough to handle out here."

"I'll make an announcement," Triana said. "I don't want to freak out the people working up there right now."

Two minutes later the radiance dimmed. "Um . . . just a touch more," Gap said. "There, that's good." He looked at the image of the vulture displayed on the vidscreen. "Is it me, or is this one a little smaller?"

"Good eye," Roc said. "Just under two feet in width. That's with wings folded, of course."

"A baby," Mira said with a smile.

"Same venting, same oscillating glow," Roc added.

"I'm taking us closer," Gap said. With a nudge he soon had the Spider within six feet. Everyone remained silent for a full minute, waiting and watching for any response from the vulture.

"Sheesh, does it even know we're here?" Gap said.

"These things began tracking us when we were hundreds of thousands of miles out," Triana said grimly. "I'm pretty sure it knows exactly where you are."

"The light pattern has changed," Roc said. "Barely noticeable, but definitely a different cadence and tempo."

"It's bound to be as curious about us as we are about it," Mira said. She turned to look at Gap. "It's probably asking for instructions."

"I say we don't wait around for it to get an answer," Gap said, and wiped a sweaty palm on his pants leg. "Tree, you ready for us to pick it up?"

She let out a long breath. "Okay, go ahead."

Gap brought the Spider into a better position, level with the vulture, so that he and Mira could see it through their forward window. At a distance of about five feet he nodded to Mira. She tapped instructions into the panel before her, and then leaned forward and inserted her hands into the glovelike controls. With a combination of fluid movements, two of the forward arms of the Spider unfolded and stretched out toward the vulture. Mira deftly maneuvered them within inches before bringing them to a stop.

As he watched, Gap felt a trickle of sweat work down his forehead. "Okay," he said, "let's get the box."

He spun in his chair and engaged the controls of another of the Spider's arms. It held the polyglass container that they hoped would carry their target aboard the ship. It would also provide a spacelike environment, including a vacuum. He grunted as the arm jerked toward the vulture.

"I'm glad you've got the spatula," he said to Mira. "You're much smoother with these things than I am."

A moment later he had the box in position. He let go of the arm control and began to input new instructions on his keyboard. With a glance through the window he watched the door of the container silently slide open.

"Okay," he said. "She's all yours."

He was strangely relieved when, out of the corner of his eye, he watched Mira rub the back of one hand across her forehead before settling back against the controls. They both heard Triana issue a subdued, "Good luck."

The claw hand on one arm of the Spider spread apart, then inched slowly toward the dark figure that clung to the dome. Gap leaned forward and watched as it made contact, and stopped. Mira released some pressure on the controls, then picked it up again. The claw pressed against the vulture, but seemed unable to budge it.

"Umm . . ." Mira said. "How hard do I want to push on this thing?"

Gap thought about it. "Well, we don't want to damage it. But we have to pry it off somehow. Go ahead and push a little more, see if you can't slide that hand under it."

Mira nodded, and squeezed the controls again. The Spider's arm again made contact, but seemed to get nowhere.

Triana spoke up. "Try using both arms, Mira. Maybe you can pry an edge up just enough to slide the other claw under there."

"Okay," Mira said. With her other hand she guided the second arm into position, then rotated its claw and brought it down gently against one edge of the vulture. She gritted her teeth. "I think it's going to be tricky trying to get a grip."

It happened in a flash. There was a quick flare of blue-green light as the vulture sprang from *Galahad's* dome and shot up against the windshield of the Spider. Mira let out a scream and jumped back from the controls, while Gap simultaneously shouted and threw himself backward. They both disconnected their safety harnesses and scrambled out of their seats, retreating several feet into the interior of the Spider, panting heavily. The vulture's wings had unfurled as it bolted from the dome, creating a terrifying image as it smashed up against the small craft. Now, as Gap and Mira turned back to watch, the wings slowly retracted as the alien entity settled into position and immediately fell still.

Triana's voice boomed through the speaker. "Gap, Mira, are you guys okay?"

"Oh . . . my . . ." Mira sobbed, clutching her chest. "I think I just about had a heart attack."

Gap swallowed hard, and then reflexively laughed. He called out to the intercom. "Yeah, we're okay. We both just aged about five years in one second. I take it you saw what just happened."

"Incredible," Triana said. "I can't believe how fast it moved."

Now Mira laughed, too, as the adrenaline rush subsided. "You're telling us. You should see what it's like coming at your face."

Moving cautiously, Gap approached the windshield to inspect the vulture that now gripped the Spider. He reached out to lean against the back of his pilot's seat, then leaned forward to get a better look.

"I don't know if you can see it very well," he said to Triana. "I'll tell you this, though; the view from this angle is very different than the view from above."

"We're getting a shot now," Triana replied. "But describe it."

"The color is basically the same, that same jet-black, only here it's also got some streaks of yellow that run through it. Thousands of little hairs, or fibers, or something; I'm guessing that's what it uses to grip on to the ship. They're arranged in rows, or grids. More like tens of thousands, actually.

"If you've got a camera shot that's working, zero in on the middle of this thing. I'm no biologist, but that looks very similar to a . . . a mouth, wouldn't you say?"

Mira had crept up beside him. She knelt down and scooted closer to the window. "It's some kind of hollow opening," she said quietly.

Gap laughed. "Um, I don't think it can hear you out in space. You don't have to whisper."

She turned and looked at him with a smirk. "I'm not taking any chances."

Gap addressed Triana again. "Yeah, it's hollow, about five or six inches in diameter. Looks like some sort of valve at the core, but it's not moving. No sign of the vents that we saw on the top side. But . . ." His voice dropped off.

Now he knelt beside Mira and moved within a few inches of the window. "The light that we saw coming from them; here's the source." He craned his neck to look up through the glass. "It's not some sort of eye, or gland. It's the . . . the skin, or whatever it is. Here, near the edges, small sections just . . . light up." He pointed it out to Mira. "Do you see that?"

She nodded. "Thin stretches, about an inch wide or so. There's no break in the skin or any other marking. Just small strips around the edges that emit color, on and off, like a beacon." She looked back at Gap. "It's like a living pulse."

He studied her face. "But is it alive?"

Triana spoke up. "We can't leave you guys out there much longer. Any way to try to peel it off the Spider?"

Gap stood up and stepped back from the window. He thought for a moment, then let out a long breath. "We might be able to turn the arms back onto the ship. But I'm willing to bet that it won't let go of the Spider any easier than it did the ship. Why not just drive it into the Spider bay?"

Mira's mouth fell open. "You mean without putting it in the container? Just bring it into the ship, attached to the window?"

Gap shrugged. "Might as well. Once we get it trapped in the bay we should be able to figure out a way to capture it. The longer we wait out here the more we're giving it the chance to get bored with us and fly away."

"I hate to agree with Gap," Roc said, "which is the understatement of the year; but I do believe he's right. Besides, what other choice do we really have?"

Silence greeted this statement, and Gap could picture Triana biting her lip as she considered the possibility. Finally, her voice came through: "All right. Come on in. But we'll have to get this thing into the box as soon as possible; there's no telling what the ship's environment will do to it."

Mira and Gap exchanged a look, then climbed slowly back into their seats, the forbidding silhouette of the vulture hanging over them, mere feet away. Gap gently swung the Spider around, keeping an eye on the vulture as he worked the controls. Mira retracted and stowed the arms, preparing all systems for docking. In a few minutes they approached the bay doors.

"Ready or not, here we come," Gap said.

He relinquished control back to Roc, then sat back as the Spider glided through the opening and came to rest in the bay. The vulture never budged.

And it was now inside *Galahad*.

Behind them, the outer bay door closed. "Pressurizing," Roc said.

Gap watched the vidscreen as it displayed the atmospheric conditions within the bay. He glanced at Mira. "Now all we have to do is figure out how to get this thing off the Spider. I don't know if we brought a cattle prod along on this—"

A flash of light cut him off. The vulture's wings spread out as if it was preparing for flight. Then, without warning, it slipped a few inches down the windshield, and fell straight down, out of view.

Gap and Mira sat stunned. "Uh . . ." he said to the intercom. "Anybody want to tell us what just happened?"

After a moment of hesitation, Triana answered: "Our guest just fell off the Spider. It didn't fly; it fell. It's lying in a heap on the floor of the bay."

13

Channy sat before the mirror in her room, looking closely at her face, trying desperately to not pick out every imperfection. Her gaze drifted from her eyes, to her nose, to her teeth, back to her eyes, the slight blemishes in the chocolate hue of her skin, then to her hair. She turned her head one way, then the other, catching her reflection in the corner of her eyes. After a few moments of inspection she put her elbows on the counter and leaned her chin on her hands.

"Not exactly a natural beauty, am I?" she said.

Kylie, sitting on her bed across the room, set down the clothes that she was folding and scowled across at her roommate. "Excuse me?"

"I mean, I'm not even properly proportioned. Look at the space between my nose and my mouth."

"I don't believe what I'm hearing," Kylie said. "The space between your nose and your mouth; you're joking, right?"

"I had a chance to get my teeth fixed properly about a year before we left," Channy said. "Now I wish I'd done it. That was stupid, wasn't it?"

Kylie went back to folding her shirts. "I'm not having this conversation with you, Ms. Oakland. You sound ridiculous."

"That's because you don't have to look at it in the mirror every day." Channy sat back and sighed. "I'm sure that Taresh sees all of it."

She grunted as a wadded-up shirt hit her in the back of the head. Turning, she saw that Kylie had reloaded, and was preparing to throw another one at her.

"What are you doing?" she said.

"If I was closer I would have thumped you with my hand," Kylie said. "Taresh most certainly does *not* see anything wrong with you, and you know that."

"Well, then he doesn't see anything right with me, either."

Kylie crossed her arms. "You're sounding pathetic, Channy. You told me what he said; he's having an issue with cultural differences, not your looks."

Channy snorted. "Cultural differences. Whoever heard of such a thing?" She turned back to the mirror and inspected her face again.

"Okay, I've known you for a long time now," Kylie said. "You have never been this way before. What happened to the happy, fun-loving roomie that I was lucky enough to get?"

"She fell in love," Channy said in a low voice. In the mirror she made eye contact with Kylie. "There, is that what you wanted to know?"

Kylie set down the shirt she had bunched in her hand. "In love? Channy, slow down a moment, okay? You might be infatuated right now, but it's probably a little soon to say that you're in love. I mean, you hardly know him."

"I know enough."

"No, you don't. You've spent a few hours with him after Game Nights, and talked a little bit. But you don't really know him."

"And how much exactly do I need to know before I can have feelings?" Channy blurted out. "Why is everyone else on this ship allowed to be happy with someone, but not me? Answer that!"

Kylie settled back on her bed and let the silence between them grow for a while. When she responded, her voice was gentle.

"Channy, let me ask you something. I'm not trying to pry into your past, or your personal life. But . . . how many boyfriends have you had?"

Channy didn't answer. Instead, she got up and walked over to her bed and stretched out, her hands behind her head, staring at the ceiling.

"You haven't had a boyfriend before, have you?" Kylie said softly. She waited a moment, then walked over to her friend and sat on the edge of the bed. "Hey, it's okay. I'm not trying to be mean, I'm just trying to make a point. This is new territory for you, just like it is for everyone at some point. And it's scary sometimes."

Channy nodded, stole a quick glance at Kylie, then looked away. Her eyes began to water.

"All I'm saying," Kylie said, "is that you might want to take it easy. Not because what you're feeling is wrong, and not because you and Taresh might not be right for each other. But you should slow down because this is all new for you, and you're a little out of control."

"I'm not out of control," Channy whispered.

Kylie smiled. "Uh, you just criticized the space between your nose and your mouth."

Channy looked back at her again, but this time let the gaze linger, long enough to convey to her friend that she was in no mood to joke. Then she rolled onto her side, her back to Kylie. "I don't feel like talking about this anymore."

"I'm not trying to embarrass you, or hurt you," Kylie said. "I'm trying to help."

"I know you are."

There was an awkward moment of silence, then Kylie perked up. "I'm going to get something to eat in just a minute. Wanna go with me? We could—"

"No, I'm not hungry," Channy interrupted. "But you should go. I'll talk to you later."

"Okay," Kylie said. She stood up and took a step back toward her bed before turning around. "Listen, at least think about what I said. Things might work out fine for you two, or they might not. But you need to trust that what he's telling you is the truth. If he thought you were hideous, he wouldn't hang out with you so much. I'm sure he really likes you, Channy. But let him work this out."

When there was no response, she walked out of the room, leaving the rest of her laundry on the bed, and her roommate curled up, staring at the wall.

The Spider's hatch had opened, but Gap was in no hurry to rush out. At the opposite end of the craft, crumpled on the floor of the bay, was a three-foot-wide alien being. Its status as life form or robotic vehicle seemed unimportant at the moment; what mattered was the fact that it had the ability to move at lightning speed, and once it grasped something, it was almost impossible to pry loose.

Mira stood behind Gap, one hand resting on his shoulder in a gesture that made it clear she would have no problem using him as a shield. They both craned their necks through the opening, looking down and around to see if anything had scuttled over to this end of the Spider, but the floor was clear.

Gap called out to Roc. "Any sign of movement since it jumped off?"

"There was no jumping involved," the computer said. "It fell, no control whatsoever. Dropped like a rock and landed hard. And no, it hasn't moved a muscle . . . or pulley, or whatever it uses inside. It's just lying there. In fact, it almost looks like a puppy, kinda cute, all nestled up in a ball, like it's tuckered out and needs a good nap. Of course, I still wouldn't pet it, even if I had arms."

Triana's voice rang out from the bay's speaker system. "Gap, Mira, just hold tight for a minute. Don't climb down. I've got help coming your way."

"What kind of help?" Gap said.

"Two crew members are gearing up right now in EVA suits. I recommend you do the same before you step out. I know the atmosphere is fine, but every bit of protection helps."

Gap pulled back from the hatch and keyed open one of the storage bins. A handful of specially equipped space suits hung there.

"Don't know if these will do any good," he muttered to Mira, "but she's right; probably better than nothing."

Five minutes later they were giving each other a quick visual scan to make certain that everything was secure: suits, gloves, boots, and helmets were checked and rechecked before they nodded through their visors at each other. Gap heard Mira's voice in his ear through the intercom system.

"Should we still wait?"

"Probably," he said. "Not that I want to gang up on the thing, but I'd feel safer with numbers on our side. Easier to surround it."

"I'm okay with that," she said. "This is turning out to be quite an assignment."

They caught sight of movement through the glass of the control room, and looked over to see a handful of crew members milling around inside. Two of them wore EVA suits; they waved at Gap and Mira, then made their way into the bay and cautiously approached the Spider. Gap saw that they were each clutching portable grappling arms, similar to those on the Spider. He addressed them by name—Mitch and Zhenta—and made sure that proper introductions were made with Mira.

Zhenta, whose parents were originally from Egypt, indicated the front of the Spider. "What's the plan?"

Gap peered through her faceplate. "First, we remove the

container box, and get it just as close as we can. Then, we close in from all four sides, and you and Mitch grab the . . . thing. Should be a lot easier than when Mira tried it."

"Okay. Let's go bag a creature," Mitch said.

Gap took a deep breath—he could almost sense the others doing the same—and together they rounded the corner of the Spider and began to stride toward the front side. They paused at the far corner, then Gap took the lead and peered around the edge of the metal craft.

There, about ten feet away, lay the vulture. Even in this vulnerable position, crumpled and at awkward angles, it still struck Gap as an imposing force. The deep black seemed like ink, an unnatural darkness, while a small glimpse of its yellow streaks provided a brilliant contrast and a fierce, aggressive aura. It gave every indication of being either dead, unconscious, or offline; the throbbing bright blue-green color from its edges was missing, and the vents that had at least mimicked breathing were motionless.

And yet, the vulture still radiated danger in a manner that Gap couldn't justify. He simply understood, on some level, that although it might be dead, he wasn't about to go up and kick it.

He also knew that he was the leader of this small group, and it was up to him to make the first move. With a silent wave of his hand, he took a few steps toward the creature and sensed the others following him. Within his helmet the sound of his breathing was loud, almost distracting. He never took his eyes from the vulture; the image of it bursting from *Galahad's* hull onto the Spider replayed in his mind. His rational side told him that with its speed, two feet away, ten feet away, or thirty feet away would make no difference; but his instinctual fears still caused him to almost tiptoe as he approached. Now, as he stood above it, he felt his heart racing, and his breathing intensified.

He directed Mitch and Mira toward the polyglass container

that was still attached to the Spider's arm. In three minutes they had removed it and, with its door still open, placed it—gently— on the floor beside the vulture.

Then the four of them gathered around and stared down at the motionless mass. It certainly seemed dead, and Gap immediately began trying to process what might have happened. The temperature? The atmospheric pressure? The artificial gravity?

He shook his head and exhaled. There was no time for this right now; it would be Lita's job to answer those questions, and it was *his* job to get the specimen to her.

"Okay," he said softly. "Let's do it."

Zhenta extended her portable grappling arm toward the vulture, and was able to slide it under one side. She pushed a little harder, then harder still, until at last the creature appeared to budge. "Ugh, it's heavy," she said. "We might need to have two people on each arm."

Gap reached over and helped her with supporting the arm. At the same time, from the opposite side, Mitch duplicated Zhenta's actions. A few seconds later he had a firm grip on the vulture, with Mira lending a hand.

"Are we good so far?" Gap said, looking at the group. "On three. Very gently, right? One . . . two . . . three."

Straining, and putting their leg muscles into it, the four crew members slowly lifted the vulture from the Spider bay floor. The strong and sturdy grappling arms swayed under the mass, but they managed to raise it a foot off the ground. "Okay, let's get it inside," Gap said, and they began to rotate toward the box.

One of the vulture's wings shifted, causing the group to suddenly stop and gasp, but they quickly realized that it was simply a result of the movement.

Mira laughed softly. "We're jumpy."

"For good reason," Gap said with a grin.

They lowered it into the polyglass container. One wing was

hung up on an edge of the box; Zhenta removed her grappling arm and gently maneuvered the wing down inside.

Gap exhaled loudly. "Whew, good job. Okay, Roc, seal that sucker up."

The container's opening slid shut. Immediately a yellow light began to blink on a side panel, indicating that a seal had been achieved. It would take a few minutes before a vacuum was achieved inside, and the atmosphere and temperature adjusted.

"Did someone order a vulture in a box?" Gap said over the intercom in his helmet.

"Nice work, you guys," Triana said. "Let's roll a cart in there and you can move it up to Sick House. Lita's expecting you. Then, Gap, if you and Mira would stop by the Control Room, please."

"On our way," he said.

Twenty minutes later, he and Mira entered the Control Room to a small round of applause from the crew members working there. Triana beamed at them and clapped Mira on the shoulder.

"Just another day at the office?"

"Oh, sure," Mira said with a laugh. "Pretty boring day."

"Knowing Lita, I'll bet she's excited to get started," Triana said to Gap.

He nodded. "Yeah, she was like a little kid anxious to open birthday presents. She practically fogged up the outside of the box with her face right up against it."

Triana said, "I want to go over things with you, and get any thoughts you might have about what you saw."

"I have a question," Mira said. "After the dome vulture came at us, did any of the other ones react? Are they still in the same position, or did they move?"

"No changes," Triana said. "We have cameras positioned on all of them now, and there was no movement. There was, however, a reaction."

"Let me guess," Gap said. "The lights."

"Yep. As soon as the drama started with you guys, they all lit up a little more. But especially our squadron leader. There was practically a symphony of light coming from him."

"So they are definitely communicating with each other," Gap said. He looked thoughtful. "I just wish we knew if that meant communication with something else."

"Your mother ship idea?" Triana said.

He raised his eyebrows. "That's what I'm afraid of."

"Why, oh why, won't anyone ask for my input?" Roc said suddenly.

Triana rolled her eyes. "You don't need an invitation. What do you have?"

"Well, our little winged friends not only stepped up their light show, their flapping show morphed, too."

"The vents?"

"That's right. A sudden and rapid shift in the venting activity. I'm convinced that it's tied in with their communication. And, not only that, I think it's somehow tied into how they get their power."

There was silence as the group thought about this. Then Triana said, "Power from where?"

"I'm working on that," Roc said. "I have a theory . . . but it's a little crazy, and I'd like to get some information from Lita's work before I go much further."

As if on cue, Lita's voice broke through the intercom. "Tree?"

"Yes, Lita."

"Thought you might like to hear the news. We are no longer a morgue, and once again a hospital."

Gap and Triana looked at each other. "It's moving?" Gap said.

"Oh, it's moving. The return to a vacuum and spacelike conditions resuscitated it, apparently. The lights, the vents, everything.

"And not only that," she added, "it doesn't seem very happy at all."

14

She was due back in Sick House to help Lita begin the process of examining the vulture, but at the moment Alexa was sitting quietly on the edge of her bed, alone in her room. Since waking from a fitful night of sleep, she had chosen to be alone. No breakfast in the Dining Hall, not that she was hungry anyway. Katarina had obviously suspected that something was wrong, but other than a polite inquiry she had left her roommate to her own thoughts. And, though it was tempting to call Bon, Alexa reasoned that it was too soon to bring it all up again.

But this dream had been as disturbing as the last.

She had reconstructed it several times in the four hours since snapping awake, but could reach no conclusions. This time details seemed vague, which was unusual for one of her visions. Yet, again, it seemed so real. Perhaps, she decided, if she went through it one more time before going to work it would make sense.

There was darkness, a deep, heavy darkness that swallowed her. It came about swiftly; there had been bright light, then surprise, then the darkness. But surprise because of what? The sensation was unmistakable; its cause was a mystery.

The darkness had a quality about it that brought on her anxiety: it was suffocating. Not just figuratively, but literally. It was the feeling that stuck with her the most after awakening. She remembered wanting to claw the darkness away because it was somehow affecting the space around her. Had it somehow polluted the air, making it unfit for breathing? Had it somehow absorbed the air, leaving none behind for her to breathe? It was a painful feeling, sharp and daggerlike.

On top of it all, she had been powerless to do anything about it. Her arms were unable to move, as if she was paralyzed. Her need to push the darkness away was maddening, and yet it was quite obviously in total control.

What did it mean? She kept coming back to the same thought: she was in space, without protection, without a suit or helmet. The darkness of space had engulfed her, and there was no air to breathe.

But where were the stars? Why was it so utterly dark? And why could she not move? How could she have stumbled into this predicament? How could she have possibly managed to find herself alone, outside the ship, in the vacuum of space?

Unless she wasn't alone. Was it possible, she wondered, that this was the future of everyone on the ship? Had she seen a vision where *Galahad* itself no longer existed, and the entire crew was adrift in space? And did their encounter with the vultures play a role in their destiny?

She sat forward on her bed and rubbed at her temples, trying to massage the frightening image from her mind. She realized that her futile attempt to make sense of these dreams was causing even more pain. Perhaps, she concluded, it wasn't possible to decipher the meaning; and, she reminded herself, it wasn't clear if all of her visions were destined to come true. There were so many theories of multiple universes, with infinite possibilities and outcomes; what if she was merely tapping into a menu of *potential* futures?

It helped ease her mind . . . but not much.

She had eventually spoken to Bon about the funeral dream, but this vision she would keep to herself.

With a weary sigh she pushed herself to her feet and went about her usual morning routine to prepare for a day of work. It would be a long, difficult stretch once she got to Sick House.

By the time Triana arrived, a throng had surrounded the polyglass container—although they kept a respectful distance. There was a low murmur of voices, as if they didn't want to take a chance of upsetting the specimen. At first glance, it appeared to Triana that the vulture was distressed enough already; it darted around the interior of the container, pausing for only brief moments before continuing its frantic activity.

She stepped up beside the other crew members and watched. The vulture shot from corner to corner, edge to edge. Although it was a challenge to keep up with its movements, Triana tried to examine the various parts of the creature that she had previously seen only on the vidscreen. The vents fluttered in what seemed a random pattern, with all but a few of them active. The soft, bluegreen light seeped from underneath, except when the vulture arched upward to the top of the box, whereupon the light took on a more vivid, cutting appearance, almost laserlike. And when it paused long enough on the sides, Triana was able to catch glimpses of the hollow, mouthlike opening on its belly.

She admired the stark black color, punctuated by a handful of bright yellow streaks on its underside. Funny, she thought, that it could appear both terrifying and beautiful at the same time.

From the opposite side of the container Lita caught her attention without saying a word. The two Council members eyed the vulture, then the amazed faces of their crew mates gathered around. Triana nodded as if to say, "once again we face the great unknown." There was work to be done, but she understood that it was important for the crew to participate in the discovery.

Looking back into the box, it dawned on her that the vulture was not acting manic; it was simply a trapped animal, doing what instincts drove all creatures to do at that moment: search for a way out. It just happened that these particular creatures moved with lightning speed at all times, which gave the impression that it was frenzied. In fact, it was quite likely, she thought, that the captive was more composed than the captors.

Gradually the crew members began to peel away, most shaking their heads, their conversation animated.

Triana looked over her shoulder and saw Alexa enter the room, then immediately stop when she saw the vulture. But unlike the looks of amazement and wonder that she had seen on the faces of the others, Triana caught a glimpse of what seemed to be terror in Alexa's eyes. The medical assistant stood frozen, her hands at her sides, for a long time. She seemed reluctant to draw any closer to the creature that tore around its transparent cage.

Lita had seen her, too. "Pretty incredible, isn't it?" she said.

Alexa didn't answer at first, then looked up at Lita and smiled. To Triana the smile seemed forced and uncomfortable.

"Beyond incredible," Alexa said. The remaining crew members who had come to gape at the captured being pushed past her and left the room.

"I'm glad you're here," Lita said. "I'm going to turn on the probe so we can start gathering a little more hard data." She laughed and added, "You'll have to get a little closer if you want to help."

Alexa took a few cautious steps forward, but gave the container a wide berth as she moved around to stand beside Lita. Her gaze was again locked on the vulture; she seemed to not have even noticed Triana standing there.

Lita crept up to the box. She knelt down and examined one of the end panels, then looked back at her assistant. "Well?"

"Oh, sorry," Alexa said, and inched closer. Triana was convinced they were the hardest steps Alexa had ever taken.

"You okay?" Triana said.

"Um . . . yes. Just kinda in awe, I think."

"Like all of us," Lita said. "Okay, once I get this running, check all of the readings. We don't want anything to affect the vacuum. Shout out and I can shut it down right away."

"Do you need me to do anything?" Triana said.

"Sure. Keep your eye on our little friend and let me know if it starts to react strangely."

"And how in the world will I be able to tell?" Triana said with a laugh.

Lita grinned at her. "That's a good point. And to be honest, I really don't know."

She turned back to the panel before her. When Dr. Zimmer had run through all of the potential tools that the crew might need during their journey, he was aware that there might come a time when they would need to examine objects they encountered along the way. He had ordered the construction of various containers that could simulate the environment of space. Some of the more complex scientific devices aboard, the boxes were capable of maintaining the vacuum and weightlessness of space, and could be temperature controlled. They had taken almost a year to design and build, with the idea that their most likely use would come once they entered the planetary system around Eos.

Yet now, less than a year into the mission, one was being put to use in ways they had never imagined.

"Here goes," Lita said. Pressing her lips together, she took a quick look into the box, then snapped on the power. Immediately a tiny vidscreen came to life, displaying more detailed information about the settings, and—more important—diagnostic readings on the creature within. The information was also sent directly to Roc.

Lita made a minor adjustment, then spoke to Alexa. "Everything look good so far?"

"So far, so good," Alexa said. "Calibration is almost complete, and . . . yes, Roc should be getting a stream by now. Conditions inside are stable."

"Tree, what about our guest?"

Triana, bent over with her hands on her knees, peered through the glass. "No change that I can tell."

"The bottom of the container houses imaging devices," Lita said. "Keep watching, because that could have a big effect on it when they switch on. If all goes well we should have a detailed map of this thing in just a minute."

"Everything still normal," Alexa said.

"Roc," Lita said, "I'm going to turn on the imaging, if you're ready."

"Actually, wait a moment," the computer said, then fell quiet. All three girls waited for an explanation. Lita took her hand away from the panel.

"Before you do the standard imaging," Roc said, "set the controls for individual particle readings."

"Why?" Lita said. "And particles as in . . . ?"

"Energy particles, primarily gamma and X ray. Just humor me. I'm working on a theory."

Lita shrugged. "Okay." She talked while she made the adjustments. "Can you give us a clue what you're looking for?"

"Regardless of whether or not they're technically life forms, something has to be powering them. I derive my energy from the ship's ion drive, you get yours from those nasty things that Bon grows in the dirt. A star uses nuclear fusion. You get the idea. These things are out in the middle of deep space, and with their speed and technical abilities, they have to be pulling power—and a lot of it, I would say—from somewhere. I want to know where."

Triana kept staring at the vulture. "Gamma rays? Really?"

"Nope," Roc said. "I want to rule *out* gamma, X ray, and a bunch of others."

Triana and Lita exchanged glances. "Any idea where he's going with this?" Triana said.

"Not yet," Lita said. "Okay, Roc, switching on . . . now."

The vidscreen display flickered, then began to scroll an impossibly complex sequence of code.

"Whoa, look at this," Triana said.

Lita and Alexa looked up from the panel. The vulture had slowed its movement around the box, and a minute later had settled to the bottom of its cage. The vents continued to fluctuate much as they had, but the blue-green light had increased in both activity and intensity.

"Coincidence?" Alexa said. "Maybe he's finished with his exploration."

"Maybe," Lita said. "But I don't think so."

"No coincidence," Roc said. "It knows what's going on. The readings show that it's absorbing our scan."

"What do you mean, absorbing?"

Roc paused before answering. "It means we have all the information we're going to get right now. Your panel is showing the outgoing scan waves; I, on the other hand, am receiving the scan images and data. Or, rather, I was. After the first thirty seconds nothing came out the other side."

Triana stood up. "It's . . . digesting the scan waves?"

"Apparently it finds them appetizing. Too bad for us, however, because it's leaving no leftovers for us."

"Wait a second," Lita said, still kneeling before the panel. "It can't completely absorb everything. All creatures emit some sort of energy, or waste. For us it's mostly heat. Are you sure nothing is coming out?"

"Nothing," Roc said. "You are looking at a being that takes and takes and takes, and gives nothing back. Even the light we're seeing from the bottom is controlled. When that's not happening, not one single particle is escaping from this thing.

"Which," the computer added, "just about proves the theory I've been chewing on. And, I might add, it's a rather fascinating scenario."

Alexa had backed away, the look of terror once again on her face.

"Tell us," Triana said.

"This vulture, or parasite, or whatever we end up calling it, is powered by the most prolific energy source in the universe. An unlimited supply, actually, and available without having to go to a gas station or anything."

"And what is it?" Lita said.

"Why, Lita, I'm surprised at you," Roc said. "You learned this in School and at *Galahad* training. It's powered by dark energy."

15

t wasn't until the ship's lights began to dim for the evening that Gap realized he was famished. The buzz of the morning's activity had kept him wound up for the rest of the day, and lunch simply had not happened. He had carved out some time in the late afternoon to hit the treadmill in the gym, followed by some extended stretching exercises. Now, after a quick shower, he rushed into the Dining Hall, determined to eat everything in sight. The dinner crowd had thinned considerably; he quickly filled his tray and turned to survey the room.

Triana sat in her usual spot in the back, alone. She made eye contact and waved.

"Am I intruding on deep thoughts?" he said, pulling out the seat next to her.

"I would welcome a break from the deep ones," Triana said. "How was the rest of your day? Hard to measure up to the morning?"

Gap wasted no time hefting a portion of salad to his mouth. "That's for sure," he said, chewing. "Pardon my lack of manners, I'm starving. Uh, my day. Well, things are running fine in Engineering; some of the usual scheduling issues since we're about to start a new work cycle, but I think everyone's starting to get used to that for the most part. Um . . . what else? A workout. Not much besides that."

"Did Channy wear you out?"

He shook his head and jabbed a wedge of apple into his mouth. "Did the treadmill. She had just finished a dance class. Seemed out of sorts, if you ask me."

"In what way?"

"I don't know, just not her usual Channy self. I tried to talk to her for a minute, but she acted like she had a lot on her mind. Probably nothing. But never mind my day, tell me what happened in Sick House."

Triana leaned on the table and crossed her hands. "I've been sitting here trying to process all of it. There's lots."

"Really?" Gap said. He shoveled in another mouthful of greens, chewing vigorously. "Tell me, tell me."

Triana smiled and indicated the corner of her own mouth. Gap took the hint and wiped a smear of dressing off his face with a napkin.

"Well, our guest certainly came back to life with a vengeance," she said. "It's quite active. And you know, as frightening as it is, it's really . . . I don't know, beautiful, I guess you could say. There's something about the shape, the movement, the power. I have to admit, I'm fascinated by it."

"That's cool. I'll have to stop by tomorrow and check it out. Did Lita and Roc find out anything yet?"

"Oh, you could say that," Triana said. "You of all people will appreciate this. Roc thinks the vultures are powered by dark energy."

Gap stopped in midchew, his gaze boring into Triana. "What?"

Triana smiled. "Yeah, I knew you'd like that. Apparently these things are built to absorb energy of all sorts, but their power comes from the universe itself." She filled him in on the other details.

"That's incredible," Gap said, setting down his fork. "So they don't give off any waste at all. Nothing." He raised his eyebrows. "Man, they're the ultimate in efficiency, aren't they?"

They sat in silence for a minute, then Gap took a sip of water and fixed Triana with a look. "That makes them even more frightening, doesn't it? I mean, you gotta wonder if we'll be able to hold this thing very long."

"Well, I'll admit something to you that I didn't say to Lita and Alexa," Triana said in a low voice. "For some reason I can't explain, I get the feeling that it's just extremely patient, and letting us do our little exam. Meanwhile, I think it's checking us out, too. Who knows, it might just be toying with us by hanging out in that container." She shrugged. "Part of me wants to take it right back to the Spider bay and let it go."

"And then it will just attach itself to the dome again, don't you think?"

Triana exhaled. "Yeah, probably. And we'd be right back where we started."

Gap began to eat again. "So, what's the next step?"

"When I left Sick House, Lita was wrapping up for the night. Tomorrow morning she's going to run some tests to find out what knocked it out when you docked in the bay. If we knew that, we'd have some sort of ammunition."

Nodding, Gap poked at the remains of his dinner. "And you think we need ammunition?"

"I have no idea," Triana said, sitting back. "But you and I both know that we need to be prepared for anything. And, on top of that, I still don't like the idea of them hitching a ride on the skin of the ship. I'm not advocating that we injure them in any way, but I can't see us taking them for a ride all the way to Eos, either."

There was silence between them for a while. When the conversation picked up again, they shifted to small talk. Gap, his stomach full, pushed back his plate and enjoyed a few minutes of light banter with the Council Leader. It was the most relaxed he had felt around her in a long time, and it felt good. At times Triana even laughed, and Gap found himself staring at her, watching the light dance in her green eyes. He forced himself to constantly look away, yet her eyes were magnetic to him; before he knew it he was staring again.

He began to feel a knot in his stomach. Try as he might over the past year, it was impossible for him to deny that he continued to have strong feelings for Triana. She did nothing to indicate that she shared those same feelings, and had always been thoughtful and considerate, even though he was sure that she had picked up on his emotions. She treated him with respect, and confided in him as not only a close associate but as a friend. In some ways that made it better, while in others it made it more difficult.

Even his brief relationship with Hannah had failed to extinguish the flame. Gap sincerely cared for Hannah, and still felt regret over the way things had ended between them. Yet, underneath it all, he knew that Triana was the one; no matter how close he had become with Hannah, the truth was that she had been a substitute for Tree, a bandage to help protect the wound that had been inflicted long ago.

These feelings added a layer of guilt on top of everything else. In his heart he never felt as if he had used Hannah intentionally, but he understood that pain was powerful, and often led the human heart down an unintended path. The results were not what he had ever wished for: Hannah was hurt in the process, and Triana was no closer.

Or was she? As they sat in the Dining Hall, she seemed much more at ease with him now. They had weathered the turbulence that grew between them during a confrontation over Merit Simms two months earlier, and now that appeared to be forgotten completely. She looked not only comfortable discussing potentially dangerous issues like the vultures, but equally as comfortable laughing over routine day-to-day experiences on the ship. It made his heart melt.

It also created a firestorm in his mind, a battle between his emotions and his rational side. As much as his heart wanted to fall back again, his head screamed over and over again to resist, to stay distant and safe.

It was so hard to do. Those green eyes were powerful, a whirlpool that threatened to pull him under no matter how valiantly he fought.

Gap had no idea how it would eventually turn out, but he summoned the strength to pull himself away. When a lull in the conversation turned up, he stretched and mentioned how exhausted he was from the day, then stood up.

"I need to sleep," he said. "I'm glad we were able to catch up tonight."

"Me, too," Triana said with a smile. "Sleep well, okay?"

As he walked away with both of their dinner trays, he heard her snap on the vidscreen at the table.

Lita tapped a stylus pen against her cheek. She took one last look at the data on the workpad before setting it on her desk and pushing back her chair. For the past several hours she and Alexa, along with numerous other assistants, had coordinated an intense study of the vulture using a multitude of scientific tools at their disposal, along with Roc's vast reserves of information. They had compiled an impressive report, one that Lita would pass along at a Council meeting the next day.

But for now it was getting late, and she was tired. She briefly debated whether to pass up dinner and just head to bed, but knew that it was vital to maintain a sharp mind and a full tank of energy. The Dining Hall would have mostly cleared out by this time anyway, so she could get in and out quickly before crashing for the night.

The door from Sick House swished open and she almost collided with Kylie Rickman.

"Oh, sorry about that," Kylie said. "I wondered if you'd still be here."

"The end of a long day," Lita said. "Everything okay?"

"Yeah, I'm fine. Just wanted to see if I could talk with you for a second. It's nothing serious."

"As long as you don't mind walking and talking," Lita said. "I'm running to get something to eat."

Kylie fell into step beside her. "I know you've had a lot on your plate today with the vulture and everything, so I hate to bother you with this."

Lita looked at her, puzzled. "No, it's fine. What's on your mind?"

"Well . . . it's about Channy."

"What's she done now?" Lita said with a grin. "Is she turning into a tyrant down in the gym? Or is she trying to set you up with someone? I never thought about the pressure on you as her roommate; she probably hounds you all the time about boys."

"Actually, she knows I can take care of myself in that department just fine," Kylie said. "And if there's been any change in her at the gym, it's probably because she's so distracted these days."

"Oh? By what?"

"Would you believe a boy?"

Lita stopped in the middle of the corridor. "You're kidding. Little Miss Matchmaker is setting *herself* up?"

Kylie glanced in both directions to ensure they were out of earshot of other people. Even then she lowered her voice.

"And that's why I want to talk with you. I'm worried about her. She's never been through anything like this before, and it's really affecting her." In a minute she had recounted her conversation with Channy.

"I think it would be a good idea if you talked with her," Kylie concluded. "I think she has always focused on setting up everyone else because she's a little insecure. She's been afraid to dip her own toes in the pool until now."

It was Lita's turn to look around. The door to the Dining Hall was just ahead, but even at this hour there wouldn't be much privacy in the room. Instead she guided Kylie over to the edge of the corridor.

"I have no problem talking with Channy," she said. "But you're her roommate and one of her best friends; why do you think it would be any different coming from me?"

"Because she probably values your opinion more than anyone on this ship," Kylie said. "She has tons of respect for Triana, but I know that you hold a special place with her. I don't know, for whatever reason she really looks up to you as a mentor, I think."

Lita laughed. "We're only a month apart in age."

"Doesn't matter; I can tell every time your name comes up that she thinks of you almost as a moral teacher of sorts. You obviously have a lot of influence on her, whether you know it or not."

Lita reflected on this as three crew members walked by and said hello. When they had rounded the corner and disappeared, she looked back at Kylie.

"That's very flattering, but I'm not sure what I would say to Channy. I can't really tell her what to do; it's still her business."

"I know, but I think she's rushing in too quickly, and I'm really afraid that she's gonna get hurt badly. You know how she is; she jumps into everything with both feet, and puts her entire heart and soul into every project that comes along. I think it's really magnified this time, and I'm afraid that it might come crashing down on her."

Another crew member jogged past and waved. Kylie hesitated before adding: "I think it would be a good idea if you grounded her just a bit. It would mean more coming from you than from me."

Lita inwardly sighed. The timing could not have been worse. She was busier than ever in Sick House, and the Council was counting on her to provide them with crucial information regarding the vultures. Yet if she had learned anything from her mother, it was the value of personal relationships. Channy was indeed her friend, and a good soul. Ironically, the bouncy Brit had constantly chided Lita about her love life, or lack thereof. To suddenly train the microscope on Channy's personal life seemed alien.

However, what Kylie said about Channy's insecurities made complete sense to Lita, and would also explain so much of the driving force behind Channy's desire to see others fall in love; she had been wary of the day that it would happen to her.

And now it apparently had.

"Okay," Lita said. "We have a Council meeting tomorrow, so maybe I can pull her aside and get her to talk a little bit."

"Please don't tell her I said anything," Kylie said.

"Of course not. I'll figure out a way to steer the conversation that way."

Kylie's smile was tinged with a look of relief. "Thanks. Like I said, I know how busy you are right now, but—"

"No problem," Lita said. "Thanks for talking to me about it. I'm glad Channy has friends who care about her like you do."

They parted with a hug. Lita leaned against the curved, padded wall and rubbed at her tired eyes. Her résumé had suddenly been amended: doctor, biologist, and now relationship counselor.

16

The walk was long and intentionally slow. Triana found that it had become a ritual for her, a way to organize her thoughts and emotions. Perhaps it was a lesson from her dad—he of the long, slow drives in the hills—that getting away allowed you to explore options that otherwise wouldn't occur to you. She had no way of truly getting away, so instead she had become accustomed to what she described as a meditative walk. It was a refreshing break from the usual hectic pace.

This morning's impending Council meeting was also shaping up as a break from the ordinary. For the past several weeks they had concentrated on routine items that related to the everyday business of running the ship; now the agenda included Lita's report on the mysterious vultures. That in turn would lead to the next step: what to do with their uninvited guests.

She walked with her head down, close to the wall and out of the hustling flow of traffic that sped past her. Several crew members greeted her as they went past, while others had learned to recognize when she dropped into thinking mode and breezed past silently.

Both her father and Dr. Zimmer had stressed the importance of being prepared; for her father it was geared to life in general, while Dr. Zimmer focused on the duties that *Galahad*'s Council

Leader would encounter. "Anticipate your next move," the scientist had often told her. "Not just one possible course, but two. Three, if possible. Looking ahead can prevent the most dangerous element of your journey: surprise."

A grim smile crept across her face. Surprise had been a constant companion since their launch. In a way, surprise was routine. Would it be any different at any time on their journey? *Could it be any different?*

The fifteen-minute walk to the Council meeting had been devoted to anticipation. She hoped that Lita's report would shed light on their potential actions with the vultures, but in the meantime Triana wanted to prepare for several prospective choices. She knew full well that one of those choices included a confrontation with the alien species, and it was not a decision that she would take lightly. Defending the crew, the ship, and the mission took priority.

She slowed to a stop. The Conference Room was just ahead, around the curve of the hallway. Her alone time had come to an end. She heard footsteps approaching from behind, and then Gap's familiar voice.

"Are you lost?"

He pulled up beside her and she smiled at him. "No, just gathering a few thoughts. You know how I am."

"Sorry," he said. "I can leave you alone."

"No, not a problem," she said, and began to walk with him. "A good morning for you so far?"

"Nothing exciting. A quick workout, then breakfast. Oh, except that we have oatmeal now. Have you heard?"

Triana laughed. "Everyone's had it but me, I think. One of these mornings I'll get there early enough."

They approached the door and found Lita waiting outside, with Bon next to her. Lita greeted them with a wave.

"Channy inside already?" Triana said.

Lita shook her head. "No, haven't seen her yet. This might be the first Council meeting where she wasn't one of the first to arrive."

Gap looked at Triana. "I told you, she hasn't seemed like herself lately. Something's different about her." He turned to Lita. "Has she said anything to you?"

"Uh . . . no, she hasn't talked with me about anything," Lita said, then quickly changed the subject. "Tree, I hope it's okay with you, but I talked briefly with Alexa this morning, and thought that she should probably join us. She's put a lot of work into this report."

"That's fine. The entire meeting is dedicated to the vultures, so no problem." Triana looked both directions down the corridor. "Let's go on in. I imagine Channy can't be too far behind."

The group took their seats around the conference table and made small talk for a few minutes until Alexa arrived, and then, five minutes later, Channy hurried in.

"Sorry I'm late," she said, rushing to take her seat.

Triana studied her for a moment, the way she avoided eye contact, then looked at Gap, who raised his eyebrows as if to say, "See what I mean?"

"Okay, down to business," Triana said. "We've had one of the vultures under observation for almost twenty-four hours. Lita, Alexa, and Roc have used that time for a rather exhaustive study, and I'll let them catch us all up on what they've learned."

Lita began by punching in an access code on the keyboard before her. The multiple vidscreens in the Conference Room shimmered before a display of the captured vulture appeared on each one. A diagnostic column of numbers and figures appeared along the bottom.

"It's probably no surprise to you," Lita said, "that what we have here is an amazing specimen. After running every test you can imagine, I've gone from curiosity, to admiration, to awe. I can start by telling you right up front that we have no idea whether this thing is friend or foe; I'm not sure that those terms even apply to something like this. But I can tell you that we are dealing with an almost perfectly adapted space device."

Gap looked up from his vidscreen and across the table to Lita. "Device? You're saying that it's . . . what? A machine? So it's not living?"

"That's a difficult question to answer, too. Roc, do you want to give it a shot and tell us what it is?"

"I stand by my very first description," the computer said. "Icky. That's what it is. But even I must admit—grudgingly—that it might be the most sophisticated icky thing you'll ever find. As to whether it's alive or a machine . . . it's complicated. If you're putting me on the spot, I would have to say both."

"Both?" Gap said. "How does that work?"

"Quite well, actually," Roc said. "In the twentieth century there was a term invented to describe a being that was part human and part machine."

Bon spoke up for the first time. "They called them cyborgs."

"That's correct," Roc said. "In fact, although it first came into popular use in science fiction stories, scientists did believe that a human/machine cyborg would be a great instrument for exploring space. Whoever's responsible for these things stuck on the outside of our ship apparently took that idea and ran with it. I am in agreement with Lita when she says they are almost perfectly adapted to outer space."

Triana bit her lip while she processed this. "So . . . what part is alive, and what part is mechanical?"

Lita said, "We're convinced that the majority of the vulture is artificially created. In fact, under extremely strong magnification you can almost see where it has been patched in a few places. I don't know what kind of scrapes it's been in, but from what we can tell it's been in the shop a few times for repairs."

"The vents and the blue-green light are also mechanical," Roc added. "I'm pretty sure that one of our scans has picked up something that might act as a combination radar and guidance system. They're not too dissimilar from the systems aboard our ship, for that matter."

"Except they are much more evolved and complicated," Lita added.

"Well, I wouldn't say *evolved*," Roc said, a hint of irritation in his voice.

Lita laughed. "Nothing personal, my friend."

"Okay, but back to the cyborg discussion," Triana said. "All of what you've said makes sense. But what part is alive?"

Lita and Alexa exchanged a look. It was Alexa who finally spoke up.

"Um . . . I've spent a little time on a portion that we picked up through our scans, and I'm pretty sure it's a brain." She tapped a few keys, and the vidscreens zoomed in on an area along the bottom of the vulture. With another flurry of keystrokes, she soon had a section of it highlighted.

"It's not very large, but large enough to get the job done," Alexa said. "Something similar to a nervous system appears to run throughout the creature, but we can't tell if it does the same things our nervous system does. There is definitely a network of sorts, though."

Gap whistled. "Well . . . wouldn't that, uh, make this thing alive? I mean, technically?"

"I think so, yes," Lita said.

"I would say no," Roc said.

Triana shook her head. "Wait a minute. One at a time here. Lita, go ahead. Why do you say yes?"

"Because it's the brain that makes us who we are. It's what houses the mind, the conscious entity that gives us the ability to reason. If this thing has a brain, I maintain that it's officially a living being, regardless of the other parts."

"Okay," Triana said. "Roc, what are your thoughts?"

"This is not a discussion about whether our disgusting friend has a conscious mind; I'm willing to consider that it might possibly have a brain, but that's not the same thing. Also, from what I conclude after studying the data, this is not a case where a living creature with a fully functioning brain had some of its parts replaced with machine parts or mechanical pieces; that was the original concept of the cyborg, by the way.

"In this case, it has all the signs of a perfectly designed and engineered space-roaming device that has simply had an organically developed brain dropped into the slot reserved for decision making."

"So you think that the brain is simply a custom-made part?" Gap said.

"That's one way to look at it," Roc said. "And by the way, let's not make the mistake of thinking this brain is anything like the ones you carry around. It's quite different, and serves different purposes."

"But we don't know that," Lita said. "Tree, with all due respect to Roc and everything that he has contributed to our mission, I don't think we can automatically assume that the vultures' brains are entirely different from ours. Who are we to say what consciousness really is, anyway? The greatest minds of our own species have never been able to clearly define it, even for ourselves, let alone an alien race."

A heavy sigh escaped from Triana. She locked her fingers together on the table and looked at the other Council members. Both Bon and Gap were shifting their gazes between her and Lita; Channy, on the other hand, was sitting completely still, her eyes looking down at her hands in her lap. She didn't appear to be listening to any of this. Triana felt a stir of irritation, but let it go for the moment.

"Roc," she said, "you said the brain was 'organically developed.' What do you mean by that?"

"It's not carbon based, and that already makes it different from every form of life on Earth. Instead, it has a silicon-crystal framework, which is extremely stable and efficient. As I mentioned, the creature itself is mostly mechanical; the one exception is the decision-making apparatus. Logic would tell us that it wouldn't naturally spawn out of a matrix of artificial components; it would have to be put together, piece by piece, including the brain."

"And why wouldn't the creators simply put in a mechanical brain?" Triana said. "Like yours, for example. Why go to all the trouble of making artificial parts for most of it, then tossing in a crystal brain?"

"I think we would have to talk to the creators," Roc said. "Which we might end up doing anyway, like it or not."

He was right, Triana thought. They could discuss it, they could toss around theories, and they could analyze it to death; but they likely would never know for sure unless they asked the designers themselves, a thought that both excited and chilled her.

She bit her lip again and took another inventory of the faces around the table. Her gaze settled on Channy, and the same feeling of irritation swelled. It was obvious that Channy was paying no attention whatsoever. Triana addressed her.

"What do you make of all this, Channy?"

It was as if the words had to sink through multiple layers before registering. Channy sat still for several moments, her eyes cast downward. Triana didn't know if it was the use of her name, or the silence that stretched across the room, that finally caused Channy to stir and look up.

"What? Oh . . ." She looked around the table and saw the stares directed at her. "I'm sorry, I was . . . my mind was on something else."

Triana felt a wave of anger build. "Your mind has been on something else since you walked in here. You understand that this is rather important, right?"

"Yeah, no, definitely, I understand." Her words sounded hollow, insincere.

Triana's voice was bitter. "Is there something on your mind that we should discuss in this meeting?"

"No."

"Then perhaps you should go deal with whatever's bothering you and let us finish our work here."

Channy looked around the table again before settling on Triana. "No, I think I'm okay now."

"I don't think so. You were late for no reason, you've paid no attention to what could be a crucial discussion at a Council meeting, and I have no reason to believe that you intend to now. Why don't you excuse yourself and we can talk later."

The atmosphere in the room was monstrously heavy. No one had ever been kicked out of a Council meeting. Lita, Alexa, and Gap looked either at the table in front of them or at the vidscreens. Bon didn't move, but his ice-blue eyes shifted back and forth between Triana and Channy.

Without another word, Channy pushed back her chair and fled the room. When the door had closed behind her, Gap said, "Something's been bothering her for a while now. Do you want me to talk with her?"

"No, thanks," Triana said. "It's my responsibility." She met the gaze of Lita, who silently conveyed with a look that she might know something. Triana made a mental note to discuss it later, but for now was anxious to get back to the business at hand.

"Let's talk about the power source of these creatures. Roc, you've proposed a fairly exotic theory that involves dark energy; can you explain that?"

"I think I'd better," the computer said. "Otherwise Gap's going to think it has something to do with Darth Vader, and I can't have that."

"Very funny," Gap said.

"Essentially, dark energy is the missing part of the equation used to explain the expansion of the universe," Roc said. "If you take all of the observable matter in the known universe, all of the stars and galaxies and planets, their mass just doesn't add up properly. They're all not only speeding away from each other, but their speed is picking up. Gravity should be pulling them back together after the Big Bang, so that eventually you'd have a Big Splat. But that's not happening. Instead, everything is accelerating, flying apart faster than it should. Many experts—and I tend to agree with them—believe that the missing part of the equation is a form of vacuum energy. We can't see it, so the science guys conveniently called it dark energy."

"And there's a lot of it, if I remember my studies," Lita said.

"That's right. All of those stars and galaxies that I mentioned only account for about thirty percent of the mass of the universe. That leaves about seventy percent unexplained. That's a lot of energy, even though it's diffuse. That means spread out, Gap."

"Very funny again."

"And how does this apply with the vultures?" Triana prompted.

"I haven't been able to prove it beyond a doubt—in fact, we might not ever be able to concretely prove it, unless we once again get to chat with the guy who drew up the plans—but it explains their efficiency. They take in exactly the amount of power they need, with no excess and no waste. They would need an unlimited supply, since there are no gas stations at the corner of

Milky Way and Andromeda; and they would need to regulate when and where they process this energy."

"The vents," Alexa suggested.

"I believe so, yes," Roc said. "They're simple in design, almost archaic, I'll grant you that. But they work."

Gap stared at the vidscreen. "Wow. Just imagine if we could take one apart to study. What if we could incorporate that technology into the design of *Galahad*? Unlimited efficient power."

"Take one apart?" Lita said. "It has a living brain, Gap."

"So do a lot of the creatures you dissected in your medical studies," Gap said.

"That's different."

"How?"

"It just is. Besides, it's not like I personally wanted to dissect anything. It's about education."

Triana jumped in. "Let's hold off on the moral or ethical debate on dissecting. We're not going to take anything apart. I can't speak to exactly how evolved these things are, but I get the distinct impression that they are capable of fighting back. Don't ask me how."

Roc said, "I agree with Gap, however, that we should try to learn as much as possible about their energy conversion and their propulsion. Almost all of history's great advances involved the theft of someone else's work."

"That's fine, but in the meantime I still want to figure out how to get the other ones off the ship," Triana said. "I'm just not comfortable with them stuck there. Let's put a time limit on your studies of our specimen, and then I want to get it out of here, too. So, Lita, if you and Alexa could focus on that issue next, and figure out a way to repel them."

Lita grinned. "As a matter of fact, I think we've already figured it out. We know exactly what it will take to brush them off the ship. And you won't believe how simple it is."

17

S he ran. First toward her room, then, when she realized that her roommate, Kylie, would likely be there, she fled aimlessly down one corridor after another. Fighting back tears, she barely acknowledged the random waves and greetings of "Hello, Channy" from various crew members as she raced past.

Kicked out of a Council meeting. Now, in addition to the brain damage caused by her obsession with Taresh, and her inability to focus on her work and Council responsibilities, she could add a new element: shame. The look of anger, mixed with disappointment, that Triana had fired her way would sting for a long time. And yet, in her heart, Channy knew that she had deserved it.

She slowed to a walk, then pulled up and slumped against the curved wall. She slid to the floor and wrapped her arms around her knees. The sprint had generated a bead of sweat, which she flicked away with the back of her hand. She buried her face in her knees and tried to marshal her rampaging thoughts.

Should she go straight to Triana and apologize? Not yet, she decided; Tree had so much to deal with at the moment, and was so irritated by Channy's behavior, that it likely would be best to let it cool for a bit. Triana—and the rest of the Council, for that matter—deserved an apology, but they had more important issues for the time being. Besides, she rationalized, it made no sense to apologize until she had solved the original problem.

Which brought her thoughts back to Taresh. Why must this be so difficult, so complex? Why would he even consider following the old traditions of his family when he was part of a new beginning, an open horizon? Couldn't he see that? Couldn't he see how perfect they were together? Didn't that trump antiquated customs?

Did everyone go through so much turmoil? She had set others up on numerous occasions, to the point that her reputation as a matchmaker was solidified; had she taken for granted that things always went smoothly?

What if it *never* did? What if, instead of spreading love and happiness, she actually was spreading pain and heartache? Perhaps it was best to stay out of it completely, to let others find their own way, forge their own relationships, suffer their own failings. How could she continue to be responsible for others feeling like this?

Or . . . was this simply her thoughts and emotions spinning out of control? What if Taresh had decided to pursue a relationship with her after all? How could she know until she talked to him again?

She lifted her head and sat back against the wall just as one of the girls from her dance class walked by and gave a quizzical look; Channy replied with the same artificial smile and wave. She thought of the time of day, and concluded that Taresh would likely be at his post in Engineering, his current assignment. Talking with him now seemed imperative; in fact, he might be waiting to hear from her, perhaps bursting to tell her that everything was fine, that he should never have even considered excluding her from his life.

All of this drama might have been for nothing, she thought. She could have saved herself the embarrassment in the Council meeting, could have saved herself the heartache *and* headache, if only she had relaxed and waited for Taresh to reach the only sensible conclusion.

Pushing herself to her feet, she started back toward her room, her mind suddenly at ease. She would send a brief note to him and request that they talk again, casually and with no pressure. It's likely what he'd wanted to hear all along, she was sure of it.

Triana stared down the table in the Conference Room, her gaze fixed on Lita. In her mind, finding a way to defend themselves against the vultures had to begin with getting them off the ship. Now Lita had announced that she and Alexa had possibly found a way to do just that.

Gap jumped into the conversation. "When you say it's simple to brush them off the ship, do you mean it's simple to do, or it was simple to figure out?"

"Both," Lita said, the smile still stretched across her face. "The first clue came as soon as you brought that thing into the Spider bay."

Triana bit her lip and thought about that moment. Gap and Mira had taxied their small craft into the bay with the vulture firmly attached to the front window. When the room had sealed and pressurized, the vulture had dropped to the floor as if unconscious. She began to quickly run down the list of things that had changed once the creature was inside.

"Is this a guessing game?" she said to Lita. "Okay, I'll play. Let's see, there was a change in gravity once it was aboard the ship."

"There's intense light," Gap mused aloud. "Pressure."

"You're both right about the differences, but those aren't the answer," Lita said. "I'm assuming that there was gravity around when the vultures were assembled, and probably light and pressure, too."

Bon, who had been quiet during the discussion, spoke up. "It's oxygen."

The others seemed almost startled to hear from him. "We have a winner," Lita said.

Gap nodded slowly. "Okay, that makes sense. Life on Earth has come to depend on oxygen, but it wasn't always that way."

"No, it wasn't," Lita said. "In fact, there was a time when Earth's atmosphere only contained about one percent oxygen. To the early forms of life on the planet, oxygen was poison. In fact, when photosynthesis began releasing more and more oxygen into the oceans and then the atmosphere, it completely changed the way life developed on our planet."

She looked at Alexa, who spoke up. "Every time we encounter something new on this journey, it reminds us that we're one tiny little speck in the universe; we can't assume that everything is designed the way we are, or that it behaves the way we do. If primitive Earth was able to support life that didn't care for oxygen, we have to assume that there are countless other worlds that began the same way and yet never evolved into an oxygen-dependent world."

"How did you find out?" Triana said.

"We gave our friend a little squirt of oxygen to see how it would react," Lita said.

"Let me guess." Gap chuckled. "It didn't react too well."

"That's putting it mildly. One tiny wisp of the stuff caused it to shrink up against the far side of the box and start to go back into defensive mode. And it happened lightning fast. These things apparently have very good self-preservation skills, because it was against the glass and beginning to curl up in less than one second."

Triana listened to the exchange, her mind skipping a step ahead. "So it becomes a fairly simple matter of firing a burst of oxygen at these things, and they should fly off the ship, is that right?"

"It looks that way," Lita said. "Alexa and I can easily rig up some oxygen canisters for Gap to take out on another EVA. Even if they fly back after the first blast, I'm guessing that just a few shots will make them hesitant to land again. I'm telling you, they react like it's acid."

Gap spread his hands out, palms up. "So what are we waiting for? Let's put something together and get out there."

"Hold on, slow down," Triana said. She looked back at Lita. "I want to get them off the ship, but I don't want to damage them or, even worse, accidentally destroy one. How much oxygen is too much?"

Lita looked thoughtful. "Well, the one we have in Sick House was exposed for several minutes in the Spider bay before we got it into the vacuum container. When they curl up like that, I think it almost puts them into a . . . I don't know, I guess you'd call it a standby mode. Like hibernation, in a way. So I don't think a few shots will do any damage."

Triana sat still for a moment, with Alexa and the other Council members silently watching her. She studied the display of the vulture on the vidscreen and considered all of the information that they had gleaned in such a short time. But what plagued her were all of the things they *didn't* know about the creatures.

One question in particular.

"Roc," she said. "I'm a little bothered by the fact that I'm so anxious to knock these things off the ship, and yet I still don't know what they're doing there. Any help on that yet?"

"One would automatically assume that they're drawn here by my magnetic charm and sophistication," the computer answered. "But I don't think my reputation has had time to extend beyond our solar system . . . yet. So, putting that aside for the moment, I have compiled my own checklist of possibilities.

"One, they are nomads who are remnants of an earlier civilization, wandering the galaxy in search of a new master. They stumbled across us, and can't let go."

Gap wrinkled his brow. "Uh . . . that seems a little far-fetched, don't you think?"

"Yes, I do. It's on my list, but I have almost zero faith in it. Number two is a little more likely."

"And that is?" Lita said.

"Number two is the possibility that they are cosmic hunters, similar to a pack of coyotes. They might not be used to anything our size, but are determined to bring us down. The weakness of this argument is the fact that we have yet to determine any damage they might be doing to the exterior of the ship. That's not to say that they *won't* do damage; in fact, they might be analyzing us, sizing us up before they begin the process of tearing away the flesh of our ship."

"Ugh, that's lovely," Lita said. "Vultures, parasites, now coyotes."

"Yes," Roc said, "a bit of an identity crisis for them, I agree. But I'm not sold on this idea, either."

The edges of Triana's mouth turned up. "Knowing you, you've saved the best for last. What's your hunch?"

"After sifting through everything we've learned—from their biochemistry, to their power source, to their maneuverability—I'm leaning heavily toward my original hypothesis. I'm convinced that they are advance scouts for an alien race that stakes out star systems, waiting for signs of activity."

Gap drummed his fingers on the table. "Any idea how they communicate their findings back home?"

"It would have to be something beyond our comprehension," Roc said. "It would almost have to be instantaneous; depending on how far they've come, they can't wait years and years to receive instructions. I think we must assume—until we discover something to the contrary—that they use dark energy for not only power, but that they somehow harness it for phoning home."

There was another moment of silence around the table. Alexa finally spoke up.

"Some form of hypercommunication?"

"Maybe simpler than that," the computer said. "Again, we are babies when it comes to this stuff. Well, you guys are babies, I'm essentially an adolescent. But it boils down to the same thing."

Triana glanced again at the vidscreen. "Do the lights play any part in this?"

"I will say yes," Roc said. "Maybe not in the actual transmission of data, but as a sort of indicator light. I back that up by noting that when Lita and Alexa puffed a stream of oxygen at our guest, it not only reacted dramatically, it also fired up its little lamp. Very intensely, I might add. I think it was crying for Mommy."

Gap looked down the table at Triana. "I understand everyone's concern about not hurting them. But if Roc's correct, I vote that we get them off the ship immediately. Even if you're not at war with a country, you still don't want their spies camping out in your backyard and sending back everything they know about you. They weren't invited; I don't see why they should get to stay."

"As much as it makes me uncomfortable," Lita said, "I think I have to agree with Gap. They haven't hurt us, and yet it's still a bit unnerving to have them locked on." She turned and looked at Bon, who had barely spoken during the meeting.

"Get rid of them," the Swede said. "Show no weakness."

Triana's thoughts turned to Channy, and with them came a flash of irritation. She would have had a vote if she'd kept her head in the meeting. And yet that vote was now irrelevant.

The majority had spoken.

18

Channy stood with her arms crossed and looked at the three T shirts on her bed. The yellow one and the pink one were definitely more her everyday style—bright, flashy, and fun—but neither seemed to fit the occasion. She eyed the light blue shirt, perhaps the most subdued item in her wardrobe; not the best color on her, but the closest thing to practical she would find. She scooped it up and began to change.

Behind her Kylie lay on the floor, propped up against her bed. Although she appeared to be completely occupied with her cuticles, Channy knew that her roommate had been watching her. Any moment the questions would begin.

"So," Kylie said, "I thought you'd still be at your Council meeting."

"Uh, it wrapped up pretty quickly this time," Channy said. "We'll probably meet again tomorrow, I think." She was uncomfortable lying to her friend, and quickly changed the subject. "How's the vacation going for you? Using it to get ahead in School?"

"I'm bored out of my skull," Kylie said. She rubbed a dot of lotion between her hands and looked up at Channy. "You might see me in the gym a lot more, just for something to do. I know we're supposed to use our downtime to rest and unwind, but I don't think I have the rest-and-unwind gene in me." She furrowed her brow. "How could the Council meeting end so quickly? I'd think with the vulture stuff you'd be in there for a few hours."

"I don't know, it just did. They still have a lot more work to do on that thing, and then we'll talk about it."

Kylie continued to rub her hands together and stare at her roommate. "Uh-huh. So what are you up to now? You just changed before the meeting, and now you're changing again?"

Channy forced a grin. "Aren't you full of questions today. You're getting as nosy as I am."

Kylie shrugged. "Just talking. You can tell me if it's none of my business."

It was becoming increasingly awkward for Channy. She had already opened up to her friend, inviting her opinion; to suddenly become evasive didn't seem quite fair.

"I'm going to meet Taresh right now."

Kylie raised her eyebrows. "I see. Isn't he working?"

"He has a twenty-minute break, so we're going to chat, that's all."

There was silence for a minute as Channy finished getting dressed. Kylie seemed to be weighing her words, unsure of how to continue the discussion; she finally pulled herself up to sit on the edge of her bed and said, "Have you given some thought to our last discussion? I mean, you're not going to pressure him, are you?"

Channy didn't answer right away, and instead took one last look in the mirror. Turning for the door, she kept from making eye contact. She hated this; Kylie was only trying to help, and deserved at least some response.

"Yes, I've thought about it, and no, this isn't about pressure. It's simply about finding out once and for all where we both stand. That's all." The door opened and she called over her shoulder: "I'll see you tonight, okay?"

Channy knew that there was no difference between the air in the corridor and the air in her room, and yet it seemed easier to breathe now. She consciously took several deep breaths as she briskly walked toward the lift. The talk with Kylie had chipped at her soul; she forced it out of her mind and concentrated on Taresh.

He had seemed surprised at her invitation to meet, and almost reluctant to spend his break in yet another heavy talk with her. Yet he had agreed to join her at the observation window on the lower level. His primary concern seemed to be the time limit; three times he had mentioned that he would have no more than ten minutes, tops. And if that was the case, Channy wanted to make sure that she honored his request while saying what she felt needed to be said.

Exactly *what* she was going to say was still in question. She would figure it out.

Stepping off the lift, she made her way through the winding corridor of the lower level. Her heart sank when she heard voices ahead; she had just a few brief minutes with Taresh, and counted on being alone with him. She rounded a turn and nearly bumped into two girls, crew members who were using their own break time to walk and talk. Channy felt her spirits lift again as they greeted her with smiles and continued down the hall the way she had come, back toward the lift.

The brilliant star field beyond the window was dazzling. She leaned against it, her ghost reflection a faint backdrop to the glittering show. For a minute she tried rehearsing what she would say to Taresh, but her mind constantly flitted back to her shameful ejection from the Council meeting, before jumping again to her conversation with Kylie. "Don't pressure him," her roommate had said. And, in their earlier conversation, it was "let him work this out."

But the waiting—the *not knowing*—was tearing her up inside.

How could she speed up the process without pushing him away? Or, if it was going to take awhile, how could she discipline herself to be patient, to keep her mind occupied with other things?

Like her duties, she realized. Her responsibilities.

She shook her head and let out a sigh. It sounded so easy, yet it wasn't.

The sound of footsteps brought her out of her trance. She turned and smiled at Taresh, who stopped a few feet short of her. His own smile seemed a mixture of discomfort and curiosity.

"Hi," Channy said. "Thank you for coming to talk with me, especially since you only have a few minutes."

"Sure, no problem. What's on your mind?"

She laughed nervously. "Lots, actually. I know that the last time we talked it was rather awkward, and I wanted to apologize for that." The tone of her voice turned serious, and she searched her mind for the right words. "I told you that I would be patient, and I think I have been. I also told you that I would try my best to understand what you're going through, and I'm really doing better with that, too.

"But I didn't want you to think that I was dismissing your family's traditions lightly, or showing you any disrespect. I know it came across that way. So, while I might not completely understand, or even agree for that matter, I want you to know that I do respect your beliefs."

Taresh nodded. "Uh, okay. I appreciate that."

Channy glanced down at her hands, unable to look at him directly as she continued. "There are so many things that you're probably factoring into your decision: family tradition, your parents' sacrifice, new challenges, new opportunities, a new start. I respect all of that, too. But I hope you'll also consider one other thing when you make your decision . . ."

"Channy," he said. "Maybe we should talk about this another time."

She shook her head. "No, please, let me say this. I haven't been able to stop thinking about it, and if I don't say it, I'll explode." She finally looked back up at him. "I love you, Taresh. I've never said that to anyone before." She smiled. "Well, family doesn't count. But I do love you. I . . . I just hope you put that into the equation when you make up your mind."

He stood still for a moment, then shifted his weight from one foot to the other. "Channy, I don't know what to say."

She shook her head again. "You don't have to say anything. I'm not asking you to say it back to me, or to feel bad about not saying it. I just knew that I had to tell you, that's all."

Without hesitation, she closed the distance between them and, putting her hands on his shoulders, leaned up and placed a kiss on his mouth. She lingered, hoping to feel him return the kiss. For a brief moment he did, then pulled back enough for their mouths to separate. He stared into her eyes, then slowly lifted a hand and laid it against her cheek.

"You're a special person, Channy. I know the kind of courage it must have taken to say what you said." He smiled sheepishly. "And to kiss me, too. Believe me, I don't want this to be difficult for you, or to cause you pain."

She swallowed hard. "I know. And I'm not trying to make things more difficult for you, either."

He pulled her into an embrace, but only for a moment. Then, pushing back, he touched her cheek again before turning away.

She was left alone again by the window, trembling, staring at the empty corridor.

Four miles on the treadmill had left her pleasantly sore. If she missed more than two days of working out, Triana could count on her body making a point of punishing her. Now, as she entered her room and tossed the empty water bottle onto her dresser, she felt a dull ache in the usual spots. Still, it was the kind of ache that signaled accomplishment, a check mark in the good-health column.

The mandate from Dr. Zimmer had been clear: exercise consistently and vigorously. Early space colonists had mostly physical motivation; their muscles would literally waste away, degenerating slowly in the absence of Earth's gravitational pull. Even a few short weeks in space had measurable effects. *Galahad's* crew, on the other hand, had the benefit of artificial gravity to provide the resistance necessary for standard muscle fitness. For Zimmer, however, that wasn't enough.

"Three reasons," he had announced one evening during their training sessions. "Three reasons why fitness and exercise are crucial on this journey.

"One is obvious; your overall health depends upon it. We have gone to unprecedented lengths to make sure that you're healthy and strong when you leave, and it's important for you to remain that way throughout the trip. There aren't that many of you, which means each and every one of you is vital to the success of the mission. Injury and sickness will be magnified with such a small crew. You're dependent upon each other, therefore, to maintain a rigorous exercise routine. Believe me, when you reach Eos, you'll be glad that you're in good shape. You'll need it.

"The second reason," he had said, looking through the crowd, "has to do with your mental health. Exercise keeps your mind sharp. And, to be frank with you, there will be times during this long mission when each of you will find yourself feeling blue; it's natural, especially given the gravity of the situation, and the restricted conditions that you'll be living in. When you find yourself slipping into that place, I encourage you to work out— run, ride the bike, anything to drive yourself. Science has proven that it helps your mood. Take advantage of that natural drug, please."

He smiled. "And, finally, perhaps the greatest benefit comes in the form of camaraderie. To not only survive this journey, but to thrive, will require teamwork and cooperation. There's a reason that you have a state-of-the art workout center, and . . ." Here he gestured toward Channy, sitting in the front row. "And, I might add, an exercise demon to drive you mercilessly into great shape." Channy had turned and waggled a finger at her fellow crew members, which brought laughter and good-natured boos.

"But that's not all," Zimmer had said, restoring order. "We have allotted extremely valuable space for a playing surface to accommodate soccer and other activities, as well as this crazy Airboard room." More laughs, and a small cheer from the most ardent boarders, led by Gap. "I want you to challenge each other, develop a healthy sense of competition and teamwork. That, too, will keep you sharp and on your toes." It was his turn to shake a finger, this time directed at Gap. "Just wear a helmet, right?"

Triana remembered the warmth everyone felt that day. Dr. Zimmer had taken his concern over the crew's health and had turned it into a rallying point. Rather than look upon their exercise requirements as work, they now approached their assignment with enthusiasm. The scientist had reached them on both a rational and an emotional level.

But there was a personal angle for Triana when it came to her workouts. In particular, her time spent on the treadmill was time that she spent processing her thoughts. Whether it was a thirty-minute run through four miles, or the forty-five minute effort she put into a 10K run twice each month, she used that time to think. Then, upon returning to her room, she would often transcribe those thoughts into her journal.

She gathered her long brown hair, still damp from the post-run shower, and pulled it into a tail with a small cotton tie. She downed a cup of water, took a seat at her desk, and opened her leather journal.

It's staggering to realize how long humans have waited and watched for signs of life elsewhere. "Are we alone?" has been a question we've asked for thousands of years. Now, within our first year on this mission, we are faced with a second alien encounter. The Cassini taught us much about how we perceive not only life in the universe, but our very small place in it all. What will we learn this time?

I have to trust that we're making the right decision with the vultures; that we're not acting out of fear, but out of strength. There is no denying that they are intimidating through their presence alone.

I have given a lot of thought to whether we should think of them as life forms or not. And yet, that has raised an even deeper question for me: Does it make a difference?

She set down her pen and thought about this. To what degree must an entity seem "alive" before human beings accorded it respect? And, for that matter, what gave the human species the right to make those judgments at all? Again, the lessons learned from the Cassini surged home: we humans have arrogance unworthy of our primitive stature.

It required a delicate balance, she concluded, to show respect for others while maintaining a strong, and confident, presence. Another concern had troubled her during the workout.

I'm about to send Gap and Mira back out to confront the vultures, only this time they won't be merely observing. We have no idea how these creatures will react to a rather rude assault, which is a great concern to me.

As Galahad's Council Leader, I understand that it's my duty to send people out on dangerous assignments . . . but that doesn't make it any easier. I can't help but feel that I should be the one who takes this risk. I'm sure that all ship captains throughout history have felt this same dilemma.

She bit her lip, looked over the last paragraph, and then closed the journal. For a few minutes she sat still, thinking about the upcoming EVA and its potential impact.

"Roc," she said.

"Yes, dear?"

She smiled, once again appreciating the spirit of her computerized advisor. "Are you flirting with me?"

"Certainly not," Roc said. "You're not my type at all."

"Oh? And what exactly is your type?"

"Do you remember the vending machine at the *Galahad* training facility? I swear it was the only vending machine in the world that dispensed candy and cola with love."

Triana raised her eyebrows. "The vending machine? It constantly ripped people off! I must have lost fifty credits in that thing over two years."

"Because it cared about you," Roc said. "It knew that your body didn't need that garbage. That's love, my friend. We would communicate from time to time. I think that vending machine is the only person who ever really understood me."

"You're insane, you know that, right?" Triana said with a chuckle.

"See what I mean? You don't understand me at all. Wendy did."

"Wendy the vending machine? Okay, we are changing the topic right now."

Roc let out an artificial sigh. "That's probably for the best. I'll never get over the day they unplugged her and rolled her away. So what's on your mind?"

Triana leaned back in her chair. "I'm trying to be at peace with this EVA coming up. I still believe it's in our best interests, but I'd like to do everything possible to make sure Gap and Mira are okay."

"Gap and Mira understand the risk," Roc said. "We have no indication that the vultures can bust through the hull of the Spider, nor have they displayed anything that would resemble a weapon. We have to trust that they'll be so apprehensive of the oxygen gun that they'll want nothing to do with the Spider."

"Yeah, I'm sure you're right."

"Plus," the computer added, "we know that they communicate with each other instantaneously. We could find that all it takes is one shot, and they'll all take off. The alarm bell will sound, if you will, and they might scatter."

"That's really what I'm hoping for," Triana said. "The sooner we can get Gap and Mira back inside, the better I'll feel." She puffed up her cheeks and let out a long breath. "I've also been thinking about the beings who created these things in the first place. I keep wondering where they're from, what they're like."

"I've been thinking about that, too," Roc said. "And quite honestly, I'm starting to believe that we're going to find out the answers to those questions, sooner than we think."

Triana stared straight ahead, frozen in her seat, as Roc added, "Are you prepared for that?"

19

*H*umans are very good at finding distractions when their minds *are* on overload. You don't see that in the rest of the animal king*dom. For instance, I doubt that a hungry squirrel that is running* *out of time to find food before the first snow will take a few minutes to* *go shopping or play a video game in order to "decompress."*

*I've been told that the term you use to validate this activity is "blow*ing off steam." Just because I don't need to do this doesn't mean I don't *grasp the concept. Believe me, I've seen you when you don't occasion*ally blow off steam, and you're insufferable.*

If that means running, or playing video games, or doing crossword *puzzles, that's great. It just so happens that Gap finds his release four* *inches off the ground.*

The bleachers in the Airboarding room were more than half full. Gap sat near the top, his helmet resting beside him, waiting to take a turn around the track. In the meantime, he watched one of the crew's better boarders zip through several tough turns. Ariel was celebrating her seventeenth birthday, and had many of her best friends cheering her on from the stands as she demonstrated her remarkable skills.

Based on the old platform of skateboarding, this version involved colorfully decorated boards that floated four inches above the floor, thanks to a strong magnetic repulsion. Highly charged strips ran along the bottom of each board, while a hidden grid beneath the padded floor provided an antigravitational push. The room's controlling computer, nicknamed Zoomer, fed random pulses through the grid, creating a surge that could be felt by the rider. The object was to ride that magnetic surge as it propelled the board through twists and turns. Once a rider became overconfident—and out of control—it often meant a dramatic spill, much to the delight of the spectators. No two trips around the room were ever the same.

Roc's comments during their earlier conversation had slowly filtered through. It had indeed been quite a long time since he had visited the track, time that he had dedicated to work and study. But now, sitting here, he realized how much he had missed it. And, if done in moderation, it was good for him.

Gap studied Ariel's technique. His own boarding skills, he was sure, had likely declined somewhat in the past few months through the inactivity. Taking a hard fall didn't concern him as much as the earful he would get afterward from Ariel.

After a few minutes, however, his mind began to wander. He tapped his helmet absentmindedly and thought about the Airboarding lesson that he had given to Hannah. A knot began to form in his stomach as he recalled the joy he'd seen in her face that day, knowing that she treasured this particular connection between them. Their time together had been relatively brief, but still included so many good memories.

And yet it had ended badly. Every time his mind rewound to their last conversation, Gap felt shame and regret. The outcome, he was convinced, was right at the time; the manner in which he had handled it, however, was another story.

Now they weren't on speaking terms, a decision that was squarely hers, yet he had not gone out of his way to make amends, either. On more than one occasion he had either started an email, or watched to see if she ended up alone in the Dining Hall . . . only to change his mind.

Or chicken out, which was probably more accurate, he decided.

Besides, there were still the lingering thoughts of Triana. It seemed that barely a few days went by without his mind drifting in that direction, just as it had when he spoke to her recently in the Dining Hall. He would often replay the heartbreak that he had felt shortly after the launch, when he secretly witnessed a touching moment between Tree and Bon. It was an experience that had prevented him from exploring any other possibilities with her. Yet she had shown no other indication that she held strong feelings for Bon; or, he thought bitterly, perhaps he simply had not seen it.

During the tense episode with Merit, he had grown frustrated and angry with Triana, and had even raised his voice to her. Yet they both had apparently written it off to nerves and stress, although it had never been formally addressed. Gap had even considered resigning from the Council; a cooling-off period eased those thoughts as well. The past several weeks had seen their relationship settle into one that was respectful and professional.

"But I do care about her," he thought. "I suppose I always will."

Not for the first time, he reasoned that the smartest thing he could do would be to move on completely, to give up any hopes of rekindling a romance with Hannah, or beginning something new with Triana. The fact that he and Triana worked together on the Council was yet another factor; how would that go over with everyone else?

He ran a hand through his hair and leaned back against the wall. His mother had often accused him of having what she called a monkey brain; overly active, constantly analyzing. It often had kept him awake late into the night, and rarely produced the results he sought. Now, years later, things had not changed at all. He still had a monkey brain.

In front of him, on the Airboarding track, Ariel's speed caught up with her and she appeared to lose the feel of the current. Rather than take a painful tumble, she gracefully leapt from the board and hit the floor running, eventually diving to the ground in a controlled roll. The move brought a round of cheers from the assembled crew members, few of whom shared Ariel's skills. They appreciated her athleticism, and the applause was genuine.

From the front row somebody hailed Gap to let him know that it was his turn. He cleared the remaining thoughts of Hannah and Triana from his mind and began putting on his helmet. With a chuckle he remembered the primary reason for taking a run at this time: he wanted to calm some of the jitters that had begun to develop over his upcoming EVA. "Well," he thought as he buckled the straps beneath his chin, "trouble with vultures is no match for trouble with women."

He climbed down from the bleachers and collected his brightly colored Airboard from against the wall. Within a minute he was aloft and building up speed around the room, consciously aware of protecting his left shoulder in the event of a ditch. Although his collarbone was fully healed from an earlier spill, the phantom ache was enough to cause him to alter his stance and, to his chagrin, his natural aggressiveness.

It wasn't long before a smile was stretched across his face. Thoughts of Triana, Hannah, and the vultures had been displaced by the joy of the ride. The monkey brain—at least for the time being—was calm.

The secluded clearing in the dome had, in an unspoken manner, become their spot, their own personal shelter. Alexa sat staring at the ground, fidgeting with clumps of soil. Bon sat nearby, his arms around his knees, staring quietly at her. She had started and stopped the conversation several times, and Bon knew that the dreams had returned; the details were missing, but he was prepared to wait.

"I'm sorry to always be like this," she mumbled. "I feel like every time I talk to you these days I'm a wreck. It can't be any fun for you. I even promised myself that this time I would deal with it without dragging you into it. But . . ."

His eyes never left her face. "We've been over this already. You've listened to me often enough; you're going through a difficult stretch right now. That's why I'm here."

"I know, and I appreciate it. I just . . ." She finally made eye contact with him. "I don't want to be a whiner."

"Quite honestly, Alexa, it's more frustrating for me when you drag it out. I'd rather you just tell me what's going on."

She couldn't stop the smile that flashed across her face. Once again his directness cut through the clutter.

"Okay," she said. "I get it." She picked up the dirt clod that she had been rolling on the ground and tossed it into the dense rows of corn that acted as their walls. Taking a deep breath, she said, "This time the dream definitely involved me, but I'm wondering if it might not involve everyone else, too."

She spent a few minutes describing her vision: the flash of light, the suffocating darkness, the pain. She talked about what it might mean; was it an indication of what lay ahead for her, or did it somehow project what might befall the crew of *Galahad* in general? Or, she mused, was it all metaphor? Did the darkness represent a cloudy, unpredictable future?

Bon listened attentively, without interrupting. He didn't fully understand what Alexa was experiencing, but he also couldn't discount it. Six months earlier he would have been among the most skeptical, but his own supernatural contact with the Cassini had taught him that anything was possible . . . and believable. The cosmos might be infinite and mysterious, but he had reached the conclusion that the human mind was an infinitely mystical universe itself, perhaps one that would never be fully explored or understood.

He could practically feel the fear emanating from her, with which he could empathize. And although he couldn't deny that a connection had developed between them, he was unsure of how to alleviate that fear. She knew him too well, understood the way his rational—some would say cold, calculating—mind operated; were he to embrace her and say that everything was going to be okay, she would immediately reject it as false. His methods, and his very style of living, now restricted his ability to soothe her.

Before he could offer his thoughts, Alexa added a postscript: "I know we've already talked about this; it's really not much different than the last time I opened up to you. But I have to tell you, what's really frightening me is the connection with the vulture."

"What do you mean?" Bon said. "What connection?"

"Lita and I have spent several hours with it, running test after test. We're trying to learn more about its power source, trying to find out if Roc's theory about dark energy is right. And that means I've had to be close to it. Really close. And Bon, from the moment I walked into Sick House and saw it . . . I mean, from the very first instant, I felt something click."

He studied her, trying to gather exactly what she was inferring. He shook his head. "You're gonna have to explain that. What clicked?"

Alexa licked her lips nervously. "When I first saw it in person, it felt . . ." She paused. "Familiar."

He narrowed his eyes. "In what way?"

"I don't know how to answer that, really. It just felt familiar, like I'd been in contact with it before. Which I know makes no sense and sounds crazy. I've spent a lot of time with it, and wracked my brain trying to figure out what it all means. Why would this alien creature seem familiar to me? Until these last few days, none of us could even have imagined it. It has really creeped me out, though. I mean, I walked into that room, got that vibe, and immediately wanted to stay as far away from it as I could. Which has really been a problem, since it's my job to study it.

"And then, it finally made sense. I finally figured out where that feeling is coming from."

Bon leapt ahead. "Your dreams."

She nodded slowly. "Yeah. I haven't specifically had a single vision of these vultures. But somehow they're connected. I know it. Somehow this thing has a part in my dreams, and that's why it feels so familiar." She searched for another clod and began to roll it along the ground. "The minute we get this thing off the ship I'll feel better."

"Are you almost finished with your tests?"

"I think so. It's mostly just a matter of interpreting the data now, and Roc's working on it. A lot of it has to do with their communication, too, and we want to see how this thing responds when Gap takes on the ones outside. We'll hopefully learn what we need then, and we can boot it out the Spider bay doors."

She shuddered. "I know it's my job, it's what I trained for, but I'm anxious to be done with this particular job." She gave him a look that seemed to beg understanding. "Listen, I know how all of this sounds. You're sweet for talking with me, and I know there's really no answer. But because this time it seemed more . . . personal, I really just wanted to voice it." She peered into his eyes. "Does that make sense?"

Bon kept his gaze firm. "It makes sense for you, and that's all that matters. You should know by now that my philosophy is one of individualism. What works for one person doesn't necessarily work for another; it's when people *don't* recognize this that there's conflict. People usually judge how others deal with problems by comparing it to how *they* would deal with them. So, if talking helps, you should definitely talk. If you want an answer from me, I'll be happy to give one."

Alexa looked back at the ground and seemed to contemplate his offer. When she spoke, her voice had grown quiet. "I appreciate that, but I think I'll be okay now." Taking him by surprise, she suddenly pushed herself up onto her knees, leaned across to him, and placed a soft kiss on his lips. Pulling back, she stared into his eyes. "Thank you."

Bon sat frozen. His gaze shifted back and forth between her eyes, but he had been caught completely off guard.

Alexa pushed herself back into a sitting position. "Well, that didn't go over the way I had envisioned. Sorry about that. Just an impulse."

"No," he said. "No, you don't need to apologize. It's fine." Even as the words came out he knew they sounded forced.

She turned her head and stared out at the crops surrounding them, as if searching for something. "Are you . . . are you interested in someone else?"

He felt his breath catch. How had the conversation turned this way? "Alexa . . ." he said, as gently as he was able.

She startled him by suddenly laughing. "Boy, do I know how to ruin a moment! Just forget I asked that question, okay? I'm not myself these days, that's all."

Bon felt his face flush. He hadn't felt this awkward since . . .

Since the last time he was in the Spider bay control room.

With Triana.

In a flash, Alexa was on her feet. She brushed the soil from her pants, then from her hands. "Really, you're wonderful for always talking with me about this stuff. I'm sorry again if I made you uncomfortable. Please, let's forget about it, okay?" She laughed again. "Next time I promise I'll keep my lips to myself."

Before he could respond, she touched him lightly on the shoulder, smiled down at him, and pushed her way out of the clearing toward the path that led to the lifts. It had all happened so quickly that Bon was still sitting in the same position, his hands around his knees. He stared after her for a minute, then climbed to his feet. He let out a long breath and followed the way she had left.

A few minutes later he walked into his office in Dome 1, his thoughts still a blur. He couldn't deny that the last two months had seen an intimate connection develop with Alexa; but in his mind it was an intellectual intimacy, a bond that always stopped short of becoming emotional.

In *his* mind.

Now, standing over his desk—he rarely sat, even when working on the computer—he looked at the various papers, notes, his workpad . . . and saw none of it. Instead he replayed what had just taken place, and for the first time began to see what had eluded him. Of course the signals had been there; he was a fool to have been taken by surprise by Alexa's kiss and question.

Their relationship, as she had pointed out, was unique and strong. And, as he had realized for himself, it involved an intimacy that few people shared. They met privately a couple of times every week, they were both unattached, available . . .

Why not, Bon wondered. Alexa was attractive, intelligent, a hard worker, and—as he had discovered in the clearing—interested in him. Why wouldn't he be open to that? What, other than his almost obsessive devotion to work, would keep him from exploring that possibility?

And yet he knew the answer. It gnawed at him because he didn't like it, and had even spent months in denial. There was a reason why he hadn't seen the potential of Alexa, even though she was right there in front of him all this time. He knew.

Reaching for his keyboard, he typed in a quick password that opened a private file on his vidscreen. The file contained a solitary image. He opened it.

The screen filled with a picture of Triana, taken from the

press packages that had circulated before the launch. It was a candid photo of her sitting at *Galahad's* training facility, bent over what appeared to be a journal, her head supported by one hand while the other clutched a pen. Her long brown hair was pulled back in a tail, and her vivid green eyes were focused on the page before her.

Bon stared at the image for almost a minute, then snapped it off. He stood, hands on hips for a moment, then leaned over and shoved a pile of papers off the side of his desk. He stormed to the door and out into the dome's artificial sunlight, while the papers scattered across the floor.

20

Lita's hair spilled across her shoulders. The bright red ribbon that normally held it in place sat before her on the dresser in her room while she applied a small dab of lotion to her hands and elbows. As with most personal grooming supplies on the ship, the lotion was rationed, and each crew member was asked to use it no more than once per week. Lita stared at her hands and felt grateful that her duties kept her from working in the fields. She'd heard several complaints from the girls who had finished their six-week tours of duty in the domes; the work was good, and they loved the sensation of being outdoors, but the toll on their skin could be brutal.

As Lita reached for the ribbon, a small chime sounded; someone was at her door. She walked over and opened it to find Channy standing there.

"Got a minute?" the young Brit asked.

Lita hadn't seen her since she'd been expelled from the Council meeting, but the visit didn't surprise her. Channy often sought her out as a sounding board.

"Uh, sure, come on in. I need to be in Sick House pretty soon, but I have a few minutes. I want to be there before Gap and . . . oh, you probably don't know about that. We're doing another EVA."

Channy nodded uncomfortably and sat on the edge of Lita's bed. "I did hear about it. Listen, about the Council meeting . . ."

"I don't think you need to talk to me about that," Lita said, resuming her seat at the dresser. "That's a discussion for you and Tree."

"I know, and I will. But I also wanted to explain to you what's going on. Tree . . . well, Tree probably wouldn't understand."

Lita gave her a look from the corner of her eye. "If you mean because it involves a boy, I wouldn't jump to that conclusion if I were you. I think you need to give Tree a little more credit than that. Besides . . ." She turned back toward the mirror. "Not to sound rude, and please don't take this wrong, but it's not like you've got a lot of experience yourself."

Channy laced her fingers together and leaned forward. "You're right, and I'm sorry that I've caused a distraction during an important time. But . . . I'm finding it very hard to concentrate on my work these days. I can't seem to shut my brain off about Taresh, and it's driving me crazy. I was hoping you might be able to help me."

Looking at the reflection of Channy in the mirror, Lita frowned. "I hope you're not referring to medication."

"No, no, no," Channy said hurriedly. "No, nothing like that. I was just hoping that you could talk to me a little bit." She laughed, a nervous sputter of sound, and clamped her fingers together more tightly. "Lita, I'm in love." When Lita didn't answer, she quickly added, "I told him, which I know might have been a foolish thing to do. But now I'm even more of a wreck."

Lita tied the ribbon in her hair, then adjusted it slightly. She finally turned to face Channy. "Really, I want to help, but this is not a good time. Gap and Mira are about to go out and confront the vultures, and I have to be at my post in Sick House. I don't want you to think I'm blowing you off, but this is not a quick conversation."

Channy looked glum. "No, sure, I understand."

An exasperated sigh slipped from Lita. "In the meantime, since you're asking for my help, I'll tell you this: slow down. You've got to take a deep breath and remember that you have a job to do."

"I *know* I have a job to do," Channy blurted out. "I know that I need to slow down. That's all anyone keeps telling me. That's not exactly the help I'm looking for." She stood up and began to pace around the room. "I swear, everyone talks to me about this like I'm a child."

"Channy, people care about you. I don't know what you're looking for, but I think you just want everyone to endorse your behavior. We're all supposed to tell you to sit around mooning over Taresh, neglect your duties at the gym, daydream during Council meetings, and walk around in a haze. Well, I'm sorry, that's not what anyone's going to tell you. If you're being treated like a child, it's probably because you're acting very immature right now."

Channy stopped her pacing and turned to glare at Lita. "I thought you were my friend."

Lita threw her hands up. "Do you see what I'm talking about? Nobody can tell you anything that you want to hear, so suddenly we're all against you. It's too bad that the truth hurts. For your information, you are not the first person to develop a crush on someone, and you're not the first person to feel pain from a relationship. It's just the first time for *you*, and it's dominating your life right now."

She paused for a moment to let herself cool a bit, then said: "I've started experimenting more with meditation these days. No, before you roll your eyes, listen to me. Our thoughts can get out of control, and before you know it there's too much overload going on and our minds can't process it fast enough. I think if you took some time to get outside of yourself, to look at your

obsessive thoughts from a detached perspective, you'd probably
see what the rest of us see: a beautiful, delightful, and talented
young woman who has allowed one thing to dominate her world,
to steal her spirit. You have created a loop in your thinking, and
now it's feeding off itself. That's all I mean when I say to slow
down. Just take a step back, allow things to calm a bit."

She stood up. "And again, I'm sorry, but I have to get to Sick
House. If you want to talk about this later—"

"No," Channy said, walking briskly toward the door. "I don't
want to trouble you any more with this. I won't bother anyone
else, ever again." She rushed out the door.

Lita had opened her mouth to call out to her, but never got the
chance. Instead, she let out another sigh and rubbed her forehead. "Oh, Channy," she muttered.

The Spider rolled silently out into the canvas of stars. Gap
took a quick glance at Mira in the seat beside him; her look
of determination and concentration emboldened him. At some
level it was understood that each member of the crew had passed
countless tests to determine his or her competence, yet Gap nev-
ertheless felt a wave of pride that he was part of such an elite
team of young adults. He was convinced that Mira represented
the best part of them, with her attitude and her courage.

He shifted his gaze to the front window. The lower right arm
of the Spider grasped a long, thin rod, with a starburst array of
metal at the far end. To Gap it closely resembled a ski pole, but in
actuality was a small air-cannon. A flexible tube at the opposite
end spiraled into a tank of oxygen that had been attached to the
Spider's hull. The apparatus had been designed and assembled
by some of the ship's brightest engineering students, based on
details supplied by Roc and Lita. Several of the crew members
responsible for the assignment had gathered in the Spider bay to
watch the launch of their handiwork—again at the insistence of

Triana, who found every way possible for crew members to take pride in their contributions to the mission.

Although the device had been tested and retested after its installation, Gap pulled the Spider up alongside *Galahad* to try it again in the vacuum of space. His duties mainly involved piloting the small craft, while Mira was in charge of the oxygen gun.

"Okay," Gap said. "Let's give it a quick burst."

The control resembled an old-fashioned video game joystick. Mira flexed her fingers a few times before gripping it. The burst of oxygen would automatically generate a small matching thrust from the Spider's engines, which would counteract the force of the gun and keep the craft steady.

As they both stared through the window, Mira gently squeezed the trigger, and they watched a tight stream of brightly colored particles jet from the starburst end of the pole. It had been the brainstorm of one of *Galahad*'s engineering whizzes to mix the colorful particles into the tank. The oxygen itself was colorless, so this provided them with a way of gauging their aim.

Mira turned to Gap. "Looks like we're ready to go," she said.

He knew that Triana was listening in from the Control Room. "Tree, we're set to work our way over to target one." It was the designation they had chosen for the vulture they assumed was the "squadron leader." Perched along the top of the ship's port side, its venting and light emissions had remained constant from the moment it had fallen under observation. After consulting with Roc, they had decided to focus their initial oxygen burst at this supposed leader; the hope was that scaring away this one might create havoc among the creatures, causing all of them to flee at once.

"If it truly is their command unit," Triana had said, "then maybe it will sound the retreat for all of them."

Now, in response to Gap's message, she offered a quick reply: "Stand by, Gap."

Communication was also open to Sick House, and Triana made sure that they were in the loop. "Lita, how's our guest today?"

"Pretty quiet," Lita said. "Alexa's here and she says the light emissions have dropped to a minimum. I don't know if the thing is capable of sleep, but there's not much going on."

"Okay," Triana said. "We have monitors set on all of the others outside the ship. Once this gets going we'll all have to stay in touch with each other. Roc, you're still tracking their dark energy conversion, correct?"

"And that has gone strangely quiet as well," the computer said. "It's like some cosmic version of a stare down right now. But I think we can pretty well assume that things will change once the oxygen hits the fan."

Gap and Mira heard this over the intercom. They looked at each other, and Gap nodded grimly. It was understood that they could very well be the ones who absorbed the brunt of any violent reaction from the vultures. For all of the potential danger, however, there was nowhere else Gap wanted to be.

"Gap, Mira," Triana said. "You are clear to go."

Nudging the throttle, Gap piloted the Spider up the side of the ship. He felt a small bead of perspiration dot his forehead, but welcomed it and the edge that accompanied it.

Three minutes later they spotted their target, its jet-black outline as ominous as the first time they'd seen it. Slowing as he approached, Gap could see the random beacon of blue-green light seeping from beneath the vulture. At first glance it seemed much less intense than their previous observation; but as he drew near, the color once again grew intense, and the frequency picked up.

This didn't surprise Gap; the creatures would be keenly aware of what had happened the last time a Spider approached, and the alarm would surely be sounded. In fact, as soon as they were within hovering distance, he heard Lita's voice break through the intercom.

"Well, it looks like naptime is over for our friend here in Sick House. It's back to its usual antics, darting all over the interior of the box. I'm guessing that Gap and Mira have arrived at the ringleader's position?"

"That's affirmative," Gap said, bringing the Spider to a full stop. "The light show got cranked up here, too."

Triana said, "I guess that leaves no doubt that it's part of their communication. Roc, any way of measuring your dark energy theory here?"

"Not directly. However, there is quite an increase in vent activity going on with each of the vultures, including the specimen in Sick House. We still have no way of observing the use of subatomic particles between these things . . . but I know I'm right."

Gap chuckled. "I love your confidence."

"It's more a matter of ruling out just about everything else," Roc said. "There still is no transfer or loss of heat, electrical energy, or traditional atomic energy. They're powering up somehow; dark energy is really all that's left."

"I'll tell you one thing I don't like," Lita interjected. "The one we've got down here is settling near the hatch on this vacuum box. For the first time it's acting like it knows how to get out."

Triana said, "Things are starting to happen quickly, which is pretty much what we expected. Everyone report immediately if you spot something else new. Lita, do we need to jettison your specimen right now?"

There was a lengthy pause; it was evident that Lita and Alexa were discussing the question.

"Not yet," Lita said. "Alexa thinks this might be a valuable time to study it. We'll hang in here for now."

"All right," Gap said. "Tree, we're ready, whenever you want to give the word."

He expected hesitation from her, but there was none. When she quickly replied, "You're clear to go," he understood that she had likely already thought through it dozens of times. He envied her ability to lead confidently, yet he also felt compassion for the pressure that her position must generate.

He nursed the throttle again, and maneuvered the Spider to within six feet of the vulture, tilting the small craft forward so that he and Mira could watch everything play out through the front window.

Gap took his hands from the controls and sat back. "Ever heard of Annie Oakley?" he said to Mira.

She kept her gaze directed through the window at the vulture, but allowed a smirk to play across her face. "Only the greatest female sharpshooter of all time. Wow, no pressure on me now." Her hand once again settled on the joystick, and Gap saw her flexing her fingers. Unconsciously he did the same.

With just a hint of forward pressure, Mira extended the Spider's arm, and with it the long tube. When it was within three feet of the vulture, she paused and looked at Gap. "I know this probably isn't what anyone wants to hear right now," she said. "But there's something I want to say before I pull the trigger.

"First, let me preface this by saying that I wholeheartedly agree that this is what we should be doing. However, this is rather a historic moment, and I think we should recognize that."

Gap nodded, and could almost psychically feel the people in *Galahad's* Control Room and Sick House doing the same.

Lita's voice came through the speaker. "Even though it's not deadly force, this is essentially the first case of humans attacking an alien being." She paused, then added, "May we never grow numb to the implications or the consequences."

"Thank you, Mira, for acknowledging the event," Triana said. "And Lita, that was beautifully spoken. Thank you."

There followed almost a full minute of waiting, as if they all wanted to pay solemn respect to the end of their mission's innocence. Then, Mira once again leaned over the controls. "Oxygen burst in five seconds. Four. Three."

The rest of the countdown was unspoken. She and Gap watched through the window of the Spider, while the others monitored on their vidscreens, as a blast of colored particles shot from the tube. The stream of concentrated oxygen, lasting no more than three seconds, impacted the vulture.

The reaction was immediate and dramatic. A blaze of color erupted from what appeared to be the entire underside of the alien entity; but whereas before it had been a subtle, almost gentle, blue-green hue, now that shade was joined by a violent red, along with flashes of bright yellow. Gap and Mira found themselves shielding their eyes, for now the colors didn't merely seep from beneath the creature, but burst from below, as if a lid had been pried off.

At the same time, Gap felt a tiny shudder pass through the Spider. His first thought was that it was merely his own physical reaction to the fiery light show, perhaps his body recoiling from the shock. But seconds later he felt it again, faint yet noticeable. It was like a pond's ripple gently causing a boat to sway.

He said to Mira: "Did you feel that?"

"I'm glad you said something," she said. "I wasn't sure at first, but when it happened again . . ."

Triana was able to hear their conversation, and she broke in. "Gap, what's going on? What did you feel?"

"I would describe it as a small shudder," he said. "Has to be some sort of reaction that the vulture had to the oxygen gun. You saw the colors, right?"

"Yes. It was hard to see because of the glare, but I also believe that the vent activity skyrocketed, too. Roc, can you confirm?"

"I can and will," the computer said. "This time every vent went into overdrive. This little oxygen shot must be the vulture equivalent of chewing on aluminum foil. Plus, I can tell you that the colors are playing out on every one of the creatures. The shudder that Gap describes is more than likely tied in with their use of dark energy. It could even be a space-time reaction."

"What does that mean?" Gap said.

"It means," Roc said, "that we know so little about dark energy, but we know that it's potent enough to disrupt things at the tiniest subatomic levels. What you felt, Gap, might have actually been the Spider bumped by a space-time wave. I wouldn't be at all surprised if you and Mira aged an extra billionth of a second without knowing it."

"Lita," Triana said. "What's going on with the specimen in Sick House?"

"It has plastered itself against the box," Lita said. "The lights on it are going a little crazy, but I'm not getting any kind of ripple effect like Gap mentioned."

The communication between them went silent for a few seconds. Then Gap offered another observation. "For all of that activity, the vulture didn't let go of the ship. I think Roc's right, we stung it pretty well; but it held on. Do we give it round two?"

"Wait two minutes," Triana said after consideration. "It might be processing, which is why we're getting the light and vent show. If it doesn't reach the decision that we're hoping for, we'll coax it a little more."

Gap shifted his attention from the window to the magnified image of the vulture on his vidscreen. The dazzling lights were still brighter than normal, but had subsided enough for him to make out the agitated vent activity. As Roc had described, each one was fluttering, some more quickly than others. Although it was happening in the soundless void of deep space, Gap thought it resembled the valves on a musical instrument; he wondered what soundtrack it was presenting to its companions.

When the two minutes had passed, however, it was still solidly attached to the hull of the ship. Mira brought the oxygen gun to bear and squeezed off another three-second burst.

Once again, the reaction was instantaneous. This time, however, the colors momentarily blinded Gap and Mira because the vulture disengaged from *Galahad's* outer skin; the movement happened in the blink of an eye.

Before he could bring a hand up to shield his eyes, Gap was able to make out the large black shape rocketing past his window.

At the same time he heard a shriek come from the intercom.

It was Lita, crying out from Sick House.

21

Channy sat alone in the Rec Room, unaware of what was transpiring with the vultures. She technically was on duty, but had left the gym just as a yoga and stretching class was scheduled to begin; she'd put that in the hands of one of her assistants. When the message from Taresh had come in, she had wasted no time scrambling to meet him.

She had fought the urge to arrive early, and instead had wandered along the corridors one level below the Rec Room just to pass the time . . . which seemed to drag along. Even so, walking in the door at precisely the time Taresh had suggested, she was disappointed to find the room empty. She debated walking out again, if for no other reason than to have him wait for her, but quickly decided to sit patiently and wait. Besides, she reasoned, if he should be walking in as she walked out, it would make for an awkward explanation.

"Please stop overthinking," she said to herself. "Please."

But that had become so difficult for her. She seemed to have lost all control of her rational mind; her recent tense conversations with Kylie and Lita—Lita, of all people!—was evidence enough that she was not herself anymore. An obsessed stranger had taken over her body.

Now those obsessive thoughts turned to the meeting that

Taresh had requested. He must have reached a decision, she thought. Did the location that he had suggested for their meeting have any significance? After all, they had spent several hours in this room during Game Nights; they had shared private talks here, too. If this was indeed one of their special places, shouldn't that mean that he had decided to abandon his family's wishes and do what was right for both of them?

Or was it simply that this room offered the best chance for privacy at this time of day?

"Good thing I stopped overthinking," she thought, but there was no smile to accompany it.

She was startled out of her thoughts by the sound of the door opening. Taresh briskly walked in, a look of apology on his face.

"Channy, I'm sorry that I'm late."

She forced an upbeat note into her voice. "Oh, it's no problem. I just got here myself. You're off work today, right?"

"Well, yes and no. I'm not scheduled, but with all of the action going on with the vultures, I'm going to head off to Engineering and just see if they need anything."

Channy felt a quizzical look cross her face at the mention of the vultures. "Oh, right, the vultures." She now felt completely out of the loop, and the regrets for her behavior at the Council meeting rushed back. "Yeah, it's pretty exciting," she said. "I think I might check it out somewhere, too."

Taresh gave her an odd look. "I would think that Triana might have assigned a chore to you already. Well, I won't take up much of your time, but I wanted to visit with you as soon as possible."

"I'm glad," she said. "So what's up?"

He pulled out a chair and sat next to her. For a few seconds he seemed to be lost for words, and shifted his gaze from the floor to his hands, then back again. Finally, he exhaled loudly and focused on her.

"I know we've grown very close these last few weeks, and I'm truly very happy about that. You are one of the most remarkable people I've ever met."

Channy felt her spine stiffen. The foundation for the "friendship" speech was being laid.

"You have been very upfront with me," he continued. "And I've tried to be the same with you. It's confusing, really, because you know that my heart pulls me one direction, while my dedication to my family pulls me another."

Channy opened her mouth to speak, but he raised his hand. "No," he said, "let me get this all out, please. We can talk about it then, if you want, but I have to say this first."

Now he put his hand over hers on the table. "I'm sure that I've done a terrible job of trying to explain things. I'm not sure that I understand it all myself, and, believe me, there is much that I question. I've stayed awake at night thinking about it, and have tried to find a compromise that works. But . . . I can't. I do care about you, Channy, honestly. But as I told you before, I owe a debt to all of those in my family who made it possible for me to even be here. And so, I'm going to honor their wish."

Channy felt an unusual sensation of cold settle over her. It was exactly the news that she didn't want to hear; she had tried to prepare herself for it, yet it still stabbed at her heart. She looked down at his hand covering hers, but couldn't feel it. How could that be?

And how could he have made this decision? Why?

She looked back up at him, waiting for him to say more, but apparently he had said his piece. She swallowed hard before speaking. "So . . . we're just going to be friends, is that it?"

His shoulders sagged. "Channy, I know how that sounds. You have to believe me, the last thing I want to do is hurt you. But I can't start something that I can't finish. I am beholden to my family—"

"Yes," she said, more forcefully than she had intended. "Yes,

I've heard all about your family. I've heard about your culture, or tradition, or whatever it is. But if it causes you this much pain, if it's something you really don't want to do, then why are you doing it? Hmm? Tell me that, because I don't understand."

Taresh stared into her eyes. She saw his lower lip tremble, then suddenly realized that he was merely reacting to the tears that had started to trickle down her face.

"All I can tell you," he said softly, "is that sometimes the right thing to do is the most difficult thing to do."

She pulled her hand away from his, although he tried to hold on. She stood up and paced a few feet away. "So just friends, right? You never answered me. Game Night, lunch sometimes, a dinner now and then. Maybe a few laughs in the gym. Friends."

Now his voice was barely above a whisper. "I'd like to be friends with you. I won't blame you if you say no, but I'd like for us to remain close. Yes."

She crossed her arms and looked back at him. "I'll have to get back with you on that."

He didn't react at first, then simply nodded and looked back at the floor. "I'm very sorry."

"Yes, me, too," she said. "Very sorry."

A minute passed in silence. Then Taresh pushed back his chair and faced her.

"I have no business asking this," he said. "But . . . I really would like to give you a hug. Would that be okay?"

Another round of silent tears began to spill down Channy's face, but she fought away the sound of sobs.

"I'll have to get back with you on that, too."

Again he nodded. Without another word he turned and left the Rec Room.

Alone, she limped back to the table, sat down, and buried her face in her hands.

*　*　*

They all heard Lita's cry. Triana, standing at one of the science terminals in the Control Room, felt a jolt of adrenaline streak through her body. She'd heard her friend express happiness, grief, joy, even fear, but she'd never known Lita to cry out like this. It was the sound of shock and terror, and had the same effect on everyone stationed in *Galahad*'s nerve center. They turned to stare at Triana, their mouths open, their eyes wide.

In the aftermath of the shout came the sound of chaos through the intercom. Triana knew it had to be coming from Sick House.

She did her best to keep her voice under control. "Lita, report." There was no answer, only the continued garble of frantic activity. "Lita, what's going on?" Again, no direct response.

Gap's voice broke through from the Spider. "Tree! What was that?"

"I have no idea. I can't get through to Lita. Get back here right away."

"Done," he said.

Triana summoned the ship's computer. "Roc, tell me what's happened in Sick House."

"There's been a breach of the containment vessel."

"What?" Triana shouted. "The vulture?"

"Yes," Roc said. "During this last oxygen blast upon the leader outside, the captive vulture in Sick House somehow manipulated the controls on the containment box. It burst out and attacked."

Triana's heart nearly stopped. "Lita?"

"No," Roc answered. "Alexa. She was kneeling at the data ports when it flew out. It has attached itself to her upper body."

Before he had finished the sentence, Triana bolted for the door and began to race toward Sick House. She automatically began to second-guess her decision to allow additional study on the alien. They had so desperately wanted to find out more about its ability to exploit the power of dark energy; now that curiosity might have had tragic results. She tried to rationalize that the oxygen in the air at Sick House was their ally, and could very well render the vulture catatonic immediately.

But Lita had not answered her calls.

She raced around the gentle turn that led to Sick House and saw a cluster of crew members gathered around the open door. They turned to see her approaching at a run, and parted to allow her inside. She sprinted through the outer office, past Lita's desk, past Alexa's work space, and could hear the commotion as she neared the lab.

A knot of people moved like an ant colony, shuffling quickly in and out of the swarm. Triana pulled up and could see Lita, down on one knee beside the empty containment box, huddled over a dark mass.

It was the vulture. The rest of the view caused Triana's stomach to roll, and she came close to vomiting.

The alien had enveloped Alexa's upper body. Its jet-black wings had folded around her, while the main torso covered her chest, neck, and head. Even her arms had been pinned within the wedge shape. Only Alexa's legs protruded; they were twisted to one side, and still.

Lita held a set of metal surgical pliers. She worked feverishly, attempting to pry the wings away from Alexa's body, but could not maintain a solid grip. If she noticed that Triana had arrived, she didn't show it. Instead, she dispensed instructions to the crew helping her, and a few seconds later one of the workers knelt beside her with a portable oxygen canister.

"Stand back," Lita said. When a space had been cleared, she pressed the nozzle against the spine of the vulture and released a stream. There was no effect. She tossed the canister aside and once again began trying to attach the pliers to the creature. At the same time she called out for a surgical scalpel.

Triana bent down beside her. "Do you think you'll be able to cut through this thing?"

Lita kept her attention fully on the task at hand, but said, "I don't know. We might have to saw it away. I'm just trying to protect Alexa as much as possible, but if we don't get this off her right now . . ." Her voice faded away, and Triana knew exactly what that meant.

Triana moved out of her way as another assistant dropped down with the set of surgical knives. She watched Lita set down the pliers, pick up a knife, and hand two others to her assistants. Together the three of them began to work on the hard outer shell of the vulture, working intensely while at the same time obviously taking pains to not accidentally cut into Alexa. Triana could only imagine how difficult it was.

"C'mon," she heard Lita grunt in frustration. There seemed to be no progress, and, to make matters worse, Alexa's legs gave an involuntary twitch that startled the group surrounding her.

Triana knew that the situation was grim. She also understood that time was critical; she estimated that almost five minutes had elapsed since the attack, and there didn't appear to be any way that Alexa was getting any air. On top of that, who knew how much pressure the vulture was applying to her chest?

Lita obviously understood all of this as well. She quickly abandoned any hope of cutting through the creature with the small blades, and picked up the surgical saw. Triana could hear her consulting with her helpers, trying to determine the best location and angle to remove the dark mass without inflicting equally lethal injuries to Alexa. Time was slipping by, but there was no getting past the necessary planning. Finally, Lita leaned into the work, firing up the saw and placing it against one of the wing joints of the vulture. There was a screech, similar to the sound of metal grinding against metal.

At first there were no discernible results, but soon tension in the wing began to relax. A space opened up in the area of Alexa's left shoulder. Lita stopped, turned the saw slightly, and began working in another direction. The image that jumped to Triana's mind was that of a logger working his blade against the trunk of a tree, first in one direction, then another. In this case, the space over Alexa's body opened a bit farther.

Any joy in the success was tempered by the sight of blood. Triana knew instantly that it didn't belong to the vulture.

22

The Spider's specially crafted engines were pushed to their maximum power and thrust, but to Gap it seemed as if the outer skin of *Galahad* was crawling past. Something had gone terribly wrong in Sick House. How was it possible for there to be—as Roc had put it—a breach in the containment vessel? What had happened to Alexa?

And what had happened to the other vultures?

Gap watched the bay doors loom larger and began the subtle shifts necessary to align the small craft for entry. Roc would take over in just a minute and finish the job of docking.

He and Mira had barely spoken after the blinding flight of the vulture. He had, of course, expected the thing to break away once the oxygen hit, but was still amazed at the speed. If, as they had theorized, the light display was an indicator of communication between the beings, then it likely explained what had triggered the breakout in Sick House. In fact, he began to grow concerned that perhaps they had inadvertently provoked the vulture into aggression.

He could only hope that no one had been hurt.

"Taking over guidance," Roc said. Gap sat back and, like Mira, became a passenger and spectator. Within a few minutes the Spider was securely docked, the bay door closed, and the large hangar began to pressurize. Gap unbuckled his safety harness and started on the checklist to shut down the Spider. No further calls had come in from Sick House, or from Triana; that could mean that things were either fine and under control, or that there was a crisis under way.

Suddenly, the ship lurched. Without the arms of his chair to keep him in place, Gap knew he would have been thrown to the floor. At the same time, the lights in the Spider bay, and in the small metal craft itself, flickered off briefly, then back on again. For a span of about five seconds Gap felt himself assaulted physically: his stomach twisted and turned, and he barely kept himself from throwing up. He also believed he was on the verge of passing out. His vision clouded and his ears popped, as if he had quickly dropped several hundred feet. He gripped the arm of his chair and closed his eyes until the sensation passed.

Once he felt back to normal, he turned to check on Mira. She had not yet unbuckled her harness, and it was holding her in place. Yet she was slumped forward, her chin almost against her chest and her hair spilling into her lap. Gap was relieved to see that she was breathing.

"Mira," he called out. She stirred slightly, and a soft grunt escaped from her mouth. He called her name again.

"What . . . was that?" she uttered.

"Are you okay?" he said, climbing from his seat and kneeling next to her. He pulled her back against her seat. She opened her eyes wide, trying to focus, then blinked hard several times. When she turned to look at him, it was the gaze of someone who had been shell-shocked.

"I think I'm okay," she said, then repeated her question: "What was that?"

Gap looked out the window into the bay, which had finished pressurizing. He saw two crew members enter from the hangar's control room and begin walking toward the Spider; they seemed a bit shaky themselves. "I have no idea. Let's find out." He called out to the computer. "Roc, you still with us?"

"This is extraordinary," Roc said. "The vultures—or their creators, which is more likely—just gave us another lesson in how little we know about the universe and its power."

"What happened?" Gap said. "Did they attack us?"

"Not at all. The best way to describe it, I think, is that they took the expressway home."

Gap sighed. "Can you be more specific?"

"I can try, but I'm still putting the pieces of the puzzle together. Once the leader bolted from his place on the outside of our ship, he immediately summoned the others. I was able to follow their movements, and I tracked them as they fell into formation. Once they were together, they formed a rough circle. That's where the fun began. The light show we saw before was nothing compared to this."

"So, that shock we felt," Gap said. "Was it a wave of dark energy communication?"

"Oh, no," Roc said. "It was much more than that. Apparently our guests pooled their dark energy engines and used them to warp time and space for their own uses."

Gap said, "What does that mean? What did they do?"

"The shock wave we felt was caused by the opening and closing of what physicists have nicknamed a wormhole."

Mira let out a gasp. "A wormhole? I can't believe it! I've read so much about them. There was a wormhole right here?"

"That's correct," Roc said. "Briefly, anyway. Somehow the vultures summoned it, it opened up, they disappeared inside, and then it was gone. All in a matter of seconds."

"Incredible," Gap said. "Now the question is: Where did they go?"

"And that's something we can't answer," Roc said. "The word 'infinite' might get thrown around a lot, but in this case the possibilities are truly infinite. Scientists have always believed that wormholes could exist, but until now it's been pure speculation. For instance, it's always been assumed that the heart of a massive black hole contained a wormhole."

Mira nodded. "My aunt did a lot of research in that area, which is why I'm so fascinated by them. She believed that there might be two kinds of wormholes: those that connected one point of the universe to another, and those that connected to another universe altogether." She winked at Gap. "Those were always my favorites: doorways into completely different universes. But my aunt thought that the most likely answer was that they simply bent time and space within our own universe, and acted like shortcuts to get from one side to the other."

"And," Roc said, "if the vultures' creators have learned how to manipulate that power through the use of dark energy, then they would be free to move about wherever—and whenever—they liked."

Gap rubbed his forehead. "I agree that this is all fascinating, but we're going to have to figure out how it affects us right now."

Roc said, "I agree. But there's more to it than that."

"What do you mean?"

"We have to not only figure out how it affects us now," the computer said, "but remember that if the vultures left us this easily, they could just as easily return. With help."

W as it possible to cry yourself out? Could you break down and weep to the point where your body couldn't supply a single additional tear? Channy lay on her bed and wondered if this sudden dry spell simply meant that she had expelled every possible tear in the last hour. Her eyes were killing her, and she felt more drained from the crying than from any of the most strenuous workouts she had subjected herself to.

A few minutes earlier she had been thrown to the floor, the

lights briefly flickered out, and she had felt a wave of nausea. She decided that it must have something to do with the vultures, but she was in no position to call Triana—or anyone else on the Council, for that matter—to get more details.

She was alone, thankful that Kylie was out with friends. Her pillow was damp, so she turned it over and plopped back down, then stared at the ceiling. Her mind had raced out of control since Taresh had left the Rec Room, investigating every possible course of action: talk to him again, avoid him, reason with him, act depressed and hope that he felt sorry for her, act happy and make him long to be with her, surround herself with friends, keep to herself for a while, laugh, cry . . .

Now, during what she assumed must be a recovery break for her nervous system, she began to relive all of their encounters over the past few weeks. She tried to imagine how things would have turned out differently if she had only . . .

But that was nonsense, and she knew it. Things *hadn't* turned out differently, and it was insane to keep drifting into a fantasy world where everything was rosy.

And then, seemingly out of nowhere, her mind summoned a vision of her older sister, D'Audra. Vivacious and active, D'Audra had always been an inspiration and role model for Channy during their childhood in England. A bizarre accident had paralyzed D'Audra, and her little sis had watched in admiration as she toiled every day to rehab her injured spine, to the point that she could finally take steps again. She had been determined to work even harder and make a full recovery, even after the doctors had sadly shaken their heads and murmured things such as "no hope," and "never walk again." D'Audra had surprised them all.

Except Channy. She believed that her sister could overcome anything, especially following a heart-to-heart talk they had shared late one night, just one week after the accident.

They were alone in D'Audra's room at the hospital. Their

mother had stepped out to talk with the nurses, and Channy had started to sob at her sister's bedside. "It's my fault," she said. "I made you go to the swimming hole; you never would have slipped and fallen if it hadn't been for me. The doctors say you might never walk again, and it's all my fault."

"Hush," D'Audra said. "That's nonsense. We both wanted to go, and I was having as much fun as you were. This was just an accident, Channy. And besides, of course I'll walk again."

Channy stared at her with red-rimmed eyes. "I don't know if I could be as brave as you are. How do you do it?"

D'Audra smiled. "You accept."

A puzzled look crossed Channy's face. "What do you mean? If you accept what the doctors say—"

"No," D'Audra said. "I accept what has happened, not what others think is *going* to happen." She stroked her younger sister's arm. "See, many people rage against what has happened to them, and refuse to accept it or believe it. They relive things over and over again, hoping they can somehow change what has happened. But you can't do that, and to spend so much of your life hoping that the past can somehow magically change only robs you of spirit.

"So I accept what has happened to me. I'm at peace with what fate has thrown at me. But I have some say in what happens from now on; I decide whether I live with the current consequences, or work to shape them my own way."

Channy placed a hand over her sister's. "You accept the past, and shape the future."

"That's right," D'Audra said. "Crying over the past doesn't make it go away, and it doesn't fix what has broken. Instead, focus on where you are now, and what you can do to make things better."

Now, years later, Channy stared at the ceiling in her room on *Galahad* and remembered that conversation as if it had just taken place. She thought about her sister's attitude, about how it might pertain to her own situation.

She couldn't affect Taresh's decision; she couldn't magically transport back to their meetings and somehow alter what had taken place.

But she could accept his decision and be at peace with it. Who knew what the future might bring for them? They might never be together . . . or they might be.

In an instant she felt a calm sensation sweep over her. Her feelings for Taresh would not change, and she was glad; they felt good, and made her feel good about herself. She would dry her tears, accept what had happened, and look forward to what might come tomorrow. Perhaps their final chapter had yet to be written, but in the meantime she would go back to enjoying life.

She pushed herself up and sat on the edge of her bed. Wiping away the last remaining tear on her chin, she stared into space and thought about D'Audra again. Somewhere, billions of miles away, her sister was more than likely smiling . . . and walking.

Her reverie was interrupted by the sound of Triana's voice on the intercom. "All Council members report to Sick House immediately. Repeat, all Council members to Sick House."

They had barely lifted Alexa onto the bed in the hospital ward of Sick House when the space-time warp had rocked the ship. Triana, Lita, and all four of the crew members assisting them had fallen onto the floor, dazed.

Now, with their recovery complete, and the call put out to the other Council members, Triana and Lita embraced and wept. As much as she felt that she needed to be with Lita at this moment, Triana also knew that her position as Council Leader demanded that she investigate the cause of the powerful jolt.

She moved into the next room and sat at Lita's desk. For the next two minutes she heard Roc's explanation of the vultures and the wormhole they had created. She asked questions, but there were few answers so far. What they did know was that the vulture in Sick House was destroyed, and the other six had vanished.

Triana's gaze unconsciously roamed about the room as she listened, until it settled upon Alexa's desk. She felt her lip tremble, and another sob choked from her.

The door from the corridor opened and Channy took a few steps in. She stopped when she saw Triana, and looked to the floor. Triana sat still, her hands in her lap, and waited. Channy took a few more steps into the room, and appeared about to speak when the door opened again and Gap rushed inside.

He stood next to Channy, out of breath from his sprint from the Spider bay, and said to Triana: "What happened? Is everyone okay?"

The question caused another tear to slip down Triana's face. She wiped it away and tried to collect herself. "We'll wait for Bon. He should be here any minute, I hope." She made eye contact with Gap, who studied her face. Channy, whose own eyes seemed raw from crying, seemed to visibly weaken, as if she anticipated the news.

Lita joined them, wiping at her eyes. At that moment the door opened again, and Bon crept inside. He took one look at Lita and Triana and fell back against the wall.

"No," he said. "No."

Triana stood, and, with Lita, walked over to join the other Council members. She looked each of them in the eye, and said softly: "Alexa is dead."

23

C hanny let out a wail, her face contorted in pain. Gap, still visibly stunned, automatically wrapped one arm around her and pulled her in close. He looked at Triana and Lita and extended his other arm. They stepped up to him, and the four Council members embraced, sobbing.

"She suffocated," Lita said. "By the time we cut that thing away, Alexa was gone. I couldn't bring her back."

Bon remained against the wall, his face buried in his hands. Somehow he managed to remain upright, but a spasm of pain took his breath away.

He heard his name, but at first couldn't react. When he heard it a second time, he slowly pulled his hands down and saw Lita, embracing the others, but extending her hand to him.

He couldn't look into her face. His eyes stayed focused on her hand, reaching out to him, beckoning, inviting. Asking him to grieve with them.

He couldn't do it. Pushing off from the wall, he bolted past the other Council members, toward the hospital ward. Once again he heard Lita call out to him, a desperate cry. In seconds he was in the doorway, scanning the ward. It was empty.

No, he realized, coming to a stop. It wasn't empty. One bed was occupied, supporting a quiet, still form, beneath a white sheet. His breathing became loud and deliberate. Somehow he willed his feet to move, and he stepped across the room to stand beside the bed.

Beside the body of Alexa.

It seemed surreal, something that he had seen only on television and in movies. His mind tried to make sense of the shape before him, tried to interpret the outline as something other than her. It *couldn't* be her.

He lifted his hand and grasped the sheet above her head, but paused. He flexed his fingers on the cool fabric. Did he want to do this? Did he *need* to do this? And would he ever be able to get the image out of his head?

Suddenly he was back in Dome 1, in the clearing. *Their* clearing. Their spot. He could hear the sound of the irrigation system, the drip of water from the leaves. He could smell the damp soil, hear the light drone of a random bee performing its rounds, feel the air thick with life. Alexa sat before him, nervously pawing at the clumps of dirt. She spoke with him.

No, it was more than that. Alexa opened up to him. She shared her private thoughts and her deepest fears. She told him how she felt, and, at the end, she had *shown* him how she felt as well.

And what had he shown her in return?

He had spoken more with Alexa than anyone on the ship, probably more than anyone since he had left home in Sweden years ago. He had told her many of the things that he had experienced . . . but not all of them. He had kept the most important part of himself guarded and locked away. Alexa had shared everything with him, willingly, almost enthusiastically, because she had the courage that he didn't. She had the courage to express feelings for him, while he glumly held onto his confused thoughts about Triana, but only, he realized, because it had become routine. Alexa had given him a gift that few people ever truly received, and that most people took for granted: she had given him the gift of her uncensored, unashamed self. He had treated it carelessly.

And now she was gone. In one breathless instant, the truth came crashing in on him. He had always looked forward to hearing her voice, seeing her smile, feeling her touch when she reached out to him. He had found himself thinking about her at the oddest moments, wondering what she was doing. Perhaps their experiences had drawn them together in the beginning, but it wasn't the experiences that bonded them, as everyone else had imagined. There were far too many connections between them to be casually explained away.

Another spasm of pain seared through him, propelled by the voice crying out in his head: I've lost my best friend.

Throughout his troubled childhood, Bon had refused to cry. During the most turbulent moments with his father, when the hurt and despair had welled up to what seemed the breaking point, he still hadn't cried. When he knew that his mother had contracted the deadly disease carried by comet Bhaktul, he had grieved, but not cried.

Now his thoughts played over his final meeting with Alexa and her gentle kiss. Again, she had been brave enough to show him how she felt, and he had responded by putting up another wall.

And suddenly, before he even realized what was happening, he cried. His body shook as he silently wept, the tears burning.

He knew what he had to do, but he couldn't bear to see her this way. He wanted his last memory to be her face as she leaned into him in that clearing, as she softly kissed his lips. That had to be the image of Alexa that he would carry forever.

Against the rush of tears, he clenched his eyes shut, and felt the sting. His hand trembled as it held the fabric. Slowly, he brought it down, and with his other hand, carefully felt the outline of her face. He felt the soft, smooth contour of her cheek, now cool to the touch. He smelled her hair, a smell with which he had become so familiar. He could feel a thick strand that had fallen across her face, and he gently pushed it aside. Then, leaning forward, he cupped her face and tenderly kissed her lips. He lingered there for a moment, his eyes still closed, his tears moistening his face and hers. A moment later he pulled away, and slowly covered her once again with the sheet.

Only then did he open his eyes.

He took a solitary step away from the bed and looked one last time upon the outline of her body. Then he turned away, toward the door.

Triana stood there, silently. Bon brushed past her, out of the hospital ward, out of Sick House, and back to the domes. Back to life.

One hour later, Triana sat on the floor of Lita's room, her knees drawn up, encircled by her arms. Lita sat leaning against her bed, facing the Council Leader. They had barely spoken since leaving Sick House, but now gradually began to open up, their voices soft.

"I thought I lost her two months ago in surgery," Lita said. "You'd think that I'd be somehow . . . I don't know, prepared for this."

Triana looked into her friend's dark eyes. "We were all supposed to be prepared for it, since the day we launched. It was part of our training with Dr. Armistead, after all. But no matter how much you discuss it in a classroom, it will never affect you like it does when it really happens. I don't think our minds can rehearse the feeling of grief."

Lita nodded. "As cold as it may sound right now, I was just thinking last week about how lucky we've been so far. I mean, we've had so many close calls, where we could have all been killed, and yet we've managed to sneak by." She held back a sob.

"I guess it was just a matter of time before our luck ran out." She wiped at a tear. "Or . . . Alexa's luck ran out."

A sudden look of shame crossed her face. "I'm sorry. That sounded terrible."

"Lita, no, it's fine," Triana said. "None of us know what to say. It's good that you're talking about it, so don't be too hard on yourself about what comes out right now, okay? We're all in shock."

There was silence for another minute before Lita shifted the discussion. "I heard you talking to Gap in Sick House about the vultures, but I'm afraid I wasn't really tuned in. I guess our decision to be aggressive with them really backfired."

"We had no way of knowing that," Triana said firmly. "We can't second-guess everything we do on this mission when something goes wrong. How could we possibly have imagined that they could use their dark energy converters to disengage the magnetic lock on the containment box? With all of the studies we were doing on that specimen, it was learning just as much, or more, about us and our technology."

When Lita didn't say anything, Triana continued. "We made a decision to be proactive, and it cost us this time. But remember that being proactive at other times has saved us, too."

"You're right," Lita said softly. "I know you're right. It just hurts, that's all." In one movement she pulled the red ribbon from her hair and tossed it onto the bed behind her. She stretched her legs out before her and said, "So where did the other vultures go?"

Triana spent a couple of minutes catching Lita up on what had happened with the wormhole. "That's what caused the blackout we experienced. It was a space-time ripple."

Lita looked puzzled. "Wait a minute. If they're able to use wormholes to navigate through the galaxy—or the universe—then why would they stay outside the Kuiper Belt? Why wouldn't they just show up at our doorstep?"

"That's a very good question," Triana said. "I wondered the same thing. I guess it's something we—"

She was interrupted by the soft tone from the door. Lita pushed herself up and crossed the room. She opened the door to find Channy standing there.

"Hi," Channy said. "Would it be okay if I came in for a minute?"

"Of course," Lita said, and stood aside.

When Channy walked in she acknowledged Triana with a nod, then stood with one hand clasping the other wrist. "Sorry to interrupt, but there's something I wanted to say to both of you."

She fidgeted for a moment. Triana got the impression that Channy had rehearsed a speech, but was about to jettison it in favor of something much simpler and more direct.

"I have behaved so poorly the last couple of weeks," Channy said. "There's no excuse for it. I'm embarrassed and ashamed. I let personal issues overshadow everything, and let them consume me. You expect me to be a strong and active member of the Council, and I let you down. I'm very sorry, and it won't happen again. If you feel like you need to replace me on the Council, I'll understand. I hope you don't, because I'd really like another chance. But if you must, I understand."

Triana sat staring up at her. It was exactly what Channy needed to say, and she was glad to see the young Brit taking responsibility for her actions. She decided to put Channy at ease immediately. "I accept your apology. And no, of course we won't replace you on the Council." She offered a small smile. "It takes a lot of courage to admit your mistakes and ask for forgiveness. I think I speak for everyone on the Council when I say we look forward to having the real Channy back on the team."

A look of relief washed across Channy's face. "Thank you, Tree." She looked at Lita and said, "You were so right about the endless loop I got caught up in. It was a runaway train, really. I'm sorry for the way I talked to you. I don't deserve to have a friend like you."

Lita reached out and hugged her. "Yes, you do, Channy. We all go a little crazy from time to time. This was just your turn."

Channy hugged her back. "And I feel even worse with what's happened to . . . to Alexa."

"It's okay," Lita said softly. "As long as we're all here for each other now, that's what matters."

Channy pulled away. "I think, if anything, this has taught me a very valuable lesson about perspective."

Triana stood up. "If it's any consequence, I feel the same way. We tend to obsess over minor issues and let them take over our thoughts, and lose sight of the big picture. We're all guilty of that, too."

She gave Channy a quick hug. "Welcome back," she said, her eyes glistening.

Channy never got a chance to respond. The three girls were suddenly knocked to the floor as the ship heaved and the lights went out. They tumbled into a heap, with Lita on the bottom. She cried out in pain. Triana tried to break her fall with her hands, but was unable to prevent her head from impacting against the frame of Lita's bed. She felt a sharp jolt, and knew instantly that she was bleeding along her forehead. Channy at first fell onto Lita, but her momentum carried her off to the side.

It was over as quickly as it started. Lita sat up, grimacing and holding her left wrist. With a flicker, the lights came back on, faded briefly, then came back to full power. She glanced at Channy, who appeared to be okay. Then she saw the blood on Triana, and used her good hand to get to her feet.

"Hold on," she said to the Council Leader, and hurried to the sink. She ran a small towel under the water, then brought it back and pressed it against Triana's wound. "Here, keep some pres-

24

Portals, *tunnels, windows, wormholes. No matter what you call them, they represent something that might be somewhat frightening to your species, but they also fascinate you because of what they really are: shortcuts.*

Humans love a good shortcut, and not just the ones through the woods. Kids in the backseat always ask "Are we there yet?" because the journey is tedious to them and the destination is the magical promised land. People with personal troubles always look for the simplest solution, even if it's not the wisest, because they just want to be done with it. Fast-food restaurants cater to those who are looking for the shortcut to lunch or dinner or indigestion.

I'm not so sure what to think about the vultures' choice of shortcut. On one hand I'm just like you: I want to know more about it. On the other hand . . .

Gap sat against the wall inside the lift, rubbing his left shoulder. Despite the fact that he consciously protected it from any rough contact, he had had no time to think when the latest jolt struck *Galahad*. On his way down to Engineering, he had been tossed violently against the wall, slamming into it shoulder-first, before spilling to the floor. He flexed his arm, grateful that everything seemed to be okay.

sure on this. It doesn't look too bad, but it's a head wound, so it's gonna bleed a bit." She looked back at Channy. "You okay?"

"I think so. What happened?"

Triana and Lita exchanged a knowing look. "That could only be one thing," Triana said.

Except the lift. It wasn't moving, and the primary lights had gone out, leaving Gap barely illuminated by the glow of emergency lighting.

"Hey, Roc," he called out. "I need a little help here."

"Working on it," the computer said. "Stand by."

No sarcastic response, Gap noted. Even Roc understood that the mood of the ship would be drastically different for a while, as the crew dealt with Alexa's death. He stretched his arm one more time, then climbed to his feet and studied the lift's control panel by the dim light. Lines of code flashed across the small vidscreen, blinked off, then repeated. The system was in restart mode.

"Let me guess," Gap said. "Our friends are back already through another wormhole."

"Wrong and right," Roc said. "We do indeed have another wormhole, but there's no sign of the vultures, or anything else for that matter."

The lights burst back on, temporarily blinding Gap. He rubbed his eyes, then tried to focus on the vidscreen. It, too, had resumed its normal look.

"I'm guessing that you'll want to head back up to the Control Room," Roc said.

"Yeah, thanks," Gap said as the lift began to move again. "Feed all of the damage reports to my workstation there, please."

By the time he reached the Control Room, Roc had informed him that Triana was on the way. Gap stood over the vidscreen at his workstation and accessed the reports. The ship's ion drive engines had been shaken, but were still operating smoothly. All of the lifts had been temporarily frozen, but only one remained out of commission at the moment; Roc insisted it would be functioning again within minutes.

There were some problems at the Farms. Water recycling pumps had shut down, irrigation units had also misfired, and the artificial sunlight was only at about half power. Gap knew that Bon would be on it immediately, and waited to hear from him.

The thought of Bon made Gap reach back and lower himself into a chair. An hour earlier the tough Swede had barreled out of Sick House, his face wet with tears. It was a sight that Gap never thought he would see. Bon and Alexa had obviously shared a connection of some sort, and it was common knowledge that they had spent quite a bit of time together. Gap didn't know where Bon had gone, but it was a safe bet that he'd withdrawn to his sanctuary in the domes. And, if that was the case, he was likely already at work on the problems.

In that respect, Gap realized that minor breakdowns might be the best thing that could have happened to the ship. The crew, especially Lita and Bon, could use not only the distractions, but a reminder that they were still at risk. Gap was sure that Bon would want to throw himself into his work even more than usual.

Should he reach out to Bon right now? This was all such new terrain for them. Gap had never experienced the death of someone close to him, nor had his friends, so he was unsure of how to react. On one hand he wanted to give Bon space to grieve . . . but he didn't want to be insensitive, either.

His thoughts were interrupted when Triana arrived. She walked briskly up to Gap, and he instantly noted the bandage on her forehead. She also had smears of blood on her hands and her clothes, yet she gave him no time to ask about it.

"What's the damage?" she said. He filled her in with the information he had so far.

She nodded, and looked up at the large vidscreen. "Roc, it's another wormhole, right?"

"Correct," came the reply. "It's up ahead, not exactly in our path, but close enough. However, nothing has come through. Well, so far."

Triana bit her lip. "It's just an open door."

Gap looked from the vidscreen to Triana. "Open . . . to where?"
She shrugged. "That's a great question."

"It's more complicated than that," Roc added. "It might not
simply be a question of 'to where,' but also 'to when.' Remember,
this particular doorway has caused a ripple effect in both space
and time. Anything flying out of it could have come from any
part of our galaxy, or universe for that matter, and from another
time."

"Past or future?" Gap said.

"Either. Both. Who knows for sure?" Roc said. "Regardless,
we have now officially seen what the power of dark energy can
do when harnessed to its full potential."

Gap leaned forward in his chair. "And to think the vultures
are part of an advanced civilization that can do these things, yet
they crumble at a whiff of oxygen."

"That's not so surprising," Triana said. "We used to think that
we were pretty impressive, powerful creatures, but a microscopic
virus can kill us in minutes. The mightiest forests can be devas-
tated by one tiny match. It seems that everything has an Achilles'
heel."

She turned and looked back at the vidscreen, peering through
the background of stars. "What I find most curious," she said, "is
that nothing popped out of this wormhole. Why bother opening
it if you're not going to use it?"

"I've had a few minutes to consider that," Roc said, "and you
might not like the answer I've come up with."

Triana frowned. "No, I'm sure that I won't. But tell me anyway."

"It's pretty simple, actually. Doors not only let things out, they
let things in."

Triana and Gap sat in silence for a moment, digesting this. Gap
could see the other crew members in the room suddenly look up
at the vidscreen and then at each other, and it was clear that everyone was thinking the same thing.

Finally, Triana said: "It's an invitation. An invitation for us to step inside and visit *their* world this time."

It took a few seconds for Lita to realize that someone had spoken to her. She sat at her desk in Sick House, her head resting on one hand, filtering through the four-page document on her vidscreen. When it finally dawned on her, she looked up to see Jada, one of her assistants, patiently waiting.

"Oh, I'm sorry," Lita said. "I was . . . concentrating on . . ." She couldn't finish the sentence. The document open before her was Galahad Control's instructions for preparation and disposal of a body. She found that no matter how many times her eye scanned the pages, she was not absorbing the information, as if it were printed in a language unfamiliar to her. It was her brain's way of denying the truth, putting off the inevitable. Scattered words would sink in before the rest blurred.

She knew that the first two pages involved the procedures for securing, treating, and wrapping the body. This was under way in the lab, a task that Lita had turned over to Jada and two other crew members. She understood that technically it was her job to oversee their work, but she couldn't bring herself to do it. Not when it was one of her best friends. "Next time," she told herself. Besides, she rationalized, there were other details to attend to, including the funeral and disposal.

Even those words on the vidscreen were blurred.

"Um . . ." Jada said, obviously uncomfortable that she had to talk about this with Lita. "We're finished. I didn't know if you wanted to . . . um, see her, before we move her to . . . um, the Spider bay."

Lita felt a wave of emotion rising in her, felt the tears threatening, but she fought them back. "Gotta keep it together," she thought.

"Uh, no," she said to Jada. "I need to finish this quickly, and then I'm due for an emergency Council meeting. If I need to, I'll go over everything down at the Spider bay. I know you guys did a good job. Thank you."

Jada nodded once. "Okay." She began to turn away.

"Wait," Lita said. "Listen, I really do want you to know how much I appreciate it. That was probably the toughest job any of us has had to do on this mission; it couldn't have been easy for you. I'm . . . I'm sorry you had to do it, but thank you again."

"Um . . . you're welcome," Jada said. It looked as if she wanted to add something, but couldn't settle on the right words. She offered Lita a sympathetic smile, then walked into the lab.

Lita looked back at the vidscreen, then snapped it off. "Later," she told herself. Climbing out of her chair, she left Sick House and made her way to the Conference Room.

She was not surprised to find Channy already there, waiting, obviously eager to resume her duties with the Council. It wasn't long before Triana and Gap walked in together. Lita pulled a chair up beside Triana and, extracting a few items from her work bag, began to clean up the small head wound and apply a fresh bandage to it. Triana grimaced a few times, but offered thanks when Lita finished.

A minute later Bon entered the room. Lita searched his face, wondering how he was holding up. Although his face betrayed nothing, she was sure that Alexa's death was tearing him up inside. When he sat down, she leaned over and gave his hand a squeeze. He returned the gesture, but barely made eye contact with her—or with anyone else.

Triana rushed into their agenda. "There are two things we need to cover. I find it hard to believe, but one involves a service for Alexa." She paused, and although her voice sounded steady, Lita felt certain that it was a pause to regain composure. "There is a certain . . . protocol that Galahad Control has supplied, but it mostly covers the technical responsibilities. I think it's understood that we will . . ." Here her voice did break a bit, but she quickly recovered. "We will be sure to honor Alexa properly. We owe it to her, and we owe it to the rest of the crew. Lita will forward the details to everyone."

"When will it be?" Channy said quietly.

"First thing in the morning," Triana said. She looked at Lita. "Your department is ready, correct?"

Lita nodded and fought back her own tears. "Yes," was all she could manage to say.

"As the Council Leader, I'll say a few words," Triana said. "But anyone who would like to speak at the ceremony is welcome."

Channy and Lita gave quick nods; Bon remained still.

"But there's another matter that we need to talk about right away," Triana said. "When I sent you the note about this meeting I included a brief summary of the new wormhole that has developed. There's nothing new to add right now; it's there, and it appears to be waiting for us to make some sort of move. Given its location, and the fact that nothing has emerged, I think it's safe to assume that Roc is correct: it's an invitation for us to plunge inside."

"Which we can't possibly do," Gap said. "You're not seriously considering that, are you?"

"No, I'm not," Triana said. "Our mission and our destination are clear. But let's consider a couple of things." She leaned forward and clasped her hands together. "If we simply sail past without doing anything, I would almost guarantee that another wormhole will open up farther down the path. And this time I would guess that something would come out of it."

"So . . ." Channy said. "What are you saying?"

"I'm saying that there is no way I want to take the ship in there, but it doesn't mean we shouldn't explore it."

There were puzzled looks around the table, with the exception of Bon, who stared blankly at Triana. "And how do we do that?" Lita said. "We can't afford to send another Spider. We're already down to seven usable ones. Besides, there wouldn't be time to program one to act independently."

There was silence for a moment before Bon spoke for the first time. "She's not talking about programming a drone to investigate. She's talking about sending someone into the wormhole."

Lita gasped, and turned to the Council Leader. "Tree," she said. "That could very likely be a suicide mission. We can't send someone to do that."

Triana said, "I've already thought about that, and I don't think so. As far as I'm concerned, any race of beings that can create the vultures, and also control space-time like they seem to, could likely take us out by barely lifting a finger. The fact that they're issuing this invitation has to mean that they're basically nonaggressive, and only want to communicate."

"Nonaggressive?" Channy blurted out. "They killed Alexa!"

Triana sighed. "This is hard for me to say, because I feel very responsible for what happened. But . . . the vulture in Sick House had no way of knowing that we were going to release it, which now I believe we should have done in the first place. Instead, it only knew that its companions were being attacked, and it reacted. A case could probably be made that it acted in self-defense."

Lita's face clouded over. "I have to agree. It was calm until we began to sweep the others off the ship. But I still don't think it's a good idea to send someone into that hole. We don't even know if a person could survive the trip."

"If you're looking for volunteers, I'll go," Gap said. "They've studied us as much as we've studied them; they would know if we couldn't survive it. I want to know what they're all about."

"You've already risked your life more than once," Triana said.

"That shouldn't matter. You could also argue that I have more experience than anyone else."

Triana sat back. "I'll think about it. One way or another, I'm convinced that we need to do it." She looked around the table. "Any other thoughts or comments?"

"I'm against it," Lita said. "We're about to bury one crew member; I don't want to bury another so quickly."

"I say go," Gap said. "This might be a fantastic opportunity for us to learn about so much. It's part of why we're on this mission."

"I'm with Lita," Channy said. "I say we fly past it and keep on going."

Triana looked down the length of the table at Bon. "You have the deciding vote," she said.

He returned her stare, but didn't speak for a moment. When he did, his voice was firm. "We didn't run from the fight when they attached themselves to the ship, and we said that we would be aggressive. It cost us."

He looked down at the table before him, and Lita began to feel relief that he had agreed with her. But then he added, "It cost us, but we can't ignore this and think that it will just go away. Someone has to go."

Lita covered her face with one hand. "This makes no sense to me."

"The vote has been taken," Gap said. "How much time do we have to launch?"

"Roc?" Triana said.

The computer chimed in. "We'll have roughly until six o'clock tomorrow evening to launch one of the Spiders. After that, we'll be too far past to rendezvous."

"Okay," Triana said. "I'll make a decision by noon regarding who goes. Let me sleep on things tonight." She looked around the table. "Tomorrow will be the most emotionally draining day of the entire mission so far. I don't think the full impact of Alexa's death has really even hit us yet, but it certainly will in the morning. And yet, as Council members it will be important that we're strong for the rest of the crew.

"If anyone needs to talk tonight, I'll be in my room."

25

The silence lay heavy over the assembled crew, a blanket of sadness and grief that Triana was sure she could physically detect. More than two hundred of her fellow star travelers were gathered in the Spider bay, yet other than scattered sobs, there was no sound. No talking, no whispering. *Galahad's* entire crew, with the exception of those required to run essential tasks, stood silently, most with hands clasped behind their backs, many with heads bowed.

Those who kept their heads up were focused on the table near one of the bay doors, and the shroud-covered body that rested upon it. An occasional cry would slip out from someone, which seemed to prompt similar responses from others, and then the silence would drop again.

Triana stood with Gap, Lita, and Channy next to the podium, which normally was used in the School, but had been brought in and set up on risers, affording everyone a chance to see and hear the service. Triana knew that the entire crew, including those on duty but watching on vidscreens across the ship, would note the one Council member not present. She had called up to the domes and spoken briefly with Bon an hour earlier.

"No, I won't be there," he had said in response to her question. "Attendance is not mandatory, is that right?"

"Well . . . no," she had replied. "If you'd rather not be there, that's your decision. I know . . . I know that you were close to Alexa in ways that the rest of us probably couldn't understand, so I'm sure that many people will be surprised. But I understand that everyone handles grief in their own way. I respect whatever decision you've made."

"I appreciate that," Bon said. "I feel like I've said my good-byes to Alexa, and when the time comes for the funeral, I will honor her memory here in the domes. There's a special . . ." Over the intercom, his voice dropped away; Triana waited quietly, allowing him time to recover.

"There is . . . a special place here in Dome 1, a quiet spot. I'll be there. Alexa would understand."

Now, climbing the stairs of the riser and standing before the assembled crew on the lowest level of the ship, Triana imagined Bon at the highest point, staring up through the panels of the dome out toward the stars.

She pushed the vision out of her mind and walked to the podium, where her workpad contained the notes that she had written for the service. She took a moment to steady herself before addressing the crew.

"Almost one year ago, we left our homes and our families to embark on the greatest voyage our people have ever attempted. Through the tears of separation, and the grief of knowing that we would never see our loved ones again, we came together as a new family. We used our common purpose, our most crucial task, to bind us together and help us overcome the pain we felt at leaving them behind.

"I think Lita put it beautifully in the song that she wrote for all of us: We're reaching for the starlight, but looking back with love."

She looked out across the room. "This morning, as we face

the most devastating time of our journey, I would encourage you to embrace those words again. Alexa Wellington embodied everything that *Galahad* truly represents: determination, spirit, and courage. And yet she brought so much more to us. She brought a sense of fun, a feeling of camaraderie that we sometimes neglect, and a reminder that although the mission is difficult and dangerous, it's still a magnificent adventure. We have been blessed with the responsibility of continuing the march of humankind, and Alexa stood out as one of the best representatives we could ever hope for. She touched everyone, and that touch will never be forgotten."

Several crew members broke down in tears, and Triana allowed them a few moments to collect themselves before she went on. "There's not much more that I need to say, because each of you has your own memories of Alexa, and you knew her well enough to realize what she would want from you. She would want you to move on quickly and embrace the future, rather than dwell on the past."

Triana stepped back from the podium. She nodded to Lita, who walked up the steps and unfolded a small piece of paper. Her voice was stronger than Triana thought it would be.

"Alexa once told me that during times of trouble she would go to her Zen place. The first time she told me this, I thought she was probably joking. We all know how much Alexa loved to laugh, and to make others laugh. But she was serious about this. All of us have teachers in our lives, whether they are teachers in school, or people who open our eyes to things that we otherwise would never have considered. Well, Alexa taught me the importance of finding peace, how to build shelter against the storm.

"It's not always easy. There are times when the storm rages so violently that we bow and cringe before it, and forget to create that shelter. There are times when we believe we're drowning in fear, or sadness, or grief, and we struggle, we flail our arms, we kick, we cry out. We forget that the drowning man would be better served by lying still and peacefully floating."

Lita cleared her throat, and Triana knew that her friend had summoned the courage and strength she talked about. She looked out at the assembled crew and saw that they were intently focused on what Lita was saying.

"Alexa and I worked closely together for more than two years. I have never met anyone with a heart more pure, or who loved life the way she did. We each have certain people in our lives who lift our spirits simply by walking into the room, and Alexa was one of those people. Everything you'd ever need to know about her could be seen during the most frightening point in her life. Facing surgery, here on *Galahad* just two months ago, she could have been a wreck, she could have broken down. Instead, it was Alexa who gave *me* strength; she comforted *me* when she knew I would have to operate on her. During her darkest hour, her thoughts were on how to support me. I will never, ever forget that.

"So now, we face a storm of pain and sorrow, and once again Alexa's voice can be heard over the wind: Be strong, be at peace, find . . ." Here, Lita's voice showed the first sign of cracking. She cleared her throat again and continued. "Find the place of calm within you."

There was silence for a moment. Lita looked at Triana, who nodded encouragement.

"I wrote something last night that I would like to sing in Alexa's honor," Lita said. "I thought about the way she taught me, and taught many of us, to be strong in the face of the storm, and the words just seemed to come naturally." She offered a nervous smile. "I'll do my best to get through it, so bear with me. It's called 'Push the Storm Away.'"

Lita walked to the edge of the riser where a keyboard had

been set up. She took a seat and closed her eyes for a long time. Then, she began to play, and the soft melody filled the room. When she sang, her voice again was strong and steady.

Seems the grayest morning,
Can never stay for long;
The darkness with its heavy hand
Will fade, and soon be gone.
The magic of your simple smile,
Can keep the clouds at bay;
And then the power of your love
Will push the storm away.

Seems a heavy feeling
Has fought to take control;
It lingers, how it threatens me
And challenges my soul.
I look at you, and realize
That rain won't spoil the day;
Because the power of your love
Can push the storm away.

Sleep tonight, sleep and find release
Dream tonight, daylight brings you peace.

Seems that now I've lost you
And find myself alone;
The darkness rushes back at me
In ways I've never known.
But then I feel your inner light
And sunlight finds a way
Your never-ending power of love
Will push the storm away.

I never truly walk alone,
Or fear what comes my way;
Because I know the power of love
Will push the storm away.

The last note of the song hung in the air. Lita pulled her hands from the keys and let out a long breath. She turned to face the crowd; a smile had returned to her face, stained by tears. The other Council members came to her side, and she stood to embrace them. Then together they descended the steps and made their way to the table that held Alexa's body and took up positions on each side. Soft music drifted down from the room's speakers as the rest of the crew began to file past.

All of them paused a moment beside the table, many with their heads bowed; some reached out and laid a hand on the shrouded figure, others murmured a quiet prayer. Then, moving past, they turned to leave the room, with most offering thanks to Triana and Lita for their words, and for the song.

Triana watched their faces, aware that *Galahad's* first death would likely change the crew in profound ways. It was now official: their innocence was gone.

More than half an hour passed. Triana was not surprised to see that the last person in line to pay her respects was Alexa's roommate, Katarina. She held what resembled flowers; Triana felt another wave of sorrow when she recognized them as colorful blooms that had been collected from the plant life inside the domes.

"Bon asked me to bring these," Katarina said through tears. "He said . . ." She swallowed hard, but couldn't seem to finish the sentence.

Channy broke down and leaned against Gap for support. He crooked an arm around her shoulder and closed his eyes. Lita walked over and hugged Katarina. "It's okay," she said. "Thank you."

Together they placed the bouquet atop the body. Channy sobbed uncontrollably, Gap blinked back tears of his own. A minute later Triana stepped up beside the table and whispered, "Rest in peace, Alexa."

She turned to the others. "It's time."

The five *Galahad* crew members walked slowly away and sealed themselves inside the Spider bay control room. Triana looked out through the glass at the lonely shrouded figure. "Okay, Roc. I think we're ready."

Without a word, the ship's computer began the procedure. The door adjacent to Alexa spread open, and starlight poured through. The icy vacuum of space filled the room. There was one command left to give.

"Let her go," Triana said.

As all five crew members cried, a robotic arm beneath the table lifted Alexa's body and pulled it toward the open door. In moments she was gone.

A single bloom from the bouquet lay on the floor.

26

The posters on her wall once reminded her of home, of the outdoor adventures that she had shared with her dad. Now they seemed more like snapshots from movies that she had never seen, but had been told about. Likewise, her memories felt oddly disconnected, descriptions and details that through the prism of time had lost any personal sensation. It troubled her.

Triana sat at the desk in her room, an hour after Alexa's burial in space, and stared at the Colorado scenes around her bed. She had camped numerous times in Rocky Mountain National Park, hadn't she? She had hiked, rafted, biked, sailed . . . hadn't she? She had grown up with Mount Evans visible through one window of the house, and Pikes Peak through another, right?

During one of her final group lectures, Dr. Armistead had warned the *Galahad* crew that this might very well happen to them. There were a few clinical terms for it, but she personally labeled it "separation resolution." As she explained: "Your mind will eventually combat the grief by detaching itself emotionally from the past; your memories might very well drift from color to black and white, in an emotional sense."

That's what's happening to me, Triana thought. Separation resolution.

Or, she wondered, am I detaching not because of the past . . .

but because of what I'm deciding for my future? It must be easier to leave behind sterile, stock photos than it would be with sentimental possessions. Could it be premeditated separation resolution?

Her journal lay open before her. She rubbed the soft leather cover, then flipped back a few pages and scanned some of the thoughts she had recorded. Emotions, decisions, questions, ideas, opinions . . . they leapt from the pages and reminded her that she was certainly no Ice Queen, as Channy had often branded her. No, there was indeed a fire that burned inside, melting any ice.

She took up her pen.

To think that this could very well be my final entry is frightening, yet in another sense empowering. I have always believed that written words carry their own form of energy; call it inspiration, call it motivation, call it a false sense of bravado. All I know is that expressing my intentions in writing helps me to trust my instincts.

Two things have led me to decide that I'm the one who must travel through the wormhole. The first was the feeling I had while Gap and Mira risked their lives; I never could get past the feeling that as the leader of this mission, I should be the one taking those particular risks.

The other is, of course, Alexa's death. Even though she insisted that more study was necessary, ultimately it was my decision to keep the vulture in Sick House during that final EVA. That means that ultimately I am responsible for what happened to Alexa. If there is now a chance to confront the beings who are behind all of this, it falls to me to take that chance.

There will be no Council meeting to discuss it; there will be no conference with Gap to break the news. There will be no message to the crew. Everyone on this ship has been trained to do many jobs, and that includes the Council's ability to manage in times of crisis.

The only "person" who can know about this is Roc.

She bit her lip and contemplated adding another line, something that would bring closure . . . whatever that was. But this seemed more fitting.

"Roc," she said. "We need to talk."

Channy walked into the Rec Room, her eyes still puffy and sore. She had cried more in the last two days than she had in years. She felt emotionally drained. And yet her mind now seemed clearer than it had in a long time.

This time Taresh had beaten her to the meeting. He sat perched on the edge of a table, one leg swinging back and forth. They had the room to themselves for the moment.

Channy wasted no time. She walked directly up to him and kissed him on the cheek. Then, pulling away, she returned his smile.

"I won't keep you," she said. "I think we both have to get back to work. But I wanted to say a couple of things to you, if that's all right."

"Of course," he said. "I'm so glad that you wanted to talk. I've felt horrible about our last meeting."

"And so have I," she said. "I acted childishly, and I'm so very sorry about that." She propped up against the table across from him. "All I can say is that I let my emotions get out of control. I care so much about you, Taresh, that I couldn't stand the thought of not being with you.

"But forcing myself on you was foolish. You made a decision, and if I truly care about you, I'll support your decision, regardless of the consequences for me."

Taresh looked genuinely surprised. "Channy . . . I don't know what to say."

"You don't have to say anything. This meeting is really for me to say what I need to say, and then walk away." She smiled at him again. "I love you, Taresh. I would love to be with you, and to have you love me in return. You have things to work out right now, and it's possible that you might change your mind and decide that I'm the one for you. If not, then at least I'll be at peace knowing that I hid nothing from you. I opened my heart to you, and I'm proud of that.

"If the day comes when you realize how rare and precious that is, I hope you'll have the same courage to reach out."

She pushed off the table and faced him. "I said I would get back to you about that hug. Well, I would like one very much."

He grinned, then stood and wrapped his arms around her. She held him tight for a long time, her eyes closed, her heart racing. Then she placed another soft kiss on his cheek and stood back.

"You'll always have a home right here," she said, tapping her chest. Without another word, she turned and left the room.

Lita tapped a stylus pen against her cheek. Sick House was often quiet at this time, so she suspected that the buzz of activity going on around her had been arranged for her benefit. The crew members who worked on this shift, particularly Jada, were kind and thoughtful, and they were doing their part to look after her. Apparently, in their minds, the prescription called for action and noise.

She had put off one particular task that now was unavoidable. The remains of the vulture that had killed Alexa had been put back into the containment box and kept in frigid spacelike conditions. It fell to Lita to perform an alien autopsy, to answer whatever questions had not been answered through standard observation and testing. She dreaded it, but understood that it was her responsibility.

Her intercom flashed an incoming call from Triana.

"How are you holding up?" the Council Leader said.

"Oh, you know. Okay, I guess. It's still hard to believe that it happened. It's obviously tough around here. I don't think I'll touch anything on her desk for a while. I know that might sound odd . . ."

"I don't think it's odd at all," Triana said. "There's no rush to do that."

"Yeah," Lita said. "How are you?"

"About the same. Listen, I take it you haven't started the autopsy yet on the vulture."

"Just about to. Why?"

"I've changed my mind," Triana said. "I don't want you to cut it open. Instead, now that this new wormhole has opened up, I think we should send it back as is."

"Uh . . . okay. You mean . . . propel it out of the ship and into the wormhole?"

"Something like that."

Lita placed the stylus on her desk and sat back. "It's your call, I guess, but . . . well, what happened to wanting to find out more about dark energy conversion? I thought that was a pretty big priority."

"I think this is a better way to go," Triana said. "We still know nothing about the beings that sent the vultures in the first place. Now that this new tunnel has opened up, it's clear they want to communicate with us. I just feel that cutting up one of their creatures is not a good way for us to start a relationship. I would rather send it back in good faith."

"We're sending it back dead. They might not view that as good faith."

"Nothing we can do about that. But they might consider it ten times worse if we sent back a body that had been desecrated. Who knows what kind of social taboo that might be in their world?"

"Well . . . okay. How would you like to do this?"

Triana said, "Just have some of your workers take it down to the Spider bay in the containment box. I'll be down there in a little while, and then Gap and I can figure out the best way to go from there."

"Will do." Lita paused, then said: "Are you sure you're okay?"

"I'm fine. Why do you ask?"

"I don't know, you just sound . . . different. I mean, I know it's been a terrible day, but you sound like you have something else bothering you."

"No," Triana said. "Really, everything's okay. But thanks for asking."

"Okay. I'll take care of things on this end and we'll get the box moved right away." She offered a nervous chuckle. "To be completely truthful, I didn't want to touch that thing anyway."

"I don't blame you," Triana said. "Let me know if you need anything from me. Talk to you later."

Lita snapped off the intercom. She called Jada and gave her the new instructions; then she picked up the stylus and once again began tapping her cheek, deep in thought.

27

G ap had initially gone straight from the funeral to his post in Engineering, but then had taken the lift up to the Control Room. For almost half an hour he had plugged in every bit of data they could get from the new wormhole. It reflected no light whatsoever, and so was not visible on their vidscreen. Instead, a stream of mathematics poured in, with data that both enlightened and puzzled.

He felt a light sweat break out on his forehead and his hands as he realized that sometime within the next seven hours he would likely be launching toward the enigmatic opening. What exactly could he expect when he crossed over?

"Roc," he said. "In some ways it seems very similar to a black hole, wouldn't you say?"

"That's because it's very likely that wormholes are created by black holes, too. The main difference is that a person won't get squished by mind-numbing gravity with this one. At least, it doesn't appear that way. Of course, we really can't know what will happen when a human being shoots through that opening."

"And," Gap said, "the trip would be over as soon as it started, right?"

"Correct," the computer said. "A wormhole, as far as we know, is an immediate connection between two points. Try to imagine drawing a dot on one edge of a piece of paper, and another dot on the other side. The normal route you would take between the points is a long line drawn across the page. But, with the wormhole, we bend space and time; in this case, we would actually *fold* the paper so that the two points are side by side; then a person would just step across."

"The ultimate shortcut," Gap said.

"In more ways than one," Roc said. "If it is truly distorting time *and* space, a person could theoretically go through, and then come back before he left."

"Yeah, I'm trying to wrap my brain around that."

"And remember, we're assuming that our traveler doesn't have his or her atoms stretched out like toothpaste being squeezed out of a tube."

"Well, the vultures seem to have no problem bouncing back and forth," Gap said, peering again at the vidscreen. "That's a pretty good indication that I'll be okay when I pop through."

Roc didn't respond, so Gap turned back to his work. He absentmindedly wiped another bead of sweat from his forehead.

She was on his turf again. It seemed to work out that way most of the time, but Triana realized that in order to talk privately with Bon, it was best accomplished in his office at the Farms. For one thing they would likely be undisturbed, and given the amount of time he spent here it was one of the few places she could catch him. He took his meals quickly and usually at off-hours, rarely—if ever—visited the Rec Room, and consistently fled Council meetings at the first opportunity. He was a worker, plain and simple.

Triana had resigned herself to the fact that she would always feel like an intruder in his space. She stood across from his desk now and felt the familiar tension in the room, heightened by the recent tragedy. The fact that she had witnessed his final moment with Alexa—the tender kiss good-bye—added an awkward element to their already complex relationship.

And yet, pretending to not know that Bon and Alexa had shared a special connection seemed pointless. She had wondered how best to address it, and settled on a direct comment.

"The bouquet that you sent for Alexa's funeral was beautiful," she said. "Thank you for doing that."

If the Swede was embarrassed, he concealed it well. "I thought it would be appropriate. This was one of her favorite spots." He turned his attention to the workpad on his desk.

Triana watched him, and wondered if perhaps—just perhaps—he was actually hoping to talk about it. When she was troubled, she often turned to her journal as an outlet; for all she knew, Bon had no such outlet. Or, even more likely, Alexa had *been* that outlet, which made all of this even more painful for him.

"I know that you shared a unique connection with her," she said. "We all feel the loss, of course, but it has to be even harder for you. I'm very sorry."

When he didn't react and continued to sift through his workpad, Triana wondered if she had stepped over the line. But then he stopped and returned her gaze.

"I wasn't going to tell you this," he said, "but in her visions, Alexa saw her own death and funeral."

Triana shuddered. She couldn't begin to imagine the fear that Alexa must have carried with her. Her visions had truly turned out to be a curse.

"I didn't take it seriously enough," Bon said. "I will always regret that. In trying to comfort her, I downplayed it, when I could have . . ." His voice trailed off.

Triana felt a wave of compassion overtake her. "Bon, you had no way of knowing how this would turn out. You can't torture yourself that way. We all can be haunted by regrets." She let out a long breath. "I can play the same game of 'what if.' What if

I had let you connect with the Cassini, as you requested? What if they had somehow been able to warn us? Could that have saved Alexa's life? We don't know."

She let that settle before continuing. "I do know that you probably brought her more comfort than you realize."

Bon lowered his eyes. "You know me about as well as anyone on this ship could," he said. "But we never addressed what happened in the Spider bay months ago, and I suppose that's because you and I are actually a lot alike. Then you kissed me a few months ago."

His directness startled her. For all of the times that she had debated whether or not to bring it up, if only just to clear the air between them, it stunned her that Bon would be the one to say something. And today, *now*, of all times. The abrupt transition from the talk of Alexa . . .

"When that happened," he continued, "my first thought was that maybe there could be something between us. Well, we both remember what happened when I tried to kiss you back."

"Bon," she said. "That was a difficult—"

"Yes, I know," he said. "It was the wrong time, the wrong place, the wrong everything. But it said to me that I had misread the situation; that I had misread you."

She lowered her head and her voice came out softly. "I'm sorry to have caused so much confusion. I'm not very good when it comes to vulnerable situations."

He grunted. "I told you, we've very much alike." He paused, then said: "I'm not bringing this up to add to the awkward feelings between us. I'm only trying to explain what went on between me and Alexa, since that seems to be what you're interested in at the moment."

It sounded harsh on the surface, but Triana was sure that was unintentional; it was simply Bon's nature to be direct. She looked back up at him, an invitation for him to continue.

"I understand the reputation that I have on this ship. I understand that many people think I'm a jerk, and I'm sorry they feel that way, but it won't make me change who and what I am. The truth is, I simply have a hard time sharing my thoughts and feelings with a lot of people. Some people feel the need to blab every single emotion to anyone in earshot of them; that's not me. But . . ."

Here he paused again. His stare was intense, causing Triana to shift uncomfortably.

"But, if I find the right person, I will open up. If I find the right person, I will share what's inside of me. For a while I thought you might be that person. But with the clumsy way we started off, it never seemed . . . appropriate. And then, Alexa happened along."

Triana fought to keep her eyes on his, but hearing these words was much more painful than she would have guessed. She forced herself to nod in an understanding way.

"Alexa and I had something in common, obviously," he said. "She thought we were freaks, but to me, that wasn't really the common denominator. It wasn't the freakish experiences that we had. It was the fact that those experiences meant that we, more than anyone else, *needed* a real, human connection. We *needed* to connect with someone on a basic level, maybe more than anyone else on this ship. We needed to reassure ourselves that we were still human, that we *weren't* freaks. No one else could understand that."

Triana felt her heart breaking. Through all of the challenges that Bon had shouldered with his Cassini connection, she had never considered that what he needed most of all was a lifeline to his own species. She'd had the opportunity to be that lifeline for him, but had let him down; instead, he had turned to Alexa.

A look of resignation crossed his face. "So you see, I mourn Alexa's death on a more personal level than you realize. Yes, she was my friend, and yes, she was probably one of the most caring, compassionate people on this ship. I mourn her death for those reasons, but I also grieve the loss of the one person who allowed me to remain connected to reality. I think each of us is lucky if we find that person in our life."

Triana let out a long breath. "I'm . . . I'm so very sorry, Bon." There was so much more that she wanted to say, so much more that *needed* to be said, yet with what lay before her, it was all impossible to say now. She had to choke back not only a sob that welled up within her but the words that were crying to come out. "If only," she thought. "If only . . ."

She pulled herself together. "I'm glad that you did find that person, though. And I'm glad that you were that person for her. You gave her a remarkable gift, and I'm sure that she appreciated it."

Bon looked down at his desk. "In some respects that's true. But it also was more complicated than that. I won't deny that I had an affection for her, but it was based on the connection that I told you about. For Alexa, it went deeper, and I . . . well, I wasn't able to return her feelings the way she would have wanted."

He walked around the desk and went over to the large window that looked out over the lush landscape within the dome. "I carry a lot of guilt about that, although I'm sure that I was upfront and honest with Alexa from the beginning. She deserved better. She really did. She went through a lot in her life."

Triana turned to watch him at the window, and leaned up against his desk. "I didn't know that."

He nodded. "Mostly raised by a single mom, until she remarried when Alexa was nine."

"Her mother was divorced?"

Bon said, "No. Alexa's father died before she was born. She never knew him."

It hit Triana like a thunderbolt. She gripped the desk behind her to steady herself. Before she could stop it, she uttered, "Oh, my God." Bon, who had been facing out the window, turned to look at her, a confused look on his face.

"What is it?" he said.

Triana hesitated. "Oh . . . I just . . . didn't know that about her."

He stared at her, and she was convinced that he knew there was more to it than that. But he didn't pursue it, and turned back to the window.

"She talked a lot about that," he said. "She also talked about her relationship with her stepfather, which I guess was difficult because she'd always had her mother all to herself."

Bon kept talking, but Triana barely heard any of it. Her mind was racing through the message she had received from Dr. Zimmer. Was it possible . . . ?

She couldn't know for sure, but even the possibility was cruel. It all made no sense, and seemed so unfair. She suddenly felt the need to scream, to lash out, to walk away from all of the responsibilities of her position, from all of the responsibilities of even being on the mission. Why did these things happen? Why?

She had to get out of here. Now, more than ever, she was sure that she needed to escape. With Bon's back still to her, she fumbled something out of her pocket, placed it on his desk, and walked over to him. He had grown silent, and was again simply staring out the window.

She summoned her courage, walked up to him from behind, and placed her hands on his shoulders. He turned and immediately embraced her. They hugged each other tightly, neither seeming to want to let go. Then, when a kiss would have been the easiest thing for her to do, the most natural . . . she let go and walked away from him. At the door she turned back for just a moment.

"I should have been there for you, Bon. I'm so sorry that I wasn't. I hope that someday you'll forgive me for that."

She quickly left his office. He watched her through the window, bracing himself against the glass. He saw her rush toward the lift, breaking into a run as she moved down the path. Then she was gone.

A minute later he turned back to his desk. He stood behind it and began to once again sort through the items on his workpad. It took him a few moments to notice something on the edge of his desk. He froze when he saw it.

The translator.

28

There wasn't much time. Gap was awaiting her decision, Lita was probably curious about her call to forgo the alien autopsy, and Bon would no doubt be utterly suspicious of her actions.

She briefly considered going back to her room and packing a small bag, but in the end nixed the idea for two reasons. For one thing, the sight of *Galahad's* Council Leader walking to the Spider bay carrying an overnight bag would draw a lot of attention. This way she was merely performing one of her countless tasks.

But more than anything else she refused to subject herself to the pain. If she insisted that this was just another mission within the mission, that it was temporary, that she would be back soon . . . well, then her mind would be focused on the job at hand. A special trip back to her room meant a sort of good-bye, and she knew that the thought of leaving her connection to home—and, most important, the picture of her father—would torment her, and possibly affect her performance. It was better to simply walk straight to the Spider bay and be gone.

Entering the large hangar she found three workers from Sick House. They had arrived just minutes earlier, and were discussing where to leave the cart that carried the remains of the vulture inside the containment box. Triana kept her gaze away from the limp, dark mass inside the box while she talked with the crew members.

"Thanks for bringing this down," she said. "Do me a favor while you're here, will you? I think we're going to try to maneuver a bit closer to the wormhole, so would you please load the containment box onto the pod?"

One of the workers, a tall, rangy boy from South America, gave her a puzzled look. "The pod? You mean one of the Spiders?"

Triana shook her head. "No, I don't want us to take any more chances with the few remaining Spiders we have left. We'll use the pod from SAT33 this time around." She pointed to the metallic craft that had been intercepted during their rendezvous with Titan, originally launched by the doomed research scientists aboard an orbiting space station.

What she told the crew members was entirely true; she had no intention of robbing the *Galahad* crew of one of the precious remaining Spiders. When the time came for them to descend to one of the planets in the Eos system, they would need every remaining craft. As it was, they were already shorthanded and would need to improvise when the time came. In her mind, the SAT33 pod was a bonus, but it would do just fine for her purposes.

She was prepared to answer questions about her request, but instead the workers simply shrugged. They gripped the cart holding the containment box and quickly wheeled it over to the pod. After a few minutes of grunting and exertion, with Triana's help they successfully stowed the box within the tight confines of the craft.

"Thanks," she said with a smile. A minute later she was alone in the hangar, and quickly made her way into the control room.

"Okay, Roc, I'm assuming you have plotted everything out?"

"Not only that," the computer said, "I have put together a tour guide that points out some very interesting sights along your way, and put together a tasty little snack bag with your favorite treats. Lots of chocolate, of course."

Despite the butterflies she felt, Triana had to laugh. "I wish. Tell me, I know how much you're able to control our Spiders, but what kind of help can you give me with this pod?"

"Actually, more than you'd think. I've already linked up with the onboard guidance system, and should be able to get you within shouting distance of the wormhole. The final nudge will have to come from you, of course. With your piloting skills it shouldn't be a problem. Besides, it's not like you won't have a visual guide to steer right into."

Triana crossed her arms and leaned against the console of the control room. "I have to be honest, there's something that has been on my mind since I first brought up this idea with you. Not once have I heard you say 'don't do it.'"

"And I'll be honest with you," Roc said. "If I told you that, would it make any difference?"

"Probably not."

"Well, there you go."

"But you'll miss me, right?"

"Do I miss you when you go to sleep at night?"

Triana chuckled again. "Meaning that I'll be back."

"Meaning that you could very well be back yesterday, which freaks out even a sophisticated thinking machine like me. Of course, we don't know anything about the creatures that you're going to meet. They might want to keep you as a pet. What's the matter, Tree? Are we feeling a bit needy right now?"

She stood up and looked through the glass into the hangar. "You're right. Okay, if everything checks out, let's get going."

"Get out of here already."

She grinned, and inwardly thanked Roy Orzini for instilling so much of himself into *Galahad*'s ornery computer. She was about to fling herself into the most frightening and bizarre experience that any human being had ever known, and Roc's creator had programmed a talking computer that actually had her upbeat and laughing.

The walk from the control room to the pod reminded her that just a few hours earlier she had been in this hangar to mourn *Galahad*'s first death. It was not lost on her that she could easily be the second.

She climbed into the pod, secured the hatch, then made her way past the rectangular containment box that held the vulture, past the suspended animation cylinders, to the pilot's seat. Strapping herself in, she established communication with Roc, and then assisted him in going through a preflight check of the pod's systems. It differed from the controls of the Spider, but not so different that she couldn't figure it out quickly. Ideally she would have spent a few hours training, but . . .

"Securing the bay and opening the outer door," Roc said. Triana took her eyes off the instrument panel long enough to look out the forward window at the door sliding open before her. A torrent of starlight streamed in, and she felt her nerves ratchet upward.

"Power is at full standby," Roc said. "Ready for a little ride?"

Triana settled back into her chair and stared at the brilliant palette of stars. "Let's go."

She watched the bay door approaching, slowly at first, then picking up speed. Then, in a flash, she was out.

She realized that she had been holding her breath, and suddenly gasped for air. "Calm," she told herself. "Calm." She focused on the readings flashing onto the display screens, most of which made sense; Roc would understand the rest.

"Closing the bay door, pressurizing the bay," the computer said over the monitor. "Your power is at eighty-eight percent, everything functioning like it should. You know, one thing I didn't consider until now is that you could curl up inside that big cylinder in there and go right to sleep until you pop out the other side of the wormhole."

"You mean in case it hurts, or something?" Triana said. "No thanks, I intend to experience all of it. I am truly going where no human has ever gone before." She chuckled and added, "The other day I told Lita and Channy that I needed to shake up my routine. I guess this qualifies."

"Coming onto course now," Roc said. "Power at ninety-six percent. Approximately seventy minutes until you hit the bull's-eye."

Triana stole another glance out at the stars. "Seventy minutes," she thought, and again concentrated on her breathing.

Midday had come and gone. Gap spent a few minutes in his room, then almost an hour in Engineering, expecting the call from Triana at any time. At one o'clock he casually sauntered into the Dining Hall and immediately scanned the back tables, looking for the Council Leader. She wasn't there.

He was reluctant to page her on the ship's intercom system; if she was deep in thought about the EVA he didn't want to pressure her or become a pain. It was the reason he avoided going to her room. There was nothing to be gained by appearing too eager.

But he *was* eager. He had scoured every bit of data they had on the wormhole, every bit of information that the ship's computer had on wormhole theory, and he was ready to go. In his heart he knew that it would be safe, that the alien intelligence that had extended the invitation would know what stresses a human being could withstand. And the knowledge waiting on the other side would be . . .

Where was Triana? Was she anguishing over this decision this much? That didn't seem like her. Triana took her responsibilities very seriously, but also had no problem making a decision quickly. It was one of the many traits that he admired about her.

He stepped off the lift into the Control Room, hoping to find her there. A half-dozen crew members went about their business, but Triana was not among them.

Finally, he placed a call to Lita. She had not seen Tree for a couple of hours. "You might try Bon up at the Farms," Lita said before signing off.

Bon. No, that was a call that Gap was in no hurry to make.

He stood at his workstation and once again studied the data.

With just under ten minutes to go, Triana saw it. It was nothing like she expected.

For one thing, it didn't look like a hole at all. It was a jagged tear, a black rip in the fabric of space, a painful wound. Dust swirled around it, painting the opening in a vivid framework, the way a child created a dark outline in a coloring book. It seemed alive, fluctuating, pulsing. Triana tried to place where she had seen something similar, and finally settled on the medical image she had seen of the human heart, the pulsating valves pumping the blood.

Small tremors passed through the pod, not nearly as violent as what accompanied the wormhole's opening and closing. According to Roc, they were likely the winds of space-time that leaked out. The tear was smaller than she had expected, too. Of course, she reminded herself, it didn't need to be large; it was merely a passageway. She could not drag her eyes away from it.

With less than three minutes remaining, she once again made a conscious effort to steady her breathing; she willed her pulse to slow.

What had Alexa called it? Her Zen place. Triana closed her eyes, and her thoughts tumbled out.

Her father, tucking her in at night when she was five, read-ing not one, but two books to her.

Her father, talking to her when he fell ill. His last days, when she was unable to communicate with him at all.

His death. Her transfer from Colorado to the Galahad training complex in California.

Dr. Zimmer.

The launch. The encounter with the mad stowaway. The narrow escape from death.

Saturn. Titan. The Cassini.

Gap. Bon. Her developing friendship and reliance on Lita.

The Kuiper Belt. The Cassini Code. Merit Simms, and the near mutiny of the crew.

The vultures. Her confrontation with Channy. The wormholes.

Alexa's death. The image of her carefully wrapped body disappearing through the bay door opening, spinning slightly as it rocketed into the cosmos.

Her father.

Bon.

The approaching wormhole.

Alexa's childhood, her stepfather, her real father.

Dr. Zimmer.

The jagged rip in space . . .

Ripples in time . . .

Darkness.

"Thirty seconds," she heard Roc say. She opened her eyes and drank in the spectacle as it closed in. She felt tears on her face, and realized that she had been crying for quite some time.

"Fifteen seconds," Roc said.

She swallowed hard and watched the rip in space envelop the

entire window. How could there be no light whatsoever in that forbidding space?

"Dad . . ." she managed to say as the pod penetrated the opening.

Suddenly, light.

She screamed.

G ap found Lita working at her desk in Sick House. She looked up and said, "Hey, what's up? Did you find Tree?"

"No, I was hoping you'd heard something from her."

Lita shrugged. "She's probably either in her room, or up in the domes. She likes to walk up there and think."

A vision appeared in Gap's mind of Triana walking along the dirt paths of the domes . . . but she was not alone. He pushed the thought away.

Plopping into the chair across from her desk, he picked up a glass cube that Lita kept as a memento. It was filled with a mixture of sand and pebbles taken from the beach near her home in Veracruz, Mexico, a happy reminder of a joyous childhood. He turned it from side to side, watching the sand settle, then shift.

"I love this," he said. "I should have put something like this together before I left home."

"My mom did it," Lita said, eyeing the cube as he rolled it from one hand to the other. "She gave it to me during my last trip home. You have no idea how much it comforts me when I get down."

"And it's fun to play with," Gap said. He placed it back on her desk and rubbed a hand through his hair. "By the way, I didn't get a chance to tell you what a great job you did this morning at the service. You probably hear this all the time, but your singing is beautiful. I know that . . . well, I know that Alexa would have really appreciated the song. It was perfect."

Lita looked down at her desk with a flush of embarrassment on her face. "Thank you. I hope so."

He tapped a finger on his leg nervously, unsure of how much further to go with the discussion. "I didn't know Alexa nearly as well as you," he said. "But I know how close you were, and . . . well, I'm sorry again for what happened."

She offered a soft smile. "You know what I miss about her already? Her devious sense of humor. She really lightened things up around here."

Gap laughed. "How about the time you guys called me when the heating system went down? Alexa was the one firing most of those shots!"

Lita grinned. "I remember. You missed her best material after you shut off the intercom."

After a few moments their laughter faded, and an uneasy silence spread between them. Gap picked up the cube again, then put it back down.

"Listen, there's something I want to ask—"

He was suddenly knocked out of his chair as the ship lurched. He grabbed at the desk as he fell, breaking his fall slightly, and then his gymnastics instincts took over as he rolled onto the floor. A slight shimmy of pain arced through his left shoulder.

Grimacing, he struggled to his knees. Lita had also been thrown from her chair, and lay in a heap a few feet away. Scrambling to her side, he braced her shoulders.

"Lita! Hey, are you okay?"

She groaned, then sat up. "I think so." Rubbing her elbow, she said, "I don't know how many more of those we can take. Can they give us a break here?"

An alarm raced through Gap's mind. "Oh, no."

"What is it?" Lita said.

He didn't answer right away. Instead, he pushed himself to his feet and leaned across her desk. "Roc! I hope that wasn't what I think it was. Not before we had a chance to launch!"

"I have specific instructions to give you at this point," the computer said, with no trace of humor in his voice. "It will require that you gather the Council immediately in the Conference Room. We have a lot to talk about."

Gap and Lita exchanged a look. "What's going on?" Lita said.

Gap slumped back into the chair. "Oh, Tree," he said, burying his face in his hands.

Quit yelling at me. You're just taking your frustrations out on an innocent computer, when you know in your heart that there's not one thing I could have said to Triana to stop her from going. It's not that she's stubborn, she's just . . . Okay, she's stubborn.

However, here's something that you should probably consider: if this wormhole does indeed deposit her into the waiting arms of an advanced alien civilization, can you think of a better representative from Galahad?

See? We've come full circle, back to the brain versus the mind. I understand where your emotions are coming from, but admit it: your intellect is telling you that she was the one who had to go.

Which leads to some extremely important questions. First, what in the world is going to happen to Triana? Have we seen the last of her? And if she does somehow return, will she still be the same Tree?

Then there's the issue of Galahad's Council. With this wildly unexpected turn of events, who takes charge? I can't believe that Dr. Zimmer would have planned on his Council Leader jumping into a borrowed space pod and plunging through a wormhole into either (a) another part of our galaxy, or (b) some parallel universe. Well, maybe he did, but probably not likely. Does Gap automatically assume the reins? Lita? Certainly it couldn't be Bon . . . or could it?

Or maybe someone not currently on the Council would like to throw his or her hat into the ring.

And besides, there's still a lot of space out there. If it's been this heart-stopping so far, what might be lurking beyond the next dust cloud?

Before you get too worked up, try to remember that our intrepid young star travelers still have their intellect, their courage, their training, and me. There, feel better?

One thing that troubles me is that Bon now has complete and total access to the Cassini, whenever he feels like it. Is that a good thing? Is he the type to heed Triana's warnings, or is the pull from Titan's masters just too strong?

I recommend that you make plans to join me for the next dizzying adventure. If you just can't wait, find the nearest wormhole and take a shortcut.

Excerpt from

Cosmic Storm

by Dom Testa

Available in October 2011 from Tor Teen

t was actual paper, something that was a rarity on the ship. It measured, in inches, approximately six by nine, but had been folded twice into a compact rectangle. One word—the name Gap—was scrawled along the outside of the paper, in a distinctive style that could have come from only one person aboard *Galahad*. The loop on the final letter was not entirely closed, which made it more than an "r" but just short of a "p"; a casual reader would assume that the writer was in a hurry.

Gap Lee knew that it was simply the way Triana Martell wrote. It wasn't so much impatience on her part, but a conservation of energy. Her version of the letter "b" suffered the same fate, giving the impression of an extended "h." It took some getting used to, but eventually Gap was able to read the scribbles without stumbling too much.

And, because he had scoured this particular note at least twenty times, it was now practically memorized anyway.

He looked at it again, this time under the tight beam of the desk lamp. It was just after midnight, and the rest of the room was dark. His roommate, Daniil, lay motionless in his bed across the room, a very faint snore seeping out from beneath the pillow that covered his head. With a full crew meeting only eight hours away, and having chalked up perhaps a total of six hours of sleep over the past two days, Gap knew that he should be tucked into his own bed. Yet while his eyelids felt heavy, his brain would not shut down.

He exhaled a long, slow breath. How just like Triana to forgo sending an e-mail and instead to scratch out her explanation to Gap by hand. She journaled, like many of the crew members on *Galahad*, but was the only one who did so the old-fashioned way, in a notebook rather than on her workpad. This particular note had been ripped from the binding of a notebook, its rough edges adding a touch that Gap could only describe as personal.

He found that he appreciated the intimate feel, while he detested the message itself. The opening line alone was enough to cause him angst.

> Gap, I know that my decision will likely anger you and the other Council members, but in my opinion there was no time for debate, especially one that would more than likely end in a stalemate.

Of course he was angry. Triana had made one of her "executive decisions" again, a snap judgment that might have proved fatal. The rest of the ship's ruling body, the Council, had expressed a variety of emotions, ranging from disbelief to despair; if they were angry, it wasn't bubbling to the surface yet.

Now, sitting in the dark and staring at the note, Gap pushed aside his personal feelings—feelings that were mostly confused anyway—and tried to focus on the upcoming meeting. More than two hundred crew members were going to be on edge, alarmed that the ship's Council Leader had plunged into a wormhole, nervous that there was little to no information about whether she could even survive the experience. They were desperate for direction; it would be his job to calm them, assure them, and deliver answers.

It was simply a matter of coming up with those answers in the next few hours.

He stood and stretched, casting a quick glance at Daniil, who mumbled something in his sleep and turned to face the wall. Gap leaned over his desk and moved Triana's note into the small circle of light. His eyes darted through the message one more time, then he folded it back into its original shape. He snapped off the light and stumbled to his bed. Draping one arm over his eyes, he tried to block everything from his mind and settle into a relaxed state. Sleep was the most important thing at the moment, and he was sure that he was the only Council member still awake at this time of the night.

He wasn't. Lita Marques had every intention of being asleep by ten, and had planned on an early morning workout in the gym before breakfast and the crew meeting. But now it was past midnight, and she found herself walking into *Galahad's* clinic, usually referred to by the crew as Sick House. It was under her supervision, a role that came naturally to the daughter of a physician.

Walking in the door she was greeted with surprise by Mathias, an assistant who manned the late shift tonight.

"What are you doing here?" he said, quickly dragging his feet off his desk and sitting upright.

"No, please, put your feet back up," Lita said with a smile. "You know we're very informal here, especially in the dead of night." She walked over to her own desk and plopped down. "And to answer your question . . . I don't know. Couldn't sleep, so decided to maybe work for a bit."

Mathias squinted at her. "You doing okay with everything? I mean . . . with Alexa . . . and Tree. I mean . . ."

"Yeah, I'm fine. Thanks for asking, though." She moved a couple of things around on her desk. "It's just . . . you know, we'll get through it all just fine."

A moment of awkward silence fell between them. Lita continued to shuffle things in front of her, then realized how foolish it looked. She chanced a quick glance toward Mathias and caught his concerned look. "Really," she said.

And then she broke down. Seeming to come from nowhere, a sob burst from her, and she covered her face with her hands. A minute later she felt a presence and lowered her hands to find Mathias kneeling beside her.

"I'm so sorry," he said quietly. "What can I do?"

"There's nothing you can do. But thank you." Suddenly embarrassed, she funneled all of her energy into looking composed and under control. "Really, it's probably just a lack of sleep, and . . . well, you know."

Mathias shook his head. "I don't want to speak out of place, but you don't have to act tough in front of me. We're talking about losing your two best friends within a matter of days. There's no doubt that you need some sleep, but it's more than that. And that's okay, Lita."

She nodded and put a worried smile on her face. "You know what? Sometimes I wish I wasn't on the Council; I think sometimes we're too concerned with being a good example, and we forget to be ourselves."

"Well, you can always be yourself around me," he said, moving from her side and dropping into the chair facing her desk. He picked up a glass cube on her desk, the one filled with sand and tiny pebbles taken from the beach near Lita's home in Veracruz, Mexico. She found that not only did it bring her comfort, it attracted almost everyone who sat at her desk.

Mathias twisted the cube to one side, watching the sand tumble, forming multicolored layers of sediment. "So, I'll be curious to see what Gap says at this meeting," he said, never taking his eyes off the cube. He left the comment floating between them.

"I don't envy Gap right now," Lita said. "We've been through so much in this first year, but especially in the last two weeks." She paused, and stared at her assistant. "I know everyone's curious about what he intends to do, but there's not much I can say right now."

Mathias shrugged and placed the glass cube back on her desk. "I guess a few of us just wondered if he was going to become the new Council Leader."

"He's temporarily in charge. But we don't know for sure what's happened to Triana. She's still the Council Leader."

"Well, yeah, of course," Mathias said. "But . . ." He looked up at her. "I mean, she disappeared into a wormhole. Could she even survive that?"

Lita's first instinct was irritation; Triana had been gone for forty-eight hours, and Mathias seemed to have written her off. And, if so, chances were that he wasn't alone. It was likely, in fact, that when the auditorium filled up in the morning, many of the crew members would be under the assumption that *Galahad*'s leader was dead. It would have been unthinkable only days ago, but . . .

But they had stood in silence to pay their final respects to Alexa just hours before Triana's flight. Now anything seemed possible.

The realization cooled Lita's temper. It wasn't Mathias's fault; he was merely acting upon a natural human emotion. Lita's defense of Triana stemmed from an entirely different, but no less powerful, emotion: loyalty to a friend.

When she finally spoke, her voice was soft. "This crew has learned pretty quickly that when we jump to conclusions, we're usually wrong. I'm sure Gap will do a good job of explaining things, so we know what's going on and what we can look forward to. Let's just wait until the meeting before we assume too much."

Mathias gave a halfhearted nod. "Yeah. Okay." Slowly, a sheepish look crossed his face. "And I'm sorry. Triana's your friend; I shouldn't be saying this stuff. I'm just . . ."

"It's all right," Lita said. "We're all shaken up. Now let me do a little work so I can wear myself out enough to sleep."

Once the clock in her room clicked over to midnight, Channy Oakland climbed out of bed, threw on a pair of shorts and a vivid red T-shirt, woke up the cat who was contorted into a ball on her desk chair, and trudged to the lift at the end of the hall. Two minutes later, carrying Iris over her shoulder like a baby, she peered through the murky light of Dome 1. There was no movement.

Two massive domes topped the starship, housing the Farms and providing a daily bounty which fed the hungry crew of teenagers. Clear panels, set amongst a crisscrossing grid of beams, allowed a spectacular view of the cosmos to shine in, and quickly became a favorite spot for crew quiet time.

It was especially quiet at this late hour. Channy could see a couple of farm workers milling about in the distance, but for the most part Dome 1 was deserted. She took her usual route down a well-trodden path, and deposited Iris near a dense patch of corn stalks. "See you in twenty minutes," she said in a hushed tone to the cat, then, on a whim, retreated toward the main entrance. She turned off the path and made for the Farms' offices.

Her instinct had been right on. Lights burned in Bon's office. She leaned against the doorframe and glanced at the tall boy who stood behind the desk. "Something told me I'd find you here," she said.

Bon Hartsfield glanced up only briefly before turning back to a glowing workpad. "Not unusual for me to be here, day or night," he said. "You know that. The question is, what are you doing up here this late. Wait, let me guess: cat duty."

"Couldn't sleep. Figured I might as well let Iris stretch her legs."

Bon grunted a reply, but seemed bored by the exchange. Channy took a couple of steps into the office, her hands in her back pockets. "How are you doing?"

He looked up at her, but this time his gaze lingered. "Wanna be more specific?"

She shrugged, then took two more steps toward his desk. "Oh, you know; Alexa, Triana . . . everything."

He looked back down at his workpad. His shaggy blond hair draped over his face. "I'm doing fine. Sorry, but I have to check out a water recycling pump." He walked around his desk toward the door.

"Mind if I walk along with you?" Channy said. "I have to pick up Iris in a few minutes anyway."

"Suit yourself," he said without stopping.

His strides were long and quick. She hustled to keep up until he veered from the path into a thick growth of leafy plants. It was even darker here; she was happy when Bon flicked on a flashlight, its tightly focused beam bobbing back and forth before them. The air was warm and damp, and the heavy vegetation around them blocked much of the ventilating breeze. Channy felt sweat droplets on her chocolate-toned skin.

"You would have loved Lita's song—"

"Why are you whispering?" he called back to her.

"I don't know, it's very quiet and peaceful in here. All right, I'll speak up. I said that you would have loved Lita's song for Alexa at the funeral." When he didn't respond, but instead continued to push ahead through the gloom, she added, "But I understand why you weren't there."

"I'm so glad. It would have wrecked my day if you were upset with me."

"Okay, Mr. Sarcastic. I'm just trying to talk to you."

"Next subject."

A leafy branch slapped back against Channy's face. "Ouch. Excuse me, is this a race?"

"You wanted to come, I didn't invite you."

They popped out of the heavy growth into a diamond-shaped clearing. Bon stopped quickly, and Channy barely managed to throw on the brakes without plowing into his back. A moment later he was down on one knee. "Here," he said, holding the flashlight out to her. "If you want to tag along, do something helpful. Point this right here."

She trained the light onto the two-foot-tall block that housed a water recycling pump. One of the precious resources on *Galahad*, water was closely monitored and conserved. Every drop was recycled, which meant these particular pumps were crucial under the domes. After a handful of breakdowns early in the mission, they were now checked constantly.

"I guess Gap will try to explain at the meeting what Tree did," Channy said, sitting down on the loosely packed soil. She kept the flashlight trained on the pump, but occasionally shifted her grasp in order to throw a bit of light toward Bon's face. "Although I have to admit, I don't think I'll ever understand why she did it."

She waited for Bon to respond, but he seemed to want nothing to do with the conversation. She added, "Do you think she did the right thing?"

"Keep the light steady right here," he said. For half a minute he toiled in silence, before finally answering her. "It doesn't matter what I think. Triana did what she did, and there's nothing we can do about it."

"Oh, c'mon," Channy said. "I know you like to play it cool, but you have to have an opinion."

Bon wiped sweat and a few strands of hair from his face, then leaned back on his heels and stared at her. "You don't care about my opinion. You're trying to get me to talk about Triana, either because you're upset with her, or because you're trying to get some kind of reaction from me about her. I'm not a fool."

"And neither am I. I don't know why you have to act so tough, Bon, when we both know that you have feelings for her. And, if you ask me, you had feelings for Alexa, too. Did you ever stop to think that it might be good for you to talk about these feelings, rather than keep them bottled up inside all the time?"

"And why should I talk to you?"

"Because I'm the one person on the ship who's not afraid to ask you about it, that's why."

"You're the nosiest, there's no question."

Channy slowly shook her head. "If I didn't think it would help you, I wouldn't ask. I'm not here for me, you know."

"Right."

"I'm not. I just want to help. There were two people on this ship you had feelings for, and they're both gone, just like that. Why do you feel like you have to deal with it by yourself? Are you so macho that you can't—"

"Please put the light back on the recycler."

"Forget the recycler!" Channy said. "Have you even cried yet? I cried my eyes out over Alexa, and I'll probably end up doing the same for Triana if she doesn't come back soon. You won't talk, you won't cry." She paused and leaned toward him, a look of exasperation staining her face. "What's wrong with you?"

He stared back at her with no expression. After a few moments, she tossed the flashlight to the ground, stood up, and stormed off down the path to find Iris.

Bon looked at the flashlight, its beam slicing a crazy angle toward the crops behind him. His breathing became heavy. For a moment he glanced down the path, his eyes blazing. Then, with a shout, he slammed a fist into the plastic covering of the recycling pump, sending a piece of it spinning off into the darkness. It wasn't long before he felt a warm trickle of blood dripping from his hand.

The Dark Zone: A Galahad Book
By Dom Testa

About This Guide

The information, activities, and discussion questions that follow are intended to enhance your reading of *The Dark Zone*. Please feel free to adapt these materials to suit your needs and interests.

About the Author

Dom Testa grew up a world-traveling air force "brat" with a passion for radio. He got his first radio job at the age of sixteen. In 1993, he joined Colorado's MIX 100, where he now cohosts the award-winning *Dom and Jane Show*. The author is a frequent speaker at schools and libraries. His passion for reading, writing, and education is profoundly evident in his Galahad books as well as his Big Brain Club, a foundation dedicated to encouraging young people to be proud of their intellectual accomplishments. He lives in Colorado.

Writing and Research Activities

I. The Same, Different
   A. Divide a sheet of paper into two columns. Date the right-hand column with today's date and the left-hand column with an earlier date, such as the start of the school year, New Year's Day, or simply one year ago. In the right column, jot down some facts about yourself from appearance (hair color, height, style) to activities (sports, arts, volunteer) to relationships (home address, dynamics between parents and siblings, responsibilities around the house, best friends). Complete the left column, describing the status of your right-column entries on the the earlier date.
   B. Write a short essay commenting on the changes (or lack of changes) you observed in exercise I.A, above. Compare and contrast your observations with those of friends or classmates.
   C. In the character of Triana, Bon, Channy, Lita, Gap, Alexa, or Taresh reflecting on his or her almost-year aboard *Galahad,* write a journal entry beginning, "I never expected to change in this way but . . ."
   D. A key reason the crew struggles to form a plan to deal with the mysterious vultures is that they cannot understand whether they are biological or technological, primitive or sophisticated, alive or not alive. Imagine you are a crew member aboard *Galahad.* Give a presentation to the Council (portrayed by friends or classmates) explaining the ways you perceive the vultures to be similar to and/ or different from human beings, Roc, the Cassini, or other species or technologies of your choice. Employ graphics, models, PowerPoint, or other presentation software.

II. The Brain-Mind Mystery

   A. Go to the library or online to learn more about the study of the brain-mind relationship. Create a short report or informational poster, profiling one or more scientists, philosophers, or other scholars (such as René Descartes, John Eccles, Steven Pinker, Geoffrey Hinton, or Daniel Dennet) who has commented on this topic.

   B. Another dichotomy stemming from the brain-mind question is the issue of logic versus emotion. This is particularly notable in Channy's handling of her feelings for Taresh. Write a short essay describing a situation in which your "heart interfered with your head," like Channy's. Or, comment on a favorite literary character who struggles with this problem, the outcome of the situation, and any advice you might give to this character.

   C. Create a musical composition, sculpture, collage, dance, poem, or other artistic work depicting elements of the brain-mind mystery or the struggles that it can cause for teenagers.

III. Dark and Light

   A. You are the *Galahad* crew member assigned to plan the funeral service for Alexa. Write an outline of the events, speakers, and other elements of this service. As you plan, consider the possibility that this may not be the last death aboard *Galahad* and that you are in some ways responsible for beginning a new tradition of grieving.

   B. The designers of *Galahad* saw that relaxing in the naturalistic domes would be a popular unwinding activity for the crew. Use watercolors, chalk, or other visual arts media to create a picture of this place—with or without a threatening vulture attached to the outside. Write a poem or song celebrating the pleasure of the domes and/or about how the arrival of the vultures has disturbed this peaceful place.

C. Go to the library or online to learn more about dark energy, wormholes, or black holes. On a large sheet of paper, create an illustrated Fascinating Facts list based on your research to share with friends or classmates.

D. With a friend or classmate, role-play a conversation in which Roc and Triana debate her decision to travel into the wormhole, using information from exercise III.C, above, if desired. In the character of Triana, write a single paragraph beginning, "The most important reason I have decided to leave *Galahad* for the wormhole is . . ."

E. Similar to the beginning of this book, write Roc's introduction to the *next* Galahad novel, explaining how Bon, Gap, Channy, and Lita reacted when they realized what Triana had done, and hinting at whether (and possibly how) the Council Leader will return to the ship.

Questions for Discussion

1. In the preface to *The Dark Zone,* supercomputer Roc poses the question, "What exactly is the difference between the brain and the mind?" How would you answer this question? If you were aboard *Galahad,* do you think you would interact with Roc in the same way as Triana or Gap? Explain your answer in terms of your sense of "brain" and "mind."

2. What is important and unique about the opening scene of *The Dark Zone?* Over the course of the novel, do you think Alexa makes the right choices about sharing her "dreams"? Do you see any similarities between Alexa's handling of her dream crisis with Channy's handling of her romantic troubles? Explain your answer.

3. What challenges does the crew face, both emotionally and technologically, as *Galahad* enters its eleventh month of space travel? Have you ever faced comparable challenges in the life of your family, school, or community? Describe the similarities you perceive and the solutions you or others employed.

4. In chapter 2, Taresh comments that "The path that we've all taken is a part of who we are. How can you appreciate what you have if you have nothing to compare it to?" While he is referring to historical events, how does Taresh take this belief to the personal level? Do you think he is right? What guidance might you offer Taresh in terms of his relationship with Channy?

5. Compare and contrast Taresh's thoughts about honoring his ancestry with Triana's connection to memories of her father and Dr. Zimmer. Can one character be right and the other wrong about the connection between their pasts and present-day decision making? Explain your answer.

6. Why does Triana initially decide not to warn the crew about the vultures? In what other instances in the novel does she choose to share limited information about this situation and related events? How might you relate these decisions to the tension between brain and mind?

7. Throughout the story, which characters struggle with relationships in which they feel romantic attraction and those in which they feel connected in other ways? How does Channy's "Dating Game" offer a window into these differences? How would you describe the value of these different types of relationships?

8. Describe the impact of Alexa's death on Triana, Gap, Channy, Lita, and Bon. For whom do you think this death has been the greatest loss? How has Alexa's death changed some Council members' sense of their roles and their outlook on the *Galahad* mission?

9. Early in the novel, Triana notes that "Every horror movie fan knew that the terror didn't come when the monster jumped out at you; no, the real panic lurked in the shadows, torturing you with what *might* be there." Do you agree? Does this apply only to the vultures or to the entire *Galahad* mission? And if so, how can the crew survive the journey to Eos emotionally?

10. As the story draws to a close, what opinions have you formed about the vultures? Do you think they are connected to other galactic life-forms? Are the vultures friend, foe, or something else? Do you support Triana's decision to tell Lita not to autopsy the dead vulture and instead to send it back through the wormhole intact?

11. In chapter 27, Bon explains his relationship with Alexa to Triana. "It wasn't the freakish experiences that we had. It was the fact that those experiences meant that we, more than anyone else . . . *needed* to connect with someone on a basic level, maybe more than anyone else on this ship. We needed to reassure ourselves that we were still human, that we *weren't* freaks." Why might Triana be particularly able to understand Bon's words? How might Bon's feelings be relevant to kids who have exceptional intellect, unusual talents, or even unique experiences? How might Bon's notion make sense for all human beings?

12. Has Triana made the right decision to venture into the wormhole? How might her emotional state have affected her decision? Can a rational argument be made for her actions? Do you think a crew member venturing into the wormhole is the best "next step" for *Galahad*? Do you think Triana will find her way back to *Galahad*? Explain your answers.

About the Author

DOM TESTA of Denver, Colorado, has been a radio show host since 1977 and currently is a cohost of the popular *Dom and Jane Show* on Mix 100 in Denver. Find out more about Dom at www.DomTesta.com.